Discours sur le bonheur

Collection dirigée par Lidia Breda

Madame du Châtelet

Discours sur le bonheur

Préface d'Élisabeth Badinter

Rivages poche
Petite Bibliothèque

Retrouvez l'ensemble des parutions
des Éditions Payot & Rivages sur
payot-rivages.fr

À Robert Mauzi auquel le souvenir
de Madame du Châtelet doit tant

Préface

Parmi la cinquantaine de traités consacrés au bonheur durant le XVIIIe siècle[1], celui de la marquise du Châtelet (1706-1749) est à coup sûr l'un des plus intéressants à relire aujourd'hui. Plusieurs raisons président à ce jugement. D'abord, contrairement aux hommes qui ont écrit sur ce sujet, elle sut distinguer entre les conditions du bonheur en général et celui dont les femmes devaient se contenter, sans pour autant rester dans les limites qu'on leur assignait. De plus, le

---

1. Voir le bel ouvrage de Robert Mauzi, *L'Idée du bonheur au* XVIIIe *siècle*, Paris, Armand Colin, 1960, p. 94.

Discours de Mme du Châtelet est l'œuvre d'une femme exceptionnelle, tant par sa personnalité que par ses talents intellectuels et sa vie hors du commun. En dépit des obligations dont aucune femme de son rang ne pouvait se dispenser, Émilie du Châtelet est la personne qui s'est le moins soumise aux préjugés de son époque, et qui sut le mieux affirmer son originalité, son indépendance et son ambition contre un monde hostile à de telles prétentions.

Enfin, le *Discours sur le bonheur* présente une liberté et un intérêt particuliers car il n'a pas été écrit pour être publié[2], et donc pour

---

2. Après la mort de Mme du Châtelet, le manuscrit se trouva entre les mains de Saint-Lambert qui refusa de le laisser publier du vivant de Voltaire et du mari de la marquise. La première édition est de 1779, sous le titre *Discours sur le bonheur* par feu Mme du Châtelet, en tête du *Huitième Recueil philosophique et littéraire* de la société typographique de Bouillon. Passé totalement inaperçu, le texte fut republié par les soins de J.-B. Suard en 1796 sous le titre *Réflexions sur le bonheur*, dans les *Opuscules philosophiques et litté-*

plaire. Proche de la quarantaine, Mme du Châtelet dresse le bilan de sa vie et en tire les leçons qui ne seront connues du public que trente ans après sa mort. Des réflexions générales sur le bonheur, elle passe à son cas personnel et aux confidences les plus intimes. Ce sont ces confessions pudiques et déchirantes qui donnent à ses propos une authenticité et une actualité qui transcendent les particularismes d'une époque.

Bien que l'on ignore la date exacte de sa rédaction, le ton et le contenu du texte sont des indications précieuses sur l'état d'esprit et l'âge de la rédactrice. La tonalité sereine, mi-désabusée, mi-mélancolique, indique la femme d'expérience qui a passé les feux de la première jeunesse. Comme elle le dit

_____

raires, la plupart posthumes ou inédits. Une troisième édition fut publiée en 1806 par Hochet. Nous publions ici l'édition de 1779, reprise par R. Mauzi et publiée en 1961 avec un commentaire et un travail critique remarquables. Paris, Société d'édition « Les Belles Lettres ».

d'emblée, « on n'aperçoit bien clairement les moyens d'être heureux que lorsque l'âge et les entraves qu'on s'est données y mettent des obstacles ».

Mme du Châtelet prêche toutes les sensations et sentiments agréables, et avant tout l'amour qui est « la seule passion qui puisse nous faire désirer de vivre ». Mais c'est pour constater aussitôt que la passion dont elle rêve n'est pas de ce monde :

« Je ne sais si l'amour a jamais rassemblé deux personnes faites à tel point l'une pour l'autre, qu'elles ne connussent jamais la satiété de la jouissance, ni le refroidissement qu'entraîne la sécurité, ni l'indolence et la tiédeur qui naissent de la facilité et de la continuité d'un commerce dont l'illusion ne se détruit jamais... et dont l'ardeur, enfin, fût égale dans la jouissance et dans la privation, et pût supporter également les malheurs et les plaisirs. »

En vérité, la marquise sait bien, lorsqu'elle écrit cela, qu'il n'y a pas deux cœurs capables d'un tel amour, mais qu'il en naît un seul par siècle, comme si « en produire deux était au-dessus des forces de la divinité » ; ce cœur-là fut le sien, qui dut faire le deuil de la passion qu'elle crut pouvoir vivre avec Voltaire.

À trente ans, la marquise du Châtelet quitte Paris, mari, enfants et amants pour aller vivre avec Voltaire, dans son château de Cirey, proche de la frontière de Lorraine. Faisant fi de ses obligations sociales et de sa réputation, elle va connaître avec lui quelques années d'un bonheur sans égal. Pendant près de cinq ans (1735-1740), en tête à tête avec le grand homme, elle formera avec lui un couple digne d'Abélard et Héloïse. Période bénie pour ces deux amants qui savent si bien allier un travail intellectuel acharné aux plaisirs des sens. Tout l'amour qu'on lui avait si mal rendu jadis, elle l'éprouve à présent pour cet homme qui l'adore comme une déesse. Voltaire résumera d'une phrase leur situation paradisiaque :

« Nous sommes des philosophes très volup-
tueux[3]. »

Le temps passant, l'indolence et la tiédeur
naîtront dans le cœur de Voltaire, qui se met
à rêver d'autres horizons, de nouveaux stimu-
lants. Sa vanité l'appelle auprès du jeune roi
de Prusse, Frédéric II, et son pauvre tempérament s'endort auprès d'Émilie. Il faut bien
reconnaître que cette femme a un caractère
impossible. Dotée d'une énergie sans limite
(elle travaille, joue la comédie et chante des
opéras entiers durant la nuit), autoritaire
jusqu'à la tyrannie, maternelle jusqu'à la sur-
protection, elle le soigne, l'habille, le nourrit
à sa façon. Pour lui éviter les mauvaises nouvelles, elle ouvre son courrier, censure ses
écrits et enferme ceux qu'elle juge dangereux
pour lui. Enfin, possessive à l'excès, elle le
traîne de Cirey à Paris et de là à Bruxelles
où l'appelle un procès familial qui va
l'occuper de longues années. Voltaire la

---

3. Lettre à Thieriot, 3 novembre 1735, Bes-
terman, D 935.

16

suivra docilement jusqu'à sa mort, en 1749, et prendra toujours soin d'elle avec la plus grande amitié. Pourtant, dès le début des années 1740, la passion n'y est plus et les chaînes d'un lien trop exclusif se font sentir. En 1740, les escapades de Voltaire s'éternisent auprès du roi de Prusse. En 1743, il repart pour la Hollande et la Prusse, au grand désespoir d'Émilie, qui l'attend durant des mois, sans qu'il daigne lui donner des nouvelles… Au début 1744, une crise sentimentale éclate, qui menace gravement la stabilité du couple. Voltaire la trompe ouvertement avec l'actrice Mademoiselle Gaussin. La marquise a cette fois beaucoup de mal à le déterminer à quitter Paris. Voltaire, d'une humeur épouvantable, la traite avec la dernière dureté. Elle pleure toute la journée, et, lorsqu'ils arrivent enfin à Cirey à la mi-avril 1744, le bonheur n'est plus au rendez-vous, même si la complicité demeure.

À présent, les charmes de Mme du Châtelet ne peuvent plus réveiller les sens de Voltaire, qui n'a jamais fait mystère de la pauvreté de ses désirs. Sur ce point, ils sont aux antipodes. Dotée d'un tempérament de feu, la marquise est contrainte de faire le deuil d'un des plus grands plaisirs de sa vie, de ces moments exceptionnels où, comme elle le dit à propos du jeu : « on se sent pleinement exister ».

Dans son *Discours sur le bonheur*, Mme du Châtelet résume cette période difficile de la fin de sa vie voltairienne de la façon la plus déchirante, bien qu'elle appartienne alors au passé :

« Quand l'âge, les maladies, peut-être aussi un peu la facilité de la jouissance ont diminué son goût, j'ai été longtemps sans m'en apercevoir ; j'aimais pour deux, je passais ma vie entière avec lui, et mon cœur, exempt de soupçon, jouissait du plaisir d'aimer et de l'illusion de se croire aimé. Il est vrai que j'ai perdu cet état si heureux, et que ça n'a pas été sans qu'il m'ait coûté bien des larmes. Il faut de terribles secousses pour briser de telles chaînes... J'ai eu lieu de me plaindre, et j'ai tout pardonné... La certitude de l'impossibilité du retour de son goût et de sa passion, que je sais bien qui n'est pas dans la nature, a amené insensiblement mon cœur au sentiment paisible de l'amitié... »

À l'heure où elle écrit, Mme du Châtelet, qui ne cache pas ses frustrations, croit pourtant avoir atteint l'âge de la sérénité. Détachée de Voltaire, au sens passionnel du terme, elle n'a pas encore rencontré Saint-Lambert, avec lequel elle connaîtra une ultime et tragique passion. Ce qui permet de situer la rédaction du *Discours* entre 1746 et 1747[4].

Faute d'avoir conservé la passion qui met le comble au bonheur humain, Mme du Châtelet a cultivé très tôt une autre passion qui celle-ci cumule tous les avantages d'un

_____

4. Cf. R. Mauzi, Préface au *Discours sur le bonheur, op. cit.*, p. LXXIV à LXXXIII. Se fondant sur la citation de deux vers de *Sémiramis*, dont la première version ne fut achevée par Voltaire qu'en mai 1746 et d'autres épisodes de la vie de Mme du Châtelet, R. Mauzi conclut de façon convaincante que la composition la plus plausible du *Discours* se situe en l'année 1747.

sentiment vif sans en présenter le moindre inconvénient. Il s'agit de l'amour de l'étude qui est à la fois : « une ressource sûre contre les malheurs et une source de plaisirs inépuisable ».

Dès l'enfance, Mme du Châtelet lut les bons auteurs (Horace, Virgile, Lucrèce) et pouvait traduire les textes latins à livre ouvert. En outre, elle avait le goût des spéculations les plus abstraites. À vingt-huit ans, ayant donné trois enfants[5] à son mari, un brave militaire qui ne l'intéressait guère, et consciente des limites d'une vie mondaine qui l'amusait, Émilie décide d'apprendre les mathématiques, discipline quasiment inconnue des femmes de son temps. Contrairement aux duchesses de Chaulnes, d'Aiguillon ou de Saint-Pierre qui s'y essaieront quelque temps parce que le séduisant Maupertuis avait mis les mathématiques à la mode, Mme du Châtelet s'y attellera avec tout le sérieux et la ténacité qu'exige cette

---

5. Deux survivront, un fils et une fille.

discipline rigoureuse. Pour elle, ce n'est pas un aimable passe-temps, mais un plein-temps qui la tiendra éveillée jours et nuits à Cirey, et jusqu'aux dernières années de sa vie. Des mathématiques à la physique, et de la métaphysique à l'analyse des textes bibliques, Mme du Châtelet est la plus solide et la plus complète des « savantes » de son temps. Aussi douée pour les langues vivantes que pour les langues anciennes, elle traduit avec aisance *La Fable des abeilles* de Mandeville, et lit l'italien dans le texte. Elle découvre que le goût des études est insatiable, sans limite, et la plus puissante distraction dont l'humain puisse rêver. En outre, c'est de toutes les passions « celle qui met le moins notre bonheur dans la dépendance des autres ».

Pourtant, Mme du Châtelet ne se contente pas de cultiver ce bonheur pour lui-même. Très tôt, elle décide d'en faire l'instrument de sa gloire, « source de tant de plaisirs et de tant d'efforts ». En dépit de ses nombreuses dénégations, Émilie est une véritable ambitieuse qui rêve de laisser sa trace après la mort[6]. Pour ce faire, la société n'a donné d'autres moyens « à la moitié du monde » que l'étude dont pourtant on prive les petites filles. À ce propos, Mme du Châtelet est d'une lucidité féministe très contemporaine lorsqu'elle constate que le bonheur des hommes est infiniment supérieur en occasions à celui des femmes :

« Il est certain que l'amour de l'étude est moins nécessaire au bonheur des hommes qu'à celui des femmes. Les hommes ont une infinité de ressources pour être heureux qui manquent entièrement aux femmes. Ils ont bien d'autres moyens d'arriver à la gloire, et il est sûr que l'ambition de rendre ses talents utiles à son pays et de servir ses concitoyens, soit par son habileté dans l'art de la guerre, ou par ses talents pour le gouvernement, ou les négociations, est fort au-dessus de celle qu'on peut se proposer pour l'étude ; mais les

---

6. Cf. Élisabeth Badinter, *Émilie, Émilie, l'Ambition féminine au XVIIIe siècle*, 1983, Le Livre de poche, n° 5952.

femmes sont exclues par leur état de toute espèce de gloire, et quand, par hasard, il s'en trouve quelqu'une qui est née avec une âme élevée, il ne lui reste que l'étude pour la consoler de toutes les exclusions et de toutes les dépendances auxquelles elle se trouve condamnée par état. »

D'abord élève assidue et docile de Maupertuis (dont elle fut aussi quelque temps la maîtresse), puis de Clairaut[7], la belle Émilie, dite Madame « Pompon Newton » par Voltaire pour signifier son goût égal pour les fanfreluches et le savant anglais, va prendre peu à peu son envol. La première étape de l'ascension vers la reconnaissance scientifique est franchie lorsqu'elle concourt anonymement pour le prix de l'Académie des sciences de 1738. Le sujet, « De la nature du feu et de sa propagation », avait inspiré Voltaire

_____

7. C'est à Maupertuis et Clairaut que revient le mérite d'avoir prouvé les premiers par leur expédition en Laponie la forme aplatie de la Terre et vérifié les théories de Newton.

qui s'était mis à rédiger un Mémoire au cours de multiples discussions avec elle. En désaccord avec le parti pris de son amant, elle décida, sans l'en avertir, d'envoyer son propre Mémoire auquel elle travailla secrètement la nuit. Ni l'un ni l'autre n'eurent le prix, mais tous deux eurent la joie d'être imprimés aux frais de l'Académie. Ce qui constituait un honneur sans précédent accordé à une femme. Émilie exulte et continue, en soutenant une polémique publique sur les forces vives avec le secrétaire de l'Académie des sciences, l'honorable Dortous de Mairan. Elle l'attaque, sous les couleurs de Leibniz, avec une grande vivacité. Agacé, pour ne pas dire exaspéré, il répond sur un ton qui frise la condescendance, à la limite de la courtoisie. En 1740, elle publie les *Institutions de physique*, officiellement adressées à son fils, qui font d'elle la représentante officielle de Leibniz en France, au grand mécontentement de Voltaire, resté fidèle à Newton. Peu lui importe que se dressent contre elle la secte cartésienne (Dortous de Mairan) et les dévots de Newton, la marquise a atteint son but, être reconnue par le monde scientifique. Son livre est traduit en allemand et en italien ; Maupertuis, Clairaut, Cramer et d'autres la soutiennent. Bien sûr, toute cette gloire n'a pas été sans susciter les sarcasmes de ses amies, telles Mmes de Graffigny ou de Créqui, en tête desquelles la redoutable Mme du Deffand qui n'hésitera pas à écrire : « qu'elle s'est faite géomètre pour paraître au-dessus des autres femmes… et étudie la géométrie pour parvenir à entendre son livre » ; sans parler de l'ironie agressive de certains hommes qui ne peuvent admettre qu'une femme se mêle de sciences. Pour sa part, Dortous de Mairan répand le bruit que tout ce qu'il y a de convenable dans les écrits de la marquise est en réalité l'œuvre de Clairaut. Peu importe à Émilie ; à présent, elle correspond avec les plus grands savants de son temps : Wolff, Euler, Cramer, Jurin, Bernoulli, Van Musschenbroek, ou le père Jacquier lui parlent comme à une égale.

À l'époque de la rédaction du *Discours sur le bonheur*, Mme du Châtelet s'est attaquée à son grand œuvre : la traduction des *Principia* de Newton, dont le latin rendait l'accès au public plus difficile. Clairaut, qui la conseille, confie au père Jacquier, grand spécialiste de Newton, qu'elle travaille comme un forçat. L'année 1747 est consacrée à la correction des épreuves de sa traduction et à la poursuite du *Commentaire* qui ne devrait porter que sur le Système du monde et les propositions du premier livre des *Principia*. Il lui faudra encore les deux ans qui la séparent de la mort pour terminer difficilement ce travail exceptionnel. Même sa passion frénétique pour Saint-Lambert ne pourra la distraire de cette œuvre si essentielle pour elle. Comme si elle avait secrètement deviné que son existence se jouait sur cette tâche.

Contrairement à la majorité de ses semblables, ce ne sont pas ses enfants qui ont assumé la pérennité de son nom. Ce n'est même pas l'attachement de son célèbre compagnon. Elle dut de survivre auprès des savants à la traduction du génie anglais qui fut pendant plus de deux siècles la seule à la disposition du public français[8]. Gloire certes bien modeste au regard de celle de Voltaire, mais réussite avérée de son vœu « de faire parler de soi quand on ne sera plus », et d'en faire parler honorablement.

En 1747, Mme du Châtelet, en ayant beaucoup rabattu, peut se dire heureuse, et offrir ses conseils éclairés aux plus jeunes que « l'âge et les circonstances de leur vie leur fournissent trop lentement ». Comme si les conseils des aînés pouvaient faire gagner du temps aux cadets, et surtout comme si la vie ne pouvait plus désarçonner la belle marquise, protégée par l'expérience durement acquise.

Ironie du sort : le destin la guettait pour faire voler en éclats la belle sagesse qu'elle

---

8. La première édition, posthume, de la traduction des *Principia* date de 1759. La dernière qui porte le nom de Mme du Châtelet date de 1966. C'est une réédition en fac-similé publiée par Blancard.

étalait dans son *Discours*. À peine ses pages terminées, Mme du Châtelet, qui prônait si bien la modération, l'indépendance et la santé, va connaître à quarante-deux ans la passion la plus dévastatrice pour un jeune officier de la cour de Lorraine qui sera la cause de sa mort. En effet, elle éprouvera pour Saint-Lambert, son cadet de dix ans, un douloureux sentiment qui tient à la fois du premier amour de la jeune fille et de la passion sénile du vieillard. Jamais personne ne fut plus aliénée à une autre. Passion détestable qui réveilla sa nature possessive, tyrannique, éternellement insatisfaite. Le jeune homme, non dénué d'égoïsme, ajouta la maladresse à la légèreté : Mme du Châtelet se retrouva enceinte à l'âge où l'on ne doit plus l'être. À la honte d'être engrossée, à celle d'éclabousser le nom de ses enfants légitimes, s'ajouta une terrible angoisse de mort qui ne la quittera plus.

Comme son pressentiment l'en avait avertie, elle mourra le 10 septembre 1749, quelques jours après avoir donné naissance à une petite fille. Pleurée par son mari, son compagnon Voltaire et son amant Saint-Lambert restés à son chevet, sa mort fut saluée à Paris par une avalanche de quolibets. Tout y passa : cette grossesse ridicule pour une femme de son âge, ses travaux scientifiques jugés nuls et non avenus par les ignorants qui ne les comprenaient pas. Qu'importe ! La postérité lui réservait la plus douce revanche, celle d'être lue encore aujourd'hui par la grâce de ce petit *Discours sur le bonheur*, qui révèle une femme hors du commun, et qui ressemble pourtant si fort aux femmes d'aujourd'hui.

Élisabeth BADINTER

DISCOURS SUR LE BONHEUR

On croit communément qu'il est difficile d'être heureux, et on n'a que trop de raison de le croire ; mais il serait plus aisé de le devenir, si chez les hommes les réflexions et le plan de conduite en précédaient les actions. On est entraîné par les circonstances, et on se livre aux espérances qui ne rendent jamais qu'à moitié ce qu'on en attend : enfin, on n'aperçoit bien clairement les moyens d'être heureux que lorsque l'âge et les entraves qu'on s'est données y mettent des obstacles.

Prévenons ces réflexions qu'on fait trop tard : ceux qui liront celles-ci y trouveront ce que l'âge et les circonstances de leur vie leur fourniraient trop lentement. Empêchons-les de perdre une partie du temps précieux et court que nous avons à sentir et à penser, et de [*passer*] à calfater leur vaisseau le temps qu'ils [*doivent employer à se procurer les plaisirs qu'ils*] peuvent goûter dans leur navigation.

Il faut, pour être heureux, s'être défait des préjugés, être vertueux, se bien porter, avoir des goûts et des passions, être susceptible d'illusions, car nous devons la plupart de nos plaisirs à l'illusion, et malheureux est celui qui la perd. Loin donc de chercher à la faire disparaître par le flambeau de la raison, tâchons d'épaissir le vernis qu'elle met sur la plupart des objets ; il leur est encore plus nécessaire que ne le sont à nos corps les soins et la parure.

Il faut commencer par se bien dire à soi-même et par se bien convaincre que nous n'avons rien à faire dans ce monde qu'à nous y procurer des sensations et des sentiments agréables. Les moralistes qui disent aux hommes : réprimez vos passions, et maîtrisez vos désirs, si vous voulez être heureux, ne connaissent pas le chemin du bonheur. On n'est heureux que par des goûts et des passions satisfaites ; [*je dis des goûts*], parce qu'on n'est pas toujours assez heureux pour avoir des passions, et qu'au défaut des passions, il faut bien se contenter des goûts. Ce serait donc des passions qu'il faudrait demander à Dieu, si on osait lui demander quelque chose ; et Le Nôtre avait grande raison de demander au pape des tentations au lieu d'indulgences.

Mais, me dira-t-on, les passions ne font-elles pas plus de malheureux que d'heureux. Je n'ai pas la balance nécessaire pour peser en général le bien et le mal qu'elles ont faits aux hommes ; mais il faut remarquer que les malheureux sont connus parce qu'ils ont besoin des autres, qu'ils aiment à raconter leurs malheurs, qu'ils y cherchent des remèdes et du soulagement. Les gens heureux ne cherchent rien, et ne vont point avertir les autres de leur bonheur ; les malheureux sont intéressants, les gens heureux sont inconnus.

Voilà pourquoi lorsque deux amants sont raccommodés, lorsque leur jalousie est finie, lorsque les obstacles qui les séparaient sont surmontés, ils ne sont plus propres au théâtre ; la pièce est finie pour les spectateurs, et la scène de Renaud et d'Armide n'intéresserait pas autant qu'elle fait si le spectateur ne s'attendait pas que l'amour de Renaud est l'effet d'un enchantement qui doit se dissiper, et que la passion qu'Armide fait voir dans cette scène rendra son malheur plus intéressant. Ce sont les mêmes ressorts qui agissent sur notre âme pour l'émouvoir aux représentations théâtrales et dans les événements de la vie. On connaît donc bien plus l'amour par les malheurs qu'il cause que par le bonheur souvent obscur qu'il répand sur la vie des hommes. Mais supposons pour un moment que les passions fassent plus de malheureux que d'heureux, je dis qu'elles seraient encore à désirer, parce que c'est la condition sans laquelle on ne peut avoir de grands plaisirs ; or ce n'est la peine de vivre que pour avoir des sensations et des sentiments agréables ; et plus les sentiments agréables sont vifs, plus on est heureux. Il est donc à désirer d'être susceptible de passions, et je le répète encore : n'en a pas qui veut.

C'est à nous à les faire servir à notre bonheur, et cela dépend souvent de nous. Quiconque a su si bien économiser son état et les circonstances où la fortune l'a placé, qu'il soit parvenu à mettre son esprit et son cœur dans une assiette tranquille, qu'il soit susceptible de tous les sentiments, de toutes les sensations agréables que cet état peut comporter, est assurément un excellent philosophe, et doit bien remercier la nature.

Je dis son état et les circonstances où la fortune l'a placé, parce que je crois qu'une des choses qui contribuent le plus au bonheur, c'est de se contenter de son état, et de songer plutôt à le rendre heureux qu'à en changer.

Mon but n'est pas d'écrire pour toutes sortes de conditions et pour toutes sortes de personnes ; tous les états ne sont pas susceptibles de la même espèce de bonheur. Je n'écris que pour ce qu'on appelle les gens du monde, c'est-à-dire pour ceux qui sont nés avec une fortune toute faite, plus ou moins brillante, plus ou moins opulente, mais enfin tels qu'ils peuvent rester dans leur état sans en rougir, et ce ne sont peut-être pas les plus aisés à rendre heureux.

Mais pour avoir des passions, pour pouvoir les satisfaire, il faut sans doute se bien porter ; c'est là le premier bien : or ce bien n'est pas si indépendant de nous qu'on le pense. Comme nous sommes tous nés sains (je dis en général) et faits pour durer un certain temps, il est sûr que si nous ne détruisions pas notre tempérament par la gourmandise, par les veilles, par les excès enfin, nous vivrions tous à peu près ce qu'on appelle âge d'homme. J'en excepte les morts violentes qu'on ne peut prévoir, et dont, par consé-quent, il est inutile de s'occuper.

Mais, me répondra-t-on, si votre passion est la gourmandise, vous serez donc bien mal-heureux : car si vous voulez vous bien porter, il faudra perpétuellement vous contraindre.

À cela je réponds que le bonheur étant votre but, en satisfaisant vos passions, rien ne doit vous écarter de ce but ; et si le mal d'estomac ou la goutte que vous donnent les excès que vous faites à table vous causent des douleurs plus vives que le plaisir que vous trouvez à satisfaire votre gourmandise, vous calculez mal, si vous préférez la jouissance de l'un à la privation de l'autre : vous vous écartez de votre but, et vous êtes malheureux par votre faute. Ne vous plaignez pas de ce que vous êtes gourmand : car cette passion est une source de plaisirs continuels ; mais sachez la faire servir à votre bonheur : cela vous sera aisé en restant chez vous, et en ne vous faisant servir que ce que vous voulez manger : ayez des temps de diète ; si vous attendez que votre estomac désire par une faim bien vraie, tout ce qui se présentera vous fera autant de plaisir que des mets plus recherchés, et auxquels vous ne songerez pas lorsque vous ne les aurez pas devant les yeux. Cette sobriété que vous vous serez imposée rendra le plaisir plus vif. Je ne vous la recommande pas pour éteindre en vous la gourmandise, mais pour vous en préparer une jouissance plus délicieuse. À l'égard des personnes malades, des cacochymes que tout incommode, elles ont d'autres espèces de bonheur. Avoir bien chaud, bien digérer leur poulet, aller à la garde-robe, est une jouissance pour eux. Un tel bonheur, s'il en est un, est trop insipide pour s'occuper des moyens d'y parvenir. Il semble que ces sortes de personnes soient dans une sphère dont ce qu'on appelle bonheur, jouissance, sentiments agréables ne peuvent approcher. Elles sont à plaindre ; mais on ne peut rien pour elles.

Quand on s'est une fois bien persuadé que sans la santé on ne peut jouir d'aucun plaisir et d'aucun bien, on se résout sans peine à faire quelques sacrifices pour conserver la sienne. J'en suis, je puis le dire, un exemple. J'ai un très bon tempérament ; mais je ne suis point robuste, et il y a des choses qui sûrement détruiraient ma santé. Tel est le vin, par exemple, et toutes les liqueurs ; je me les suis interdits dès ma première jeunesse, j'ai un tempérament de feu, je passe toute la matinée à me noyer de liquides ; enfin, je me livre trop souvent à la gourmandise dont Dieu m'a douée, et je répare ces excès par des diètes rigoureuses que je m'impose à la première incommodité que je sens, et qui m'ont toujours évité des maladies. Ces diètes ne me coûtent rien, parce que dans ces temps je reste toujours chez moi à l'heure des repas, et comme la nature est assez sage pour ne nous pas donner les sentiments de la faim quand nous l'avons surchargée de nourriture, ma gourmandise n'étant point excitée par la présence des mets, je ne me refuse rien en ne mangeant point, et je rétablis ma santé sans qu'il m'en coûte de privation.

Une autre source de bonheur, c'est d'être exempt de préjugés, et il ne tient qu'à nous de nous en défaire. Nous avons tous la portion d'esprit nécessaire pour examiner les choses qu'on veut nous obliger de croire ; pour savoir, par exemple, si deux et deux font quatre, ou cinq ; et d'ailleurs, dans ce siècle, on ne manque pas de secours pour s'instruire.

Je sais qu'il y a d'autres préjugés que ceux de la religion, et je crois qu'ils sont très bons à secouer, quoiqu'il n'y en ait aucun qui influe autant sur notre bonheur et notre malheur que celui de la religion. Qui dit préjugé dit une opinion qu'on a reçue sans examen, parce qu'elle ne se soutiendrait pas. L'erreur ne peut jamais être un bien, et elle est sûrement un grand mal dans les choses d'où dépend la conduite de la vie.

Il ne faut pas confondre les préjugés avec les bienséances. Les préjugés n'ont aucune vérité, et ne peuvent être utiles qu'aux âmes mal faites : car il y a des âmes corrompues comme des corps contrefaits. Celles-là sont hors de rang, et je n'ai rien à leur dire. Les bienséances ont une vérité de convention, et c'en est assez pour que toute personne de bien ne se permette jamais de s'en écarter. Il n'y a point de livre qui apprenne les bienséances, et cependant personne ne les ignore de bonne foi. Elles varient suivant les états, les âges, les circonstances. Quiconque prétend au bonheur ne doit jamais s'en écarter ; mais l'exacte observation des bienséances est une vertu, et j'ai dit que pour être heureux il faut être vertueux. Je sais que les prédicateurs, et même Juvénal, disent qu'il faut aimer la vertu pour elle-même, pour sa propre beauté ; mais il faut tâcher d'entendre le sens de ces paroles, et l'on verra qu'elles se réduisent à ceci : Il faut être vertueux, parce qu'on ne peut être vicieux et heureux. J'entends par *vertu* tout ce qui contribue au bonheur de la société, et, par conséquent, au nôtre, puisque nous sommes membres de la société.

Je dis qu'on ne peut être heureux et vicieux, et la démonstration de cet axiome est dans le fond du cœur de tous les hommes. Je leur soutiens, même aux plus scélérats, qu'il n'y en a aucun à qui les reproches de sa conscience, c'est-à-dire de son sentiment intérieur, le mépris qu'il sent qu'il mérite et qu'il éprouve, dès qu'on le connaît, ne tiennent lieu de supplice. Je n'entends pas par scélérats les voleurs, les assassins, les empoisonneurs, ils ne peuvent se trouver dans la classe de ceux pour qui j'écris ; mais je donne

ce nom aux gens faux et perfides, aux calom-
niateurs, aux délateurs, aux ingrats, enfin à
tous ceux qui sont atteints des vices contre
lesquels les lois n'ont point sévi, mais contre
lesquels celles des mœurs et de la société ont
porté des arrêts d'autant plus terribles qu'ils
sont toujours exécutés.

Je maintiens donc qu'il n'y a personne sur
la terre qui puisse sentir qu'on le méprise
sans désespoir. Ce mépris public, cette ani-
madversion des gens de bien est un supplice
plus cruel que tous ceux que le lieutenant-
criminel pourrait infliger, parce qu'il dure
plus longtemps, et que l'espérance ne
l'accompagne jamais.

Il faut donc n'être pas vicieux si l'on ne
veut pas être malheureux ; mais ce n'est pas
assez pour nous de n'être pas malheureux ; la
vie ne vaudrait pas la peine d'être supportée
si l'absence de la douleur était notre seul but ;
le néant vaudrait mieux : car assurément c'est
l'état où l'on souffre le moins. Il faut donc
tâcher d'être heureux. Il faut être bien avec
soi-même par la même raison qu'il faut être

logé commodément chez soi, et vainement espérerait-on pouvoir jouir de cette satisfaction sans la vertu :

Aisément des mortels on éblouit les yeux ;
Mais on ne peut tromper l'œil vigilant des
[dieux,

a dit un de nos meilleurs poètes ; mais c'est l'œil vigilant de sa propre conscience qu'on ne trompe jamais.

On se rend une justice exacte, et plus on peut se rendre témoignage que l'on a rempli ses devoirs, qu'on a fait tout le bien qu'on a pu faire, qu'on est vertueux enfin, plus on goûte cette satisfaction intérieure qu'on peut appeler la santé de l'âme. Je doute qu'il y ait de sentiment plus délicieux que celui qu'on éprouve quand on vient de faire une action vertueuse, et qui mérite l'estime des honnêtes gens. Au plaisir intérieur que causent les actions vertueuses se joint encore le plaisir de jouir de l'estime universelle : car les fripons ne peuvent refuser leur estime à la probité ; mais l'estime des honnêtes gens mérite seule qu'on la compte. Enfin, je dis que pour être heureux il faut être susceptible d'illusion, et cela n'a guère besoin d'être prouvé ; mais, me direz-vous, vous avez dit que l'erreur est toujours nuisible : l'illusion n'est-elle pas une erreur ? Non : l'illusion ne nous fait pas voir, à la vérité, les objets entiè- rement tels qu'ils doivent être pour nous donner des sentiments agréables, elle les accommode à notre nature. Telles sont les illusions de l'optique : or l'optique ne nous trompe pas, quoiqu'elle ne nous fasse pas voir les objets tels qu'ils sont, parce qu'elle nous les fait voir de la manière qu'il faut que nous les voyions pour notre utilité. Quelle est la raison pour laquelle je ris plus que personne aux marionnettes, si ce n'est parce que je me prête plus qu'aucun autre à l'illusion, et qu'au bout d'un quart d'heure je crois que c'est Polichinelle qui parle ? Aurait-on un moment de plaisir à la comédie, si on ne se prêtait à l'illusion qui vous fait voir des personnages que vous savez morts depuis longtemps, et qui les fait parler en vers alexandrins ? Mais quel plaisir aurait-on à un autre spectacle où tout est illusion, si on ne savait pas s'y prêter ? Assurément, il y aurait bien à perdre, et ceux qui n'ont à l'opéra que le plaisir de la musique et des danses y ont un plaisir bien décharné et bien au-dessous de celui que donne l'ensemble de ce spectacle enchanteur. J'ai cité les spectacles, parce que l'illusion y est plus aisée à sentir. Elle se mêle à tous les plaisirs de notre vie, et elle en est le vernis. On dira peut-être qu'elle ne dépend pas de nous, et cela n'est que trop vrai, jusqu'à un certain point ; on ne peut se donner des illusions, de même qu'on ne peut se donner des goûts, ni des passions ; mais on peut conserver les illusions qu'on a ; on peut ne pas chercher à les détruire ; on peut ne pas aller derrière les coulisses voir les roues qui font les vols, et les autres machines : voilà tout l'art qu'on y peut mettre, et cet art n'est ni inutile ni infructueux.

Voilà les grandes machines du bonheur, si je puis m'exprimer ainsi ; mais il y a encore bien des adresses de détail qui peuvent contribuer à notre bonheur.

La première de toutes est d'être bien décidé à ce qu'on veut être et à ce qu'on veut faire, et c'est ce qui manque à presque tous les hommes ; c'est pourtant la condition sans laquelle il n'y a point de bonheur. Sans elle, on nage perpétuellement dans une mer d'incertitudes ; on détruit le matin ce qu'on a fait le soir ; on passe la vie à faire des sottises, à les réparer, à s'en repentir.

Ce sentiment de repentir est un des plus inutiles et des plus désagréables que notre âme puisse éprouver. Un des grands secrets est de savoir s'en garantir. Comme rien ne se ressemble dans la vie, il est presque toujours inutile de voir ses fautes, du moins l'est-il de s'arrêter longtemps à les considérer et de se les reprocher : c'est nous couvrir de confusion à nos propres yeux sans aucun profit. Il faut partir d'où l'on est, employer toute la sagacité de son esprit à réparer et à trouver les moyens de réparer ; mais il ne faut point regarder au talon, et il faut toujours écarter de son esprit le souvenir de ses fautes : quand on en a tiré dans une première vue le fruit qu'on en peut attendre, écarter les idées tristes et leur en substituer d'agréables, c'est encore un des grands ressorts du bonheur, et nous avons celui-là en notre pouvoir, du moins jusqu'à un certain point ; je sais que dans une violente passion qui nous rend malheureux, il ne dépend pas entièrement de nous de bannir de notre esprit les idées qui nous affligent ; mais on n'est pas toujours dans ces situations violentes, toutes les maladies ne sont pas des fièvres malignes, et les petits malheurs de détail, les sensations désagréables, quoique faibles, sont bonnes à éviter. La mort, par exemple, est une idée qui nous afflige toujours, soit que nous prévoyions la nôtre, soit que nous pensions à celle des gens que nous aimons. Il faut donc éviter avec soin tout ce qui peut nous rappeler cette idée. Je suis bien opposée à Montaigne, qui se félicitait tant de s'être tellement accoutumé à la mort qu'il était sûr de la voir de près sans être effrayé. On voit, par la complaisance avec laquelle il rapporte cette victoire, qu'elle lui avait coûté beaucoup, et en cela le sage Montaigne avait mal calculé : car assurément c'est une folie d'empoisonner par cette idée triste et humiliante une partie du peu de temps que nous avions à vivre, pour supporter plus patiemment un moment que les douleurs corporelles rendent toujours très amer, malgré notre philosophie ; d'ailleurs, qui sait si l'affaiblissement de notre esprit, causé par la maladie ou par l'âge, nous laissera recueillir le fruit de nos réflexions, et si nous n'en serons pas pour nos frais, comme il arrive si souvent dans cette vie ? Ayons toujours dans l'esprit, quand l'idée de la mort nous revient, ce vers de Gresset :

La douleur est un siècle, et la mort un
[moment.

Détournons cet esprit de toutes les idées désagréables ; elles sont la source d'où naissent tous les maux métaphysiques, et c'est surtout ceux-là qu'il est presque toujours en notre pouvoir d'éviter.

La sagesse doit avoir toujours les jetons à la main : car qui dit *sage* dit *heureux*, du moins dans mon dictionnaire ; il faut avoir des passions pour être heureux ; mais il faut les faire servir à notre bonheur, et il y en a auxquelles il faut défendre toute entrée dans notre âme. Je ne parle pas ici des passions qui sont des vices, telles que la haine, [*la vengeance, la colère ; mais l'ambition*], par exemple, est une passion dont je crois qu'il faut défendre son âme, si on veut être heureux ; ce n'est pas par la raison qu'elle n'a pas de jouissance, car je crois que cette passion peut en fournir ; ce n'est pas parce que l'ambition désire toujours, car c'est assurément un grand bien, mais c'est parce que de toutes les passions c'est celle qui met le plus notre bonheur dans la dépendance des autres ; [*or moins notre bonheur dépend des autres*] et plus il nous est aisé d'être heureux.

Ne craignons pas de faire trop de retranchement sur cela, il en dépendra toujours assez. Par cette raison d'indépendance, l'amour de l'étude est de toutes les passions celle qui contribue le plus à notre bonheur. Dans l'amour de l'étude se trouve renfermée une passion dont une âme élevée n'est jamais entièrement exempte, celle de la gloire ; il n'y a même que cette manière d'en acquérir pour la moitié du monde, et c'est cette moitié justement à qui l'éducation en ôte les moyens, et en rend le goût impossible.

Il est certain que l'amour de l'étude est bien moins nécessaire au bonheur des hommes qu'à celui des femmes. Les hommes ont une infinité de ressources pour être heureux, qui manquent entièrement aux femmes. Ils ont bien d'autres moyens d'arriver à la gloire, et il est sûr que l'ambition de rendre ses talents utiles à son pays et de servir ses concitoyens, soit par son habileté dans l'art de la guerre, ou par ses talents pour le gouvernement, ou les négociations, est fort au-dessus de [celle] qu'on peut se proposer pour l'étude ; mais les femmes sont exclues, par leur état, de toute espèce de gloire, et quand, par hasard, il s'en trouve quelqu'une qui est née avec une âme assez élevée, il ne lui reste que l'étude pour la consoler de toutes les exclusions et de toutes les dépendances auxquelles elle se trouve condamnée par état.

L'amour de la gloire, qui est la source de tant de plaisir et de tant d'efforts en tout genre qui contribuent au bonheur, à l'instruction et à la perfection de la société, est entièrement fondé sur l'illusion ; rien n'est si aisé que de faire disparaître le fantôme après lequel courent toutes les âmes élevées ; mais qu'il y aurait à perdre pour elles et pour les autres ! Je sais qu'il est quelque réalité dans l'amour de la gloire dont on peut jouir de son vivant ; mais il n'y a guère de héros, en quelque genre que ce soit, qui voulût se détacher entièrement des applaudissements de la postérité, dont on attend même plus de justice que de ses contemporains. On ne savoure pas toujours le désir vague de faire parler de soi quand on ne sera plus ; mais il reste

toujours au fond de notre cœur. La philosophie en voudrait faire sentir la vanité ; mais
le sentiment prend le dessus, et ce plaisir
n'est point une illusion : car il nous prouve
le bien réel de jouir de notre réputation
future ; si le présent était notre unique bien,
nos plaisirs seraient bien plus bornés qu'ils
ne le sont. Nous sommes heureux dans le
moment présent, non seulement par nos
jouissances actuelles, mais par nos espérances,
par nos réminiscences. Le présent s'enrichit
du passé et de l'avenir. Qui travaillerait pour
ses enfants, pour la grandeur de sa maison,
si on ne jouissait pas de l'avenir ? Nous avons
beau faire, l'amour-propre est toujours le
mobile plus ou moins caché de nos actions ;
c'est le vent qui enfle les voiles, sans lequel
le vaisseau n'irait point.

J'ai dit que l'amour de l'étude était la passion la plus nécessaire à notre bonheur ; c'est
une ressource sûre contre les malheurs, c'est
une source de plaisirs inépuisable, et Cicéron
a bien raison de dire : *Les plaisirs des sens et
ceux du cœur sont, sans doute, au-dessus de ceux*

de l'étude ; il n'est pas nécessaire d'étudier pour être heureux ; mais il l'est peut-être de se sentir en soi cette ressource et cet appui. On peut aimer l'étude, et passer des années entières, peut-être sa vie, sans étudier ; et heureux qui la passe ainsi : car ce ne peut être qu'à des plaisirs plus vifs qu'il sacrifie un plaisir qu'il est toujours sûr de trouver, et qu'il rendra assez vif pour le dédommager de la perte des autres.

Un des grands secrets du bonheur est de modérer ses désirs et d'aimer les choses qu'on possède. La nature, dont le but est toujours notre bonheur (et j'entends par nature tout ce qui est instinct et sans raisonnement), la nature, dis-je, ne nous donne des désirs que conformément à notre état ; nous ne désirons naturellement que de proche en proche : un capitaine d'infanterie désire d'être colonel, et il n'est point malheureux de ne point commander les armées, quelque talent qu'il se sente. C'est à notre esprit et à nos réflexions à fortifier cette sage sobriété de la nature ; on n'est heureux que par des désirs satisfaits ; il faut donc ne se permettre de désirer que les choses qu'on peut obtenir sans trop de soins et de travail, et c'est un point sur lequel nous pouvons beaucoup pour notre bonheur. Aimer ce qu'on possède, savoir en jouir, savourer les avantages de son état, ne point trop porter sa vue sur ceux qui nous paraissent plus heureux, s'appliquer à perfectionner le sien et à en tirer le meilleur parti possible, voilà ce qu'on doit appeler heureux ; et je crois faire une bonne définition en disant que le plus heureux des hommes est celui qui désire le moins le changement de son état. Pour jouir de ce bonheur, il faut guérir ou prévenir une maladie d'une autre espèce qui s'y oppose entièrement, et qui n'est que trop commune : c'est l'inquiétude. Cette disposition d'esprit s'oppose à toute jouissance, et par conséquent à toute espèce de bonheur.

La bonne philosophie, c'est-à-dire la ferme persuasion que nous n'avons autre chose à faire dans ce monde que d'être heureux, est un remède sûr contre cette maladie, dont les bons esprits, ceux qui sont capables de principes et de conséquences, sont presque toujours exempts.

Il est une passion très déraisonnable aux yeux des philosophes et de la raison, dont le motif, quelque déguisé qu'il soit, est même humiliant, et devrait seul suffire pour en guérir, et qui cependant peut rendre heureux : c'est la passion du jeu. Il est heureux de l'avoir, si l'on peut la modérer et la réserver pour le temps de notre vie où cette ressource nous sera nécessaire, et ce temps est la vieillesse. Il est certain que l'amour du jeu a sa source dans l'amour de l'argent ; il n'y a point de particulier pour qui le gros jeu (et j'appelle gros jeu celui qui peut faire une différence dans notre fortune) ne soit un objet intéressant.

Notre âme veut être remuée par l'espérance ou la crainte ; elle n'est heureuse que par les choses qui lui font sentir son existence. Or le jeu nous met perpétuellement aux prises avec ces deux passions, et tient, par conséquent, notre âme dans une émotion qui est un des grands principes du bonheur qui soient en nous. Le plaisir que m'a fait le jeu a servi souvent à me consoler de n'être pas riche. Je me crois l'esprit assez bien fait pour qu'une fortune, médiocre pour un autre, suffise à me rendre heureuse ; et dans ce cas le jeu me deviendrait insipide ; du moins je le craignais, et cette idée me persuadait que je devais le plaisir du jeu à mon peu de fortune, et servait à m'en consoler.

Il est certain que les besoins physiques sont la source des plaisirs des sens, et je suis persuadée qu'il y a plus de plaisir dans une fortune médiocre que dans une entière abondance. Une boîte, une porcelaine, un meuble nouveau, sont une vraie jouissance pour moi ; mais si j'avais trente boîtes, je serais peu sensible à la trente et unième. Nos goûts s'émoussent aisément par la satiété, et il faut rendre grâces à Dieu de nous avoir donné les privations nécessaires pour [*les*] conserver. C'est ce qui fait qu'un roi s'ennuie si souvent, et qu'il est impossible qu'il soit heureux, à moins qu'il n'ait reçu du ciel une âme assez grande pour être susceptible des plaisirs de son état, c'est-à-dire de celui de rendre un grand nombre d'hommes heureux ; mais alors cet état devient le premier de tous par le bonheur, comme il l'est par la puissance.

J'ai dit que plus notre bonheur dépend de nous, et plus il est assuré ; et cependant la passion, qui peut nous donner de plus grands plaisirs et nous rendre le plus heureux, met entièrement notre bonheur dans la dépendance des autres : on voit bien que je veux parler de l'amour.

Cette passion est peut-être la seule qui puisse nous faire désirer de vivre, et nous engager à remercier l'auteur de la nature, quel qu'il soit, de nous avoir donné l'existence. Mylord Rochester a bien raison de dire que les dieux ont mis cette goutte céleste dans le calice de la vie pour nous donner le courage de la supporter :

Il faut aimer, c'est ce qui nous soutient :
Car sans l'amour, il est triste d'être homme.

Si ce goût mutuel, qui est un sixième sens, et le plus fin, le plus délicat, le plus précieux de tous, se trouve rassembler deux âmes également sensibles au bonheur, au plaisir, tout est dit, on n'a plus rien à faire pour être heureux, tout le reste est indifférent ; il n'y a que la santé qui y soit nécessaire. Il faut employer toutes les facultés de son âme à jouir de ce bonheur ; il faut quitter la vie quand on le [*perd*], et être bien sûr que les années de Nestor ne sont rien au prix d'un quart d'heure d'une telle jouissance. Il est juste qu'un tel bonheur soit rare ; s'il était commun, il vaudrait bien mieux être homme que d'être dieu, du moins tel que nous pouvons nous le représenter. Ce qu'on peut faire de mieux est de se persuader que ce bonheur n'est pas impossible. Je ne sais cependant si l'amour a jamais rassemblé deux personnes faites à tel point l'une pour l'autre qu'elles ne connussent jamais la satiété de la jouissance, ni le refroidissement qu'entraîne la sécurité, ni l'indolence et la tiédeur qui naissent de la facilité et de la continuité d'un commerce dont l'illusion ne se détruit jamais (car où en entre-t-il plus que dans l'amour ?), et dont l'ardeur, enfin, fût égale dans la jouissance et dans la privation, et pût supporter également les malheurs et les plaisirs.

Un cœur capable d'un tel amour, une âme si tendre et si ferme paraît avoir épuisé le pouvoir de la divinité ; il en naît une en un siècle : il semble que d'en produire deux soit au-dessus de ses forces, ou que si elle les a produites, elle serait jalouse de leurs plaisirs, si elles se rencontraient ; mais l'amour peut nous rendre heureux à moins de frais : une âme tendre et sensible est heureuse par le seul plaisir qu'elle trouve à aimer ; je ne veux pas dire par là qu'on puisse être parfaitement heureux en aimant, quoiqu'on ne soit pas aimé ; mais je dis que, quoique nos idées de bonheur ne se trouvent pas entièrement remplies par l'amour de l'objet que nous aimons, le plaisir que nous sentons à nous livrer à toute notre tendresse peut suffire pour nous rendre heureux ; et si cette âme a encore le bonheur d'être susceptible d'illusion, il est impossible qu'elle ne se croie pas plus aimée qu'elle ne l'est peut-être en effet ; elle doit tant aimer qu'elle aime pour deux, et que la chaleur de son cœur supplée à ce qui manque réellement à son bonheur. Il faut sans doute qu'un caractère sensible, vif et emporté paie le tribut d'inconvénients attachés à ces qualités, et je ne sais si je dois dire bonnes ou mauvaises ; mais je crois que quiconque composerait son individu les y ferait entrer. Une première passion emporte tellement hors de soi une âme de cette trempe qu'elle est inaccessible à toute réflexion et à toute idée modérée ; elle peut sans doute se préparer de grands chagrins ; mais le plus grand inconvénient attaché à cette sensibilité emportée, c'est qu'il est impossible que quelqu'un qui aime à cet excès soit aimé, et qu'il n'y a presque point d'homme dont le goût ne diminue par la connaissance d'une telle passion. Cela doit sans doute paraître bien étrange à qui ne connaît pas encore assez le cœur humain ; mais pour peu qu'on ait réfléchi sur ce que nous offre l'expérience, on sentira que pour conserver longtemps le cœur de son amant, il faut toujours que l'espérance et la crainte agissent sur lui. Or une passion, telle que je viens de la peindre, produit un abandonnement de soi-même qui rend incapable de tout art ; l'amour perce de tous côtés ; on commence par vous adorer, cela est impossible autrement ; mais bientôt la certitude d'être aimé, et l'ennui d'être toujours prévenu, le malheur de n'avoir rien à craindre, émoussent les goûts. Voilà comme est fait le cœur humain, et qu'on ne croie pas que j'en parle par rancune : j'ai reçu de Dieu, il est vrai, une de ces âmes tendres et immuables qui ne savent ni déguiser ni modérer leurs passions, qui ne connaissent ni l'affaiblissement ni le dégoût, et dont la ténacité sait résister à tout, même à la certitude de n'être plus aimée ; mais j'ai été heureuse pendant dix ans par l'amour de celui qui avait subjugué mon âme ; et ces dix ans, je les ai passés tête à tête avec lui sans aucun moment de dégoût, ni de langueur. Quand l'âge, les maladies, peut-être aussi un peu la facilité de la jouissance ont diminué son goût, j'ai été longtemps sans m'en apercevoir ; j'aimais pour deux, je passais ma vie entière avec lui, et mon cœur, exempt de soupçon, jouissait du plaisir d'aimer et de l'illusion de se croire aimé. Il est vrai que j'ai perdu cet état si heureux, et que ce n'a pas été sans qu'il m'en ait coûté bien des larmes. Il faut de terribles secousses pour briser de telles chaînes : la plaie de mon cœur a saigné longtemps ; j'ai eu lieu de me plaindre, et j'ai tout pardonné. J'ai été assez juste pour sentir qu'il n'y avait peut-être au monde que mon cœur qui eût cette immutabilité qui anéantit le pouvoir des temps ; que si l'âge et les maladies n'avaient pas entièrement éteint les désirs, ils auraient peut-être encore été pour moi, et que l'amour me l'aurait ramené ; enfin, que son cœur, incapable d'amour, m'aimait de l'amitié la plus tendre, et m'aurait consacré sa vie. La certitude de l'impossibilité du retour de son goût et de sa passion, que je sais bien qui n'est pas dans la nature, a amené insensiblement mon cœur au sentiment paisible de l'amitié ; et ce sentiment, joint à la passion de l'étude, me rendait assez heureuse.

Mais un cœur aussi tendre peut-il être rempli par un sentiment aussi paisible et aussi faible que celui de l'amitié ? Je ne sais si on doit espérer, si on doit souhaiter même de tenir toujours à cette sensibilité dans l'espèce d'apathie à laquelle il est difficile de l'amener. On n'est heureux que par des sentiments vifs et agréables ; pourquoi donc s'interdire les plus vifs et les plus agréables de tous ? Mais ce qu'on a éprouvé, les réflexions qu'on a été obligé de faire pour amener son cœur à cette apathie, la peine même qu'on a eue de l'y réduire, doit faire craindre de quitter un état qui n'est pas malheureux pour essuyer des malheurs que l'âge et la perte de la beauté rendraient inutiles.

Belles réflexions, me dira-t-on, et bien utiles ! Vous verrez de quoi elles vous serviront, si vous avez jamais du goût pour quelqu'un qui devienne amoureux de vous ; mais je crois qu'on se trompe si l'on croit que ces réflexions soient inutiles. Les passions, au-delà de trente ans, ne nous emportent plus avec la même impétuosité. Croyez qu'on résisterait à son goût, si on le voulait bien fortement, et qu'on fût bien persuadé qu'il fera notre malheur. On n'y cède que parce qu'on n'est pas bien convaincu de la sûreté de ces maximes, et qu'on espère encore d'être heureux, et on a raison de se le persuader. Pourquoi s'interdire l'espérance d'être heureux, et de la manière la plus vive ? Mais s'il ne faut pas s'interdire cette espérance, il n'est pas permis de se tromper sur les moyens du bonheur ; l'expérience doit du moins nous apprendre à compter avec nous-mêmes, et à faire servir nos passions à notre bonheur. On peut prendre sur soi jusqu'à un certain point ; nous ne pouvons pas tout, sans doute, mais nous pouvons beaucoup ; et j'avance, sans crainte de me tromper, qu'il n'y a point de passion qu'on ne puisse surmonter, quand on s'est bien convaincu qu'elle ne peut servir qu'à notre malheur. Ce qui nous égare sur cela dans notre première jeunesse, c'est que nous sommes incapables de réflexions, que nous n'avons point d'expérience, et que nous nous figurons que nous rattraperons le bien que nous avons perdu, à force de courir après ; mais l'expérience et la connaissance du cœur humain nous apprennent que plus nous courons après, et plus il nous fuit. C'est une perspective trompeuse qui disparaît quand nous croyons l'atteindre. Le goût est une chose involontaire qui ne se persuade point, qui ne se ranime presque jamais. Quel est votre but quand vous cédez au goût que vous avez pour quelqu'un ? N'est-ce pas d'être heureux par le plaisir d'aimer et par celui de l'être ? Autant donc il serait ridicule de se refuser à ce plaisir par la crainte d'un malheur à venir que peut-être vous n'éprouverez qu'après avoir été fort heureux, et alors il y aurait compensation, et vous devez songer à vous guérir et non à vous repentir, autant une personne raisonnable aurait à rougir si elle ne tenait pas son bonheur dans sa main, et si elle le mettait entièrement dans celle d'un autre.

Le grand secret pour que l'amour ne nous rende pas malheureux, c'est de tâcher de n'avoir jamais tort avec votre amant, de ne lui jamais montrer d'empressement quand il se refroidit, et d'être toujours d'un degré plus froide que lui ; cela ne le ramènera pas, mais rien ne le ramènerait : il n'y a rien à faire qu'à oublier quelqu'un qui cesse de nous aimer. S'il vous aime encore, rien n'est capable de le réchauffer et de rendre à son amour sa première ardeur que la crainte de vous perdre et d'être moins aimé. Je sais que ce secret est difficile à pratiquer pour les âmes tendres et vraies ; mais elles ne peuvent trop cependant prendre sur elles pour le pratiquer, d'autant plus qu'il leur est bien plus nécessaire qu'à d'autres. Rien ne dégrade tant que les démarches qu'on fait pour regagner un cœur froid ou inconstant : cela nous avilit aux yeux de celui que nous cherchons à conserver, et à ceux des hommes qui pourraient penser à nous ; mais ce qui est bien pis, cela nous rend malheureux et nous tourmente inutilement. Il faut donc suivre cette maxime avec un courage inébranlable, et ne jamais céder sur cela à notre propre cœur ; il faut tâcher de connaître le caractère de la personne à qui on s'attache, avant de céder à son goût ; il faut que la raison soit reçue dans le conseil, non cette raison qui condamne toute espèce d'engagement comme contraire au bonheur, mais celle qui, en convenant qu'on ne peut être fort heureux sans aimer, veut qu'on n'aime que pour son bonheur, et qu'on surmonte un goût dans lequel on voit évidemment qu'on n'essuirait que des malheurs ; mais quand ce goût a été le plus fort, quand il l'a emporté sur la raison, comme cela n'arrive que trop, il ne faut point se piquer d'une constance qui serait aussi ridicule que déplacée. C'est bien le cas de pratiquer le proverbe, *les plus courtes folies sont les meilleures* ; ce sont surtout les plus courts malheurs : car il y a des folies qui rendraient fort heureux, si elles duraient toute la vie ; il ne faut point rougir de s'être trompé ; il faut se guérir, quoi qu'il en coûte, et surtout éviter la présence d'un objet qui ne peut que vous agiter, et vous faire perdre le fruit de vos réflexions : car chez les hommes la coquetterie survit à l'amour ; ils ne veulent perdre ni leur conquête ni leur victoire, et par mille coquetteries ils savent rallumer un feu mal éteint, et vous tenir dans un état d'incertitude aussi ridicule qu'insupportable. Il faut trancher dans le vif, il faut rompre sans retour ; il faut, dit M. de Richelieu, découdre l'amitié et déchirer l'amour ; enfin, c'est à la raison à faire notre bonheur : dans l'enfance, nos sens se chargent seuls de ce soin ; dans la jeunesse, le cœur et l'esprit commencent à s'en mêler avec cette subordination, que le cœur décide de tout ; mais dans l'âge mûr, la raison doit être de la partie, c'est à elle à nous faire sentir qu'il faut être heureux, quoi qu'il en coûte. Chaque âge a ses plaisirs qui lui sont propres ; ceux de la vieillesse sont les plus difficiles à obtenir ; le *jeu* et l'*étude*, si on en est encore capable, la *gourmandise*, la *considération*, voilà les ressorts de la vieillesse.

Tout cela n'est sans doute que des consolations. Heureusement qu'il ne tient qu'à nous d'avancer le terme de notre vie, s'il se fait trop attendre ; mais tant que nous nous résolvons à la supporter, il faut tâcher de faire pénétrer le plaisir par toutes les portes qui l'introduisent jusqu'à notre âme ; nous n'avons pas d'autres affaires.

Tâchons donc de nous bien porter, de n'avoir point de préjugés, d'avoir des passions, de les faire servir à notre bonheur, de remplacer nos passions par des goûts, de conserver précieusement nos illusions, d'être vertueux, de ne jamais nous repentir, d'éloigner de nous les idées tristes, et de ne jamais permettre à notre cœur de conserver une étincelle de goût pour quelqu'un dont le goût diminue et qui cesse de nous aimer. Il faut bien quitter l'amour un jour, pour peu qu'on vieillisse, et ce jour doit être celui où il cesse de nous rendre heureux. Enfin, songeons à cultiver le goût de l'étude, ce goût qui ne fait dépendre notre bonheur que de nous-mêmes. Préservons-nous de l'ambition, et surtout sachons bien ce que nous voulons être ; décidons-nous sur la route que nous voulons prendre pour passer notre vie, et tâchons de la semer de fleurs.

Table

Rivages poche/Petite Bibliothèque
Collection dirigée par Lidia Breda

DERNIÈRES PARUTIONS

Giorgio Agamben	*Le Feu et le Récit* (n° 904)
Épictète	*La Paix de l'âme* (n° 902)
I. de Loyola	*Exercices spirituels* (n° 818)
R.W. Emerson	*La Confiance en soi* (n° 301)
Florence Burgat	*Être le bien d'un autre* (n° 901)
Gandhi	*Du végétarisme* (n° 900)
H.D. Thoreau	*Les Forêts du Maine* (n° 771)
Plutarque	*Manger la chair ?* (n° 395)
Simone Weil	*Contre le colonialisme* (n° 898)
E. Coccia	*La Vie sensible* (n° 801)
Marc Bekoff	*Les Émotions des animaux* (n° 773)
E. Levinas	*Quelques réflexions sur la philosophie de l'hitlérisme* (n° 226)
Hannah Arendt	*Considérations morales* (n° 181)
Mme de Souza	*Adèle de Sénange* (n° 897)
Mme de Staël	*Dix années d'exil* (n° 744)
Mme de Lambert	*Avis d'une mère à sa fille* (n° 566)
Mme de Lambert	*De l'amitié* (n° 268)
Gustave Flaubert	*Lettres à Louise Colet* (n° 894)
Victor Hugo	*Lettres à la fiancée* (n° 893)
C.M. Schulz	*Peanuts* (n° 446)
C.M. Schulz	*Lucy psychiatre* (n° 369)
C.M. Schulz	*La vie est un rêve, Charlie Brown* (n° 368)
J. Jellezs - L. Meyer	*Spinoza vu par ses amis* (n° 891)
Gilberte Périer	*Vie de Monsieur Pascal* (n° 890)
Pascal	*L'Art de persuader* (n° 930)
Pline le Jeune	*L'Art d'écrire* (n° 888)

Virginia Woolf	*Elles* (n° 759)
A. Gramsci	*Pourquoi je hais l'indifférence* (n° 746)
Pétrarque	*Sur sa propre ignorance* (n° 755)
Ludwig Tieck	*Le Chat botté* (n° 754)
Edith Wharton	*Paysages italiens* (n° 753)
H. de Balzac	*Traité de la vie élégante* (n° 752)
Italo Svevo	*Court voyage sentimental* (n° 751)
S. Kierkegaard	*La Crise dans la vie d'une actrice* (n° 749)
Lola Montès	*L'Art de la beauté* (n° 748)
Marc Augé	*Pour une anthropologie de la mobilité* (n° 747)
James Joyce	*Lettres à Nora* (n° 741)
Clarice Lispector	*Le Seul Moyen de vivre* (n° 743)
Franz Kafka	*Cahiers in-octavo* (n° 742)
Mori Ôgai	*Chimères* (n° 739)
Walter Benjamin	*Critique et utopie* (n° 737)
Léon Tolstoï	*Lettres à sa femme* (n° 738)
Épictète	*Ce que promet la Philosophie* (n° 735)
Virginia Woolf	*Une pièce bien à soi* (n° 733)
A. Dufourmantelle	*En cas d'amour* (n° 732)
Charles Nodier	*Questions de littérature légale* (n° 731)
Carlo Ossola	*En pure perte* (n° 730)
Nikolaï Leskov	*Le Voyageur enchanté* (n° 728)
John Ruskin	*La Bible d'Amiens* (n° 725)
H. de Balzac	*Petites misères de la vie conjugale* (n° 724)
Jackie Pigeaud	*Melancholia* (n° 726)
William Temple	*Sur les jardins d'Épicure* (n° 720)
William Morris	*L'Art et l'Artisanat* (n° 719)
John Ruskin	*Sésame et les Lys* (n° 718)
Ippolita	*Le Côté obscur de Google* (n° 709)
Chantal Thomas	*L'Esprit de conversation* (n° 706)
G. Leopardi	*Chants* (n° 717)

Mise en pages
PCA – 44400 Rezé

Imprimé à Barcelone par:
BLACK PRINT
en juillet 2023

Imprimé en Espagne

The
Court Guide
2006/2007

The
Court Guide
2006/2007

Andrew Goodman
LLB MBA FCI Arb FLnst CPD
of the Inner Temple, Barrister
Professor of Conflict Management
and Dispute Resolution Studies,
Rushmore University

OXFORD
UNIVERSITY PRESS

OXFORD
UNIVERSITY PRESS

Great Clarendon Street, Oxford OX2 6DP

Oxford University Press is a department of the University of Oxford.
It furthers the University's objective of excellence in research, scholarship,
and education by publishing worldwide in

Oxford New York

Auckland Bangkok Buenos Aires Cape Town Chennai
Dar es Salaam Delhi Hong Kong Istanbul Karachi Kolkata
Kuala Lumpur Madrid Melbourne Mexico City Mumbai Nairobi
São Paulo Shanghai Taipei Tokyo Toronto

Oxford is a registered trade mark of Oxford University Press
in the UK and in certain other countries

Published in the United States
by Oxford University Press Inc., New York

British Library Cataloguing in Publication Data

Data available

Library of Congress Cataloging in Publication Data

Data available

Typeset by SPI Publisher Services, Pondicherry, India
Printed in Great Britain
on acid-free paper by
CPI Bath

ISBN 0-19-929749-5   978-0-19-929749-8
1 3 5 7 9 10 8 6 4 2

Introduction

Like its predecessors, this little book is intended to be a brief reference guide to the location of and facilities at the various courts and tribunals situated in the South Eastern and Western Circuit areas. It is designed to aid those who regularly attend court, including counsel, solicitors, clerks, pupils, students, and members of the media. It is particularly hoped to assist the first-time visitor to a particular court or tribunal in knowing how to find the venue and what he or she may expect of the facilities on arrival. Such facilities, and indeed the venues themselves, do change from time to time and it is wise to check the information prior to departure. However, the contents of this volume have benefited from the direct assistance of H.M. Courts Service and their employees, and may be taken as accurate as at 1 January 2006.

This edition contains Coroner's, Crown, County, Family Proceedings, Magistrates', and Youth courts, and major tribunal centres, set out alphabetically and separately for each Circuit by geographical location. An alphabetical index set out by jurisdiction is available for cross-referencing entries that the reader may not find merely by flicking through the book.

Facilities

This book is only as useful as the accuracy of its contents. Venues do occasionally change with very little notice: in 2000 Uxbridge County Court moved out to a location beyond Hayes that required an initiative test to find, and so quickly that one wondered whether the LCD had paid the rent on the old place, or if they could afford a new one within three miles of a station. Walking directions given are often affected by large-scale redevelopments in town centres, such as in Kingston and Slough. Readers are therefore positively exhorted to write or e-mail changes and constructive suggestions.

Travel

I have endeavoured to provide for each venue the optimum means of travel by rail, car, tube, and bus where appropriate. Underlined bus numbers indicate that a route actually passes the court building. The times given for rail journeys are taken from timetables, but obviously an allowance should be built into journey times for the wrong kind of leaves on the track, failing service providers, and industrial inaction.

There are still courts that appear to sit biannually in virtually open countryside (not for much longer if the DCA has its way), and it is possible to suffer a three-hour train journey only to have to take a taxi for another twenty miles. If that is the case advocates who cannot get a lift back with the judge should book their return cab trips in advance.

Deregulation of bus services has made it impossible to describe adequately the number and variety of bus routes serving the south and west of England. Apart from inner city areas the safest advice is not to travel to court by bus! If that is the only means available readers are asked to check the timetable with the respective bus company in advance of travel.

The walking routes given are not necessarily the quickest or most direct. They are the easiest to describe. There are also other considerations; for example, I do not recommend short cuts via alleyways or snickets which may feel unsafe, particularly for female advocates walking alone. Thus I accept that my directions to the courts, for example at Guildford from the station, are not the preferred route for many people.

Parking facilities offered are varied. Unless there is a domestic court car park the likelihood of free parking outside major urban areas is a thing of the past.

Local eating-out facilities
This is not an Egon Ronay guide to eating in and about the courts. Those readers who complained to me about the prevalence of McDonald's and Burger King clearly thought it was. The intention is merely to provide a convenient venue within a reasonable distance of the court to get refreshment in the time available. Those who know some local courts well will realize that it is often impossible to make recommendations where decent luncheon facilities do not exist, or those that do require a car journey. The short adjournment is just that—short! Readers who know of convenient places are encouraged to write.

This edition
I wish to express my gratitude to Oxford University Press who have decided to continue publishing *The Court Guide*, having taken over the Blackstone list. As a venture it has now reached its twenty-sixth year, and much of the credit for that goes to Heather Saward and Alistair MacQueen who helped to institutionalize it. I want also to thank Barbara Mensah who helped compile the original Western Circuit addition in 1995 together with my band of original researchers. This edition could not have been completed without the invaluable assistance of James Carter, my editor, and Annabel Moss, the editorial assistant at Oxford University Press.

A.G.

1 Chancery Lane
January 2006
agoodman@1chancerylane.com

Note on Future Planning

I am indebted to H.M. Courts Service, newly amalgamated to take in Magistrates' Courts, for its kind assistance in facilitating changes to this edition, together with the respective circuit administrators' offices, and a number of court group administrators. The centralizing of court administration has become a significant feature of change over the past few years. As this process continues, visitors to courts outside urban areas are likely to find that questions concerning listing arrangements may only be answered from offices at a considerable distance from the courthouse, and information about the courts may be less forthcoming from clerks who have never been there. Those ringing will also have to allow for the cost and inconvenience of going through digital answering systems.

During the lifetime of the 2004/2005 edition there were fewer court closures, notably Gillingham, Newquay, and Tavistock Magistrates' Courts, and, in view of the recent changes to licensing laws, the few courts dedicated to licensing sessions. The emphasis has been more on consolidation of building stock rather than on closure. The West London County Court has moved from its original home and now sits at the Magistrates' Court building on Talgarth Road.

A number of courts have moved to new premises: Cheltenham County Court and Thanet (Margate) County Court; and Southampton Magistrates' Court. In central London HM Lands Tribunal, the Transport Tribunal, and London Central Employment Tribunals have all left long-established locations; and the Exeter Employment Tribunals are to be found at a new venue.

Banbury courthouse has re-opened after a period of refurbishment.

There are new premises for Cambridge, Exeter, and Ipswich Crown Courts, and Cambridge County Court.

Abbreviations

Ar	Arriva
AV	Alder Valley
Ct.	Court
Cty	County
DCA	Department for Constitutional Affairs
DLR	Docklands Light Railway
EC	Eastern Counties
EK	East Kent
EN	Eastern National
F	Family
GL	Green Line
LC	London Country
LCD	Lord Chancellor's Department
LRT	London Regional Transport*
M&D	Maidstone and District
Mags	Magistrates'
NR	National Rail (including franchised services)
SD	Southdown
s/p	signpost/s, signposted
UC	United Counties
Und.	London Regional Transport Underground
Y	Youth

*To include franchised operators running bus services for Transport for London using the same route numbers.

To His Honour E. F. Monier-Williams in gratitude

Acknowledgements

Oxford University Press would like to thank Transport for London for permission to reproduce the map on pages 155–6. Every attempt has been made to obtain permission from the copyright holders of the map on pages 158–9.

The
South Eastern
Circuit

ACTON MAGISTRATES' COURT,
ACTON YOUTH COURT (Tues. 10.00 a.m.),
ACTON FAMILY PROCEEDINGS COURT (Fri. 10.00 a.m.)
Winchester St. Acton, London W3 8PB.
Telephone: (020) 8992 9014. Fax: (020) 8993 9647.
DX: 5166 Ealing.
Court times: Doors open 9.00 a.m. Court sits 10.00 a.m. Office
hours 9.00 a.m.–4.30 p.m.
Facilities: Advocates' room. Interview room. Drinks machine. Waiting room.
Travel: NR Acton Central (North London Line) plus 10 min. walk.
Und. Ealing Common (Embankment 28 min., Piccadilly 22 min.)
plus 207. Acton Town (Embankment 26 min., Piccadilly 20 min.)
plus 15 min. walk or E3 bus.
LRT 70, 207, 266, 607, E3.
From Acton Central turn left into Birkbeck Rd. and right into High St.
Winchester St. 3rd left. Court 150 yds on left.
From Acton Town turn right and bear 2nd right, Avenue Rd.
Continue along Avenue Rd. 800 yds. Court on corner of junction
with Winchester St.
Driving: Court situated off A4020 behind Acton Town Hall.
Parking: Limited parking in side-streets to rear. Public car park.
Eating out:

The Windmill	bar food	High St.
McDonald's	restaurant	High St.
Coffee Pot (Thai)	cafe	High St.
Acton Grill	cafe	High St.
Kings Head	bar food	High St.

AMERSHAM (CENTRAL BUCKINGHAMSHIRE)
  MAGISTRATES' COURT,
AMERSHAM YOUTH COURT
The Law Courts, King George V Rd., Amersham, Bucks. HP6 5AR.
All correspondence to be sent to The Magistrates' Court, Walton St.,
Aylesbury, Bucks. HP21 7QZ.
The business of Amersham County Court has been transferred to
High Wycombe County Court.
Telephone: Gen. enquiries: 01296 554350. Accounts: 0870
2412819. Fax: 01296 554320.
Court times: Doors open 9.30 a.m. Courts sit: Y. 10.00 a.m. fortnightly Tues.; Mags 10.00 a.m. each Weds. and Thurs., F. 2.00 p.m.
two Tues. a month.
Facilities: Advocates' room. Refreshments.
Travel: NR Amersham (Marylebone 38 min.) plus 5 min. walk.
Und. Amersham (Baker St. 40 min.).
From station turn right. 150 yds King George V Rd. 1st right. Court
25 yds on left.

AMERSHAM (CENTRAL BUCKINGHAMSHIRE) MAGISTRATES' COURT—CONTINUED

Driving: A40 to Denham roundabout then A413 to Amersham. Follow signs to station, then as for walking.

Parking: Multi-storey car park opposite court.

Eating out:

The Iron Horse	bar food	facing station
Tucker's Fish Bar	restaurant	Hill Ave.
Mans Chinese Restaurant		Sycamore Rd.

APPEALS SERVICE

(Formerly the Independent Tribunal Service.)
5th Floor, Fox Court, 14 Gray's Inn Road, London WC1X 8HN.
Telephone: (020) 7712 2600. Fax: (020) 7712 2650.

ASHFORD COUNTY COURT

The Court House, Tufton St., Ashford, Kent TN23 1QQ.
Telephone: 01233 632464. Fax: 01233 612786.
DX: 98060 Ashford (Kent) 3.

ASHFORD (CHANNEL) MAGISTRATES' COURT

The Court House, Tufton St., Ashford, Kent TN23 1QS.
Telephone: 01233 653103. Fax: 01233 611314.
Court times: Doors open 9.30 a.m. Courts sit 10.00 a.m. Office hours 10.00 a.m.–4.00 p.m.
Facilities: Advocates' room. Interview room. Vending machine.

ASHFORD EMPLOYMENT TRIBUNALS

1st Floor, Ashford House, Court Sq. Shopping Centre, Ashford, Kent TN23 1YB.
Telephone: 01233 621346. Fax: 01233 624423.
Travel: NR Ashford International (Charing Cross 1 hr. 22 min., Victoria 1 hr. 38 min.) plus 10 min. walk.

Exit station turn left past car park. Follow road to roundabout on right-hand side and take footpath into Elwick Rd. and 1st right into Church Rd. Turn left at Tufton St. and continue to County Sq. straight ahead. Ashford House on left just inside entrance to County Sq.
Cty Mags/Y: Take 1st left after Tannery Lane into Vicarage Lane. Court approx. 200 yds.

Driving: A20–M20–A20 to Ashford town centre. Proceed on inner one-way system to NCP car park on right below County Sq. shopping centre.

Parking: NCP below County Sq. shopping centre and elsewhere as indicated by road signs.

Eating out: A variety of restaurants and sandwich shops in town centre.

ASYLUM AND IMMIGRATION TRIBUNAL (Hearing Centre)

Field House, 15 Breams Buildings, London EC4A 1DZ.
Telephone: 0845 600 0877. Minicom (text phone): 0845 66 0766.
Fax: (020) 7073 4090.
Admin. from Asylum and Immigration Tribunal, PO Box 6987, Leicester LE1 6ZX. Fax: 0116 249 4130.

THE PATENTS COUNTY COURT

Field House, 15—25 Breams Buildings, London EC4A 1DZ.
Telephone: Clerk to the Patents Judge: (020) 7073 4251. Fax: (020) 7073 4253.
Court times: Doors open 8.30 a.m. Office hours: Tribunal 8.30 a.m.–5.00 p.m.; Patents Court 9.30 a.m.–4.30 p.m. Court Sits: Tribunal 9.00 a.m.–5.00 p.m.; Patents Court 10.00 a.m.
Facilities: Robing and conference rooms. Waiting areas. Disabled access and loop system. Snacks and hot and cold drinks vending machines.
Travel: Und: Holborn, Chancery Lane, Temple, Faringdon + 10 mins walk. Court situated in Breams Buildings which runs between Chancery Lane and Fetter Lane.
LRT: 4, 11, 25, 45, 501, 521, 341 to Chancery Lane.
Driving: Not recommended; Court is in congestion zone and no easy nearby parking.
Eating Out: Many restaurants, coffee shops and sandwich bars in Chancery Lane, Holborn, and Fetter Lane.

AYLESBURY COUNTY COURT

2nd Floor, Heron House, 49 Buckingham St., Aylesbury, Bucks. HP20 2NQ. (District Judge's appointments also held here.)
Telephone: 01296 393498. Fax: 01296 397363.
DX: 97820 Aylesbury 3.
Court times: Doors open 9.30 a.m. Court sits 10.00 a.m. Office hours 10.00 a.m.–4.00 p.m.
Travel: NR Aylesbury (Marylebone 1 hr.–1 hr. 30 min.) plus 20 min. walk. From station turn right. Cross at roundabout into High St., cross diagonally across Market Sq. leaving by top right. Take the 2nd on left (Buckingham St.). County Ct. is approx. 200 yds on right.
Parking: Coopers Yard next to Heron House.
Eating out: See Aylesbury Magistrates' Court.

AYLESBURY CROWN COURT

County Hall, Market Sq., Aylesbury, Bucks. HP20 1XD.
Telephone: 01296 434401. Fax: 01296 435665.
DX: 97400 Aylesbury 2.
Court times: Doors open 9.00 a.m. Court sits 10.00 a.m. Office hours 10.00 a.m.–4.00 p.m.

AYLESBURY CROWN COURT—
CONTINUED

Facilities: Advocates' room. Interview room. No on-premises catering. Public toilets. Public telephones.

Travel: NR Aylesbury (Marylebone 1 hr.–1 hr. 30 min.) plus 5 min. walk. From station follow Friar Sq. shopping centre sign— cross inner ring road over footbridge into shopping centre. Walk through, turning right down 'mall', exit into Market Sq. then turn right. Crown Ct. approx. 100 yds on, in old County Hall.

Driving: A41 to Aylesbury. Proceed from inner ring road into town centre. Court in Market Sq.

Parking: Multi-storey at Civic Centre in Exchange St. Exit opposite end to entrance. Turn left, walk 100 yds into Market Sq., Crown Ct. on left.

Eating out: See Aylesbury Magistrates' Court.

AYLESBURY (CENTRAL BUCKINGHAMSHIRE) MAGISTRATES' COURT,
AYLESBURY FAMILY PROCEEDINGS COURT (Wed.),
AYLESBURY YOUTH COURT (Fri.)

The Magistrates' Court, Walton St., Aylesbury, Bucks. HP21 7QZ.

Telephone: Gen. enquiries: 01296 554350. Fax: 01296 554320. Accounts: 0870 2412819.

Court times: Doors open 8.45 a.m. Court sits 10.00 a.m. Office hours 9.00 a.m.–5.00 p.m. (4.30 Fri.).

Facilities: Advocates' room. Interview room. WRVS coffee.

Travel: NR Aylesbury (Marylebone 1 hr.–1 hr. 30 min.) plus 10 min. walk. From station turn right. At 2nd roundabout turn right into Walton St. Court half mile on right.

Driving: A41 to Aylesbury. Proceed from inner ring road into town centre. Turn left at roundabout in town centre. Court half mile on right in Walton St.

Parking: Public car park.

Eating out:

The Aristocrat	bar food	Walton St.
Bricklayers Arms	bar food	Walton St.
The Bell	bar food	Market Sq.

BALHAM YOUTH COURT,
LAMBETH YOUTH COURT (Wed., Fri.),
WANDSWORTH YOUTH COURT (Tues.)

217 Balham High Rd., London SW17 7BS. All correspondence to be sent to 176A Lavender Hill, London SW11 1JU. (These courts are the responsibility of South Western Magistrates' Court.)

Telephone: (020) 7805 1452. Fax: (020) 8271 2241. South Western Mags Ct: (020) 7228 9201. Fax: (020) 7805 1448.

DX: 58559 Clapham Junction.

BALHAM YOUTH COURT—
CONTINUED

Court times: Doors open 9.15 a.m. Court sits 10.00 a.m. Office hours 8.30 a.m.–4.30 p.m. Payments: 9.30 a.m.–3.30 p.m.

Facilities: Advocates' room. Interview rooms. Drinks machine. Witness service. Video link. Video and tape playing equipment.

Travel: NR Balham and Upper Tooting (Victoria 12 min.) plus 5 min. walk.

Und. Balham (Embankment 15 min., Bank 19 min.) or Tooting Bec plus 10 min. walk.

LRT 88, 131, 155.

From station turn south into High Rd. and proceed under bridge. Court 600 yds on left.

Driving: Court situated on A24 (Balham High Rd.).

Parking: Parking meters. Side-streets opposite.

Eating out:

Ferrari's	Italian restaurant	Balham High Rd.
Paphos	Greek restaurant	Balham High Rd.
Chris's	cafe	Balham High Rd.
McDonald's	restaurant	Balham High Rd. (North)

Tesco Express next door to the court for sandwiches.

BANBURY COUNTY COURT

The Court House, Warwick Rd., Banbury, Oxon. OX16 2AW.
Telephone: 01295 265799. Fax: 01295 277025.
DX: 701967 Banbury 2.
Court times: 10.00 a.m.–4.00 p.m.
Facilities: Private interview room.

BANBURY (NORTHERN OXFORDSHIRE)
MAGISTRATES' COURT,
NORTHERN OXFORDSHIRE YOUTH COURT
(BANBURY)

The Court House, Warwick Rd., Banbury, Oxon. OX16 2AW.
Telephone: 01295 452000. Fax: 01295 452050.
DX: 701968 Banbury 2.
Court times: Doors open 8.45 a.m. Court sits 10.00 a.m.
Facilities: Advocates' room. CPS room. Duty solicitor's room. Two interview rooms.
Travel: NR Banbury (Paddington 1 hr. 40 min.; Marylebone 1 hr. 7 min.) plus 10 min. walk. For Mgs and Cty Cts.: From station (London-bound exit) turn left and left over railway. Cross over into Bridge St. and take diagonal exit across Market Place. Parsons St. is first right. Continue to the end of Parsons St., turn right into South Bar St. and left at lights into Warwick Rd. Court 50 yds on right.

Driving: From the south—A4260 Oxford Rd., into Banbury. From the north—M40 Junc. 11 s/p Banbury town centre.

Parking: No parking at the court. Nearest public car park is the multi-storey in Castle St. (2 min. drive away).

Eating out: Several sandwich shops on Parsons St.

BARKING MAGISTRATES' COURT,
BARKING YOUTH COURT (Mon., Thurs. 10.00 a.m.)

East St., Barking, Essex IG11 8EW.

Telephone: (020) 8594 5311. Fax: (020) 8594 4297.

DX: 8518 Barking 1.

Court times: Doors open 9.00 a.m. Court sits 10.00 a.m. Office hours 8.30 a.m.–4.30 p.m.

Facilities: Advocates' room. Two interview rooms. Witness room. No on-premises catering.

Travel: NR, Und. Barking (Fenchurch St. 13 min., Embankment 32 min.).

LRT 5, 62, 87, 162, 179, 238, 287.

From station turn right. Court 500 yds on left.

Driving: Court situated near junction of A123 and A124.

Parking: Large pay and display car park St. Ann's Rd. (to rear of Town Hall). **NB** No access from East St. to car park: one-way system s/p Town Hall parking. Multi-storey on London Rd.

Eating out:

McDonald's	restaurant	East St.
The Brewery Tap	bar food	London Rd.
Percy Ingle	bakery	East St.

BARNET COUNTY COURT

St. Mary's Court, Regents Park Rd., Finchley Central, London N3 1BQ.

Telephone: (020) 8343 4272. Fax: (020) 8343 1324. Bailiff's direct line: (020) 8343 3955. Family Direct: (020) 8371 7111.

DX: 122570 Finchley Church End.

Court times: Doors open 9.30 a.m. Office hours 10.00 a.m.–4.00 p.m. Bailiff's office open 8.30 a.m.–10.00 a.m. Court sits 10.00 a.m.–4.00 p.m. Urgent business 9.30 a.m.–4.00 p.m.

Facilities: Robing room. Consultation rooms. Children's room.

Travel: Und. Northern line to Finchley Central (Euston or King's Cross 30 min.) plus 5 min. walk. Turn up hill out of station then left along main road (signposted). Court on right-hand side at junction of Regents Park Rd. and Hendon Lane.

LRT 82, 125, 143, 260, 326.

Driving: Court car park in Victoria Ave., off Hendon Lane.

BARNET COUNTY COURT—
CONTINUED
Parking: for 40 cars only. Car park open from 9.15 a.m.

Eating out:

Catcher in the Rye	bar food	Finchley High Rd.
Taylors	wine bar	Finchley High Rd.
D.B.'s	sandwiches	Finchley High Rd.

BARNET MAGISTRATES' COURT,
BARNET YOUTH COURT (Fri. 10.00 a.m.)
The Court House, 7C High St., Barnet, Herts. EN5 5UE.

Telephone: (020) 8441 9042. Fax: (020) 8441 6753. Premier: (020) 8449 9941.

DX: 8626 Barnet.

Court times: Doors open 9.30 a.m. Court sits 10.00 a.m. Office hours 9.30 a.m.–4.00 p.m. Tues. 8.30 a.m.–4.00 p.m.: Thurs. 9.30 a.m.–5.00 p.m..

Facilities: Interview room. Hot drinks machine.

Travel: Und. High Barnet (Embankment 36 min.).

LRT 26, 34, 84A, 107, 234, 263.

Ar 84, 307.

Turn right out of station up hill. Court 300 yds on left.

Driving: Court on A1000 above Barnet Hill.

Parking: Public car park Fitzjohn Ave. (first left past court). Side-streets (Bedford Ave. a.m. only).

Eating out:

Old Mitre	bar food	Barnet Hill
McDonald's	restaurant	High St. Barnet

BASILDON COUNTY COURT,
BASILDON CROWN COURT
The Gore, Basildon, Essex SS14 2EU.

Telephone: 01268 458000. Fax: 01268 458100.

DX: 97633 Basildon 5.

Court times: Doors open 9.00 a.m. Courts sit 10.30 a.m. Office hours 10.00 a.m.–4.00 p.m.

Facilities: Advocates' robing room and dining room. Consultation rooms. Public dining room. Children's room. Witness service.

BASILDON MAGISTRATES' COURT,
The Court House, Great Oaks, Basildon, Essex SS14 1EH.

Admin: Osprey House, Hedgerows Business Park, Colchester Rd., Springfield, Chelmsford, Essex CM2 5PF.

Court times: Doors open 9.00 a.m. Court sits 10.00 a.m.

Facilities: Advocates' room. Interview rooms. Coffee bar.

Travel: NR Basildon (Fenchurch St. 35 min.) plus 5 min. walk.

For Magistrates' Court: from station cross over main road, Southern Hay, and proceed into pedestrianized shopping precinct. Cross Town Sq. into East Sq. and emerge onto Great Oaks. Court diagonally opposite on left next to police station. Continue for Crown and County Cts. across Broadmayne (A1321) into The Gore.

Driving: For Mgs Ct.: from A127 Southend Rd. take exit A176 into Basildon along Upper Mayne. At 2nd roundabout, Round Acre, take 2nd exit Town Gate and 1st left Pagel Mead. Park in car park. Follow road around to right, court 250 yds on left. For Crown and Cty Cts., from car park cross the main road Broadmayne by roundabout, turn right along Broadmayne and left into The Gore.

Parking: Car parks for shopping centre at Pagel Mead and Great Oaks.

Eating out: At Great Oaks and Town Square.

BEDFORD AND MID-BEDFORDSHIRE MAGISTRATES' COURT,
BEDFORD YOUTH COURT

The Shire Hall, St. Paul's Sq., Bedford, Beds. MK40 ISQ.
Telephone: Mags: 01234 319100. Fax: 01234 319114.
DX: 729420 Bedford 10.
Court times: Doors open 9.00 a.m. Court sits 10.00 a.m. Office hours 10.00 a.m.–4.00 p.m.
Facilities: Advocates' room. Interview rooms. Refreshments (until 1.00 p.m.). Children's area. Mother and baby room. Disabled toilets. Witness waiting area. Witness Service.
Travel: NR Bedford (Thameslink 39–55 min.) plus 25 min. walk. Recommend taking a taxi.
Driving: M1 to Junc. 13 then A5140 into town. Shire Hall immediately on left over bridge across river. Cty Ct. on A428 eastbound one-way system via Kimbolton Rd.
Parking: Cty Ct.: public car park on one-way system in Kimbolton Rd. No parking at the Mags Ct.

BEDFORD COUNTY COURT

May House, 29 Goldington Rd., Bedford, Beds. MK40 3NN.
Telephone: 01234 760400 Fax: 01234 327431. Bailiff: 01234 760402.
DX: 97590 Bedford 3.
Court times: Doors open 9.00 a.m. Court sits 10.00 a.m. Office hours 9.30 a.m.–4.00 p.m.
Facilities: Robing room. Interview rooms. Drinks machine. No smoking in building.

BEDFORD AND MID-BEDFORDSHIRE MAGISTRATES' COURT—CONTINUED

BEDFORD EMPLOYMENT TRIBUNALS SERVICE

8–10 Howard St., Bedford, Beds. MK40 3HS.

Telephone: 01234 351306. Fax: 01234 352315.

Court times: 10.00 a.m.–5.00 p.m.

Facilities: Waiting rooms.

Travel: Call for map.

NR Midland mainline from St. Pancras to Bedford fast train—35 min. 7 min. walk to Tribunal.

Parking: Large multi-storey pay and display opposite.

Eating out: Many pubs and cafes within short walking distance.

BELMARSH MAGISTRATES' COURT (Admin. from

Greenwich Mags Ct. Tel: (020) 8276 1341. Fax: (020) 8276 1398. 4 Belmarsh Rd., Western Way, Thamesmead, London SE28 0EY.)

Telephone: (020) 8271 9099. Fax: (020) 8221 9097.

DX: 35203 Greenwich West.

Court times: Doors open 9.30 a.m. Court sits 10.30 a.m. Office hours 9.30 a.m.–4.15 p.m.

Facilities: Robing rooms. Conference rooms. Vending machine. Disabled access.

Travel: NR Woolwich Arsenal (Charing Cross 28 min., London Bridge 19 min.) plus taxi or bus.

LRT 244.

Driving: Take A206 s/p Woolwich Royal Arsenal East past Waterfront Centre into Woolwich High St. At mini-roundabout 2nd exit into Beresford St. which becomes Plumstead Rd. Bear left at 2nd traffic lights s/p Royal Arsenal East into Pettman Crescent. Follow road around to right and bear left into Western Way s/p Belmarsh. At lights move into left-hand filter lane then cross lights s/p Belmarsh and court. Keep in left-hand lane and cross dual carriageway at lights going straight ahead into approach road for Belmarsh Prison and court. Turn right into car park.

Parking: Domestic car park.

Eating out: None.

BEXLEY MAGISTRATES' COURT,
BEXLEY FAMILY COURT,
BEXLEY YOUTH COURT (Wed. 9.30 a.m.)

Norwich Place, Bexleyheath, Kent DA6 7NB.

Telephone: (020) 8304 5211. Fax: (020) 8303 6849.

DX: 100150 Bexleyheath 3.

Court times: Doors open 8.30 a.m. Court sits 10.00 a.m. (**NB** 9.30 a.m. some pleas and directions.)

Facilities: Advocates' room. Interview room. Disabled facilities. Crèche facilities.

BEXLEY MAGISTRATES' COURT—
  CONTINUED
Travel: NR Bexleyheath or Barnhurst (Cannon St. 33 min. London Bridge 29 min.) plus B11, B12, B15.
LRT 89, 96, 132, 229, 269, 422.
Ar 401, 422, 469.
GL 726.
Bus 422 to Bexleyheath Broadway shopping centre. Turn right by Marks & Spencer. Court 50 yds on left.
Driving: Bexleyheath Broadway is on A207 from London via continuation from Shooters Hill, or s/p from Black Prince interchange on A2.
Parking: Car park on top of Broadway shopping centre. Access from rear.
Eating out: Good selection of pubs and restaurants within easy walking distance.

BICESTER (NORTHERN OXFORDSHIRE) MAGISTRATES' COURT

Waverley House, Queen's Ave., Bicester, Oxon. OX26 8NZ.
Telephone: 01295 452000. Fax: 01295 452050.
DX: 710968 Banbury 2.
Court times: Adult court sits 10.00 a.m. Tues. and Fri. Y: 10.00 a.m. 4th Wed. of month. Office hours 8.15 a.m.–4.30 p.m. (4.00 p.m. on Fri.).
Facilities: Vending machine. Three interview rooms.
Travel: NR Bicester Town (Oxford 25 min.) plus 10 min. walk. Bicester North (London Marylebone 1 hr. 5 min.) plus 5 min. walk. From North Station turn left into Buckingham Rd. and proceed to roundabout, 3rd exit Field St. becomes Queen's Ave. Court 250 yds on right in building by Fire Station. From Town Station turn left out of station approach into London Road. Bear left at Market Sq. into Causeway. Follow into Church St. and King's End. Turn right at T-junction into Queen's Ave. Court 200 yds on left.
Driving: M40, Juncs. 9 and 10. From either station follow walking directions.
Parking: Limited car parking at court. Car park in town centre (5 min. walk).
Eating out: Town centre within 5 min. walking distance.

BLACKFRIARS CROWN COURT (Formerly Knightsbridge Crown Court sitting at Borough.)

Pocock St., London SE1 0BJ.
Telephone: (020) 7922 5800. Fax: (020) 7922 5815.
DX: 400800 Lambeth 3.
Court times: Doors open 9.00 a.m. Court sits approx. 10.30 a.m.
Facilities: Robing room. Interview rooms. Barristers' lounge. Public cafeteria. Drinks vending machine. Disabled facilities.

BLACKFRIARS CROWN COURT—
CONTINUED

Travel: Und. Borough plus 5 min. walk, Southwark plus 5 min. walk.

NR Waterloo or Waterloo East plus 10 min. walk.

LRT 45, 63, 344, 100.

From Borough Station turn right along Borough. Turn right into Lant St. Cross Southwark Bridge Rd. to Sawyer St. and turn left into Pocock St. Court on right. From Southwark Station cross Blackfriars Rd. and turn right. Pocock St. is 2nd left. Court 100 yds on right.

From Waterloo Station turn right along Waterloo Rd. Turn left into The Cut. At the end cross Blackfriars Rd. to Union St. Proceed along Union St. and turn right into Gt. Suffolk St. Pocock St. is 3rd turning on left. Twenty-five min. walk to Inns of Court.

Driving: Use of public transport is advised due to lack of car parking facilities. Court is 25 min. walk from Inns of Court.

Parking: No car parking facilities, save for disabled drivers.

BOW COUNTY COURT

96 Romford Rd., Stratford, London E15 4EG.

Telephone: (020) 8536 5200. Fax: (020) 8503 1152.

DX: 97490 Stratford 2.

Court times: Doors open 9.00 a.m. Court sits 10.00 a.m. Office hours 10.00 a.m.–4.00 p.m.

Facilities: Robing room. Interview room. Drinks machine.

Travel: NR Stratford (Liverpool St. 8 min., Camden Rd. 19 min.).

Und. Stratford (Liverpool St. 10 min., Oxford Circus 21 min.) plus 20 min. walk.

LRT 25, 86.

From station cross into and through shopping centre. Cross High Rd., turn left to Romford Rd. Court half mile up on right.

Driving: Court situated on A118 Romford Rd. 200 yds beyond junction with B164 Vicarage Lane.

Parking: Limited, side-streets with parking restrictions.

Eating out:

Eastern Curry House	Indian restaurant	Romford Rd.
Sun Ho	Chinese restaurant	Romford Rd.
City Cafe	cafe	Romford Rd.

(See also local eating for Stratford Magistrates' Court.)

BOW ST. MAGISTRATES' COURT

28 Bow St., London WC2E 7AS.

Telephone: (020) 7853 9217. Fax: (020) 7853 9292.

DX: 40041 Covent Garden 2.

Court times: Doors open 9.30 a.m. Court sits 10.00/10.30 a.m. Office hours 8.30 a.m.–4.30 p.m.

BOW ST. MAGISTRATES' COURT—
CONTINUED

Facilities: Cold drinks machine available. Access for disabled to ground floor Court One only. Lift to upper floors if required. Two consultation rooms.

Travel: Und. Covent Garden.

LRT 6, 9, 11, 13, 77, 170, 176, 188, 501, 513.

10 min. walk Inns of Court.

Turn right out of station right along Long Acre. Bow St. 2nd right. Court 150 yds on left.

Parking: Limited meter parking. NCP car park.

Eating out:

Simeonis	Italian restaurant	Drury Lane
The Globe	bar food	Bow St.
Marquess of Anglesey	bar food	Bow St.
Brasserie du Jardin	restaurant	Tavistock St.
Sofra	restaurant	Tavistock St.

BRACKNELL (EAST BERKSHIRE) MAGISTRATES' COURT

Court House, Town Square, Bracknell, Berks. RG12 1AE.

Telephone: 0870 241 2820. Fax: 01753 232190.

Court times: Doors open 9.00 a.m. Court sits 10.00 a.m. Office hours 8.30 a.m.–4.45 p.m. (Fri. 4.15 p.m.).

Facilities: Advocates' room. Interview room. Vending machine.

Travel: NR Bracknell (Waterloo 52–6 min.) plus 15 min. walk.

AV X29, X6.

From station take footpath s/p town centre to Charles Sq. Proceed along Crossway. At the Broadway turn right. Court in Town Sq.

Driving: M4 Junc. 10 s/p Bracknell then A329 (M) into town to Town Sq.

Parking: Multi-storey car park for shopping centre.

Eating out:

Bentall's	restaurant	High St.
The Oven Door	restaurant	High St.
McDonald's	restaurant	High St.
Anna's Pantry	restaurant	High St.

BRENT MAGISTRATES' COURT,
BRENT YOUTH COURT

Church Rd., 448 High Rd., London NW10 2DZ.

Telephone: (020) 8955 0555. Fax: (020) 8955 0543. Minicom: (020) 8955 0550.

DX: 110850 Willesden 2.

Court times: Doors open 9 a.m. Court sits 10 a.m. Office hours 9.30 a.m.–4.30 p.m.

BRENT MAGISTRATES' COURT—
CONTINUED

Facilities: Advocates' room. Interview rooms. Public refreshments.

Travel: Und. Neasden (Charing X 20 min.) plus 10 min. walk.
From Neasden Station turn right down Neasden Lane, under bridge and to end. At roundabout turn left. Court 50 yds on left.

LRT 8, 52, 172, 260, 266, 297.

Driving: From North Circular A406 take Neasden exit northbound. At 1st roundabout (Dudden Hill) take 3rd exit Neasden Lane s/p Neasden Station, courthouse at very end of Neasden Lane bearing left off roundabout. From central London take A5 Edgware Rd. to Cricklewood Broadway. Turn left along Chichelle Rd. A407 s/p Willesden Green. Follow A407 to High Rd. Court mile on right after Willesden Green station.

Parking: Domestic car park.

BRENTFORD COUNTY COURT

Alexandra Rd., High St., Brentford, Middx. TW8 0JJ.

Telephone: (020) 8231 8940. Fax: (020) 8568 2401.

DX: 97840 Brentford 2.

Court times: Doors open 9.00 a.m. Court sits 9.30 a.m. Public counter opens 10.00 a.m. Building closed 4.00 p.m.

Facilities: Counsel and solicitors' rooms. Consultation rooms. Drinks machine. Public telephone.

Travel: Und. Gunnersbury (Embankment 26 min.) plus 267.

NR Brentford Central (Waterloo 26 min.) plus 10 min. walk.

LRT 203, 237, 267, E8, E2.

From Brentford turn left into Boston Manor Rd. and continue into Half Acre. Turn left into High St. Court 100 yds on left.

Driving: Court on A315. About a mile beyond Kew Bridge.

Parking: No parking facility.

Eating out:

The Beehive	bar food	High St.
Brentford Tandoori	Indian restaurant	High St.
Watermans Centre	cafeteria	High St.

BRENTFORD (HOUNSLOW) MAGISTRATES' COURT,
HOUNSLOW YOUTH COURT (Tues.),
HOUNSLOW FAMILY PROCEEDINGS COURT (Thurs.)

Market Place, Brentford, Middx. TW8 8EN.
(Entrance at rear of building.)

Telephone: (020) 8917 3400. Fax: (020) 8917 3448. Minicom: (020) 8917 3438.

DX: 133823 Feltham 3.

BRENTFORD (HOUNSLOW) MAGISTRATES' COURT— CONTINUED

Court times: Doors open 9.00 a.m.–4.00 p.m. Court sits 10.00 a.m. and 2.15 p.m. daily. Block booking/appointment system in operation—contact scheduling office for timing detail if in doubt ((020) 8917 3400). Office hours 9.00 a.m.–4.00 p.m. telephone contact 8.45 a.m.–5.00 p.m.

Facilities: Interview rooms. Drinks machine. Stair lifts. Separate witness waiting accommodation on request.

Travel: As for Brentford Cty Ct. At the High St. turn right. Court 200 yds on right.

Driving: Court on A315 1.5 miles beyond Kew Bridge. Alternatively take the Great West Rd. to junction with A302 Boston Manor Rd. Proceed to High St. Brentford and turn right for Market Place or 1st right before the High St. for parking (or from Great West Road it is 3rd on right).

Parking: Parking meters in vicinity.

Eating out: Various public houses/cafes/sandwich bars within 100 yds.

BRIGHTON COUNTY COURT

William St., Brighton, East Sussex BN2 0RF. Family Section at The Family Centre, 1 Edward St., Brighton BN2 0JD.

Telephone: 01273 674421. Fax: 01273 602138. Family: 01273 811333. Fax: 01273 607638.

DX: 98070 Brighton 3. Family: 142600 Brighton 12.

Court times: Doors open 9.00 a.m. Court sits 10.30 a.m. Office hours 10.00 a.m.–4.00 p.m.

Facilities: Robing rooms. Interview rooms.

Travel: Follow instructions for Mags Ct., William St. is adjacent to Edward St.

BRIGHTON EMPLOYMENT TRIBUNALS

Brighton Hearing Centre, St. James House, New England St., Brighton, East Sussex BN1 4GQ. (Admin. from Southampton.)

Telephone: 01273 571488. Fax: 01273 623645.

Court times: 9.45 a.m.

Facilities: Consultation rooms. Telephones. Hot drinks machine.

Travel: NR Brighton railway station 10 min. walk. Local buses— London Rd.

Driving: Follow signs to railway station and New England St.

Parking: Large public car parks in the vicinity. No public parking at the building.

Eating out: Many cafes and restaurants in the vicinity of the station and in London Rd.

BRIGHTON MAGISTRATES' COURT,
BRIGHTON YOUTH COURT

The Law Courts, Edward St., Brighton, East Sussex BN2 0LG.
Telephone: 01273 670888. Fax: 01273 790260.
Website: www. sussex-magistrates.co.uk.
Court times: Doors open 9.00 a.m. Court sits 10.00 a.m. Office hours 9.00 a.m.–4.30 p.m.
Facilities: Mags: Interview rooms. Advocates' room. Public telephone. Martletts coffee.
Travel: NR Brighton (Victoria 52 min.–1 hr. 40 min.) plus 15 min. walk. From station proceed down Queen's Rd. Take 3rd left into Church St. Proceed to bottom of hill and cross Grand Parade. Edward St. is on opposite side of traffic lights. Courts 200 yds on left.
Driving: Brighton Road A23–M23–A23 into town centre to Grand Parade. Edward St. on left just before Royal Pavilion.
Parking: Vouchers. NCP car park in Church St.
Eating out:

Beiderhoffs	sandwich bar	Edward St.

BROMLEY COUNTY COURT

Court House, College Rd., Bromley, Kent BR1 3PX.
Telephone: (020) 8290 9620. Fax: (020) 8313 9624.
DX: 98080 Bromley 2.
Court times: Doors open 9.00 a.m. Court sits 10.00 a.m. Public counter open 10.00 a.m.–4.00 p.m.
Facilities: Male/female robing rooms. Drinks vending machine.
Travel: Details as Mags/Youth Court.
LRT 61, 119, <u>126</u>, 138, 146, 162, 227, <u>261</u>, 269, 320, 336, 354, 367, 402.
Metro Bus: 351 and 352.
Turn right out of Bromley South Station and proceed to Market Sq. Cross to north-east corner and bear left into West St. West St. becomes College Rd. Court approx. 400 yds on left-hand side.
Driving: Court situated on A2212 north of town centre.
Parking: For disabled drivers only, by prior arrangement.
Eating out:

American Hamburger	restaurant	High St.
Star and Garter	bar food	High St.
Akashi	Indian restaurant	High St.
McDonald's	restaurant	Market Sq.
Cater's	coffee shop	Market Sq.

BROMLEY MAGISTRATES' COURT,
BROMLEY YOUTH COURT (Tues. and Fri. 10.00 a.m.),
IMMIGRATION APPELLATE AUTHORITY

The Court House, London Rd., Bromley, Kent BR1 1RA.
Telephone: (020) 8325 4000. Fax: (020) 8325 4006.

BROMLEY MAGISTRATES' COURT—
CONTINUED

DX: 119601 Bromley 8 (Mags/Y only).

Court times: Doors open 8.45 a.m. Court sits 10.00 a.m. Immigration sits 10.00 a.m. Office hours 9.00 a.m.–5.00 p.m.

Facilities: Advocates' room. Interview rooms.

Travel: NR Bromley South (Victoria 16–20 min.) plus 15 min. walk (**NB** Bromley North Station is nearer but trains from central London are slower and less frequent).

LRT 119, 126, 138, 146.

Turn right out of station and proceed half mile up High St. to Market Sq. Keeping to the left-hand side of Market Sq. continue past Allders and the cinema. The court is on the corner of London Rd. and Beckenham Lane.

Driving: A21 to Bromley. Follow signs for The Hill car park.

Parking: The Hill multi-storey and Glades shopping centre.

Eating out:

British Home Stores	cafeteria/restaurant	High St.
McDonald's	restaurant	Market Sq.
Clarke's	coffee shop	Market Sq.
Glades shopping centre	various	High St.

BURY ST. EDMUNDS COUNTY COURT

Entrance B, Triton House, St. Andrews St. North, Bury St. Edmunds, Suffolk IP33 1TR.

Telephone: 01284 753254. Fax: 01284 702687.

DX: 97640 Bury St. Edmunds 3.

Court times: Office hours 10.00 a.m.–4.00 p.m.

Facilities: Robing room. Interview rooms. Baby changing facilities. Payphone. Vending machine.

Travel: NR Bury St. Edmunds (Liverpool St. 1 hr. 56 min.–2 hrs. 18 min.) plus taxi or 10–15 min. walk.

EC 204, 901–19, 922–3, 925, 927, 936, 940, 943–4, 946–8, 950–8, 960, 964–5, 970–5, 979.

From station straight up hill on to Station Hill. Bear right into Tayfen Rd. and left into St. Andrews St. North. Court 250 yds on right.

Driving: M11–A11 to Newmarket then A14 to Bury St. Edmunds.

Parking: Car park near court.

BURY ST. EDMUNDS (IPSWICH) CROWN COURT, BURY ST. EDMUNDS MAGISTRATES' COURT, WEST SUFFOLK COMBINED YOUTH COURT

The Shire Hall, Honey Hill, Bury St. Edmunds, Suffolk IP33 1HF.

Telephone: 01473 220750 (Ipswich). Fax: 01473 220780. Mags: 01284 352300. Fax: 01284 352345.

DX: (Crown) 3252 Ipswich 1.

BURY ST. EDMUNDS (IPSWICH) CROWN COURT—
CONTINUED

Court times: Doors open 9.30 a.m. Courts sit: Crown 10.30 a.m., Mags/Y. 10.00 a.m.

Facilities: Robing room. Interview room. On-premises catering. East Anglian Air Ambulance refreshments, a.m. only.

Travel: NR Bury St. Edmunds (Liverpool St. 1 hr. 56 min.–2 hrs. 18 min.) plus taxi or 25 min. walk.

EC 901–19, 922–3, 925, 927, 936, 940, 943–4, 946–8, 950–8, 960, 964–5, 970–5, 979.

From station turn right into Northgate. Over roundabout and proceed entire length of Northgate St. Right into Mustow St. and left Angel Hill. Continue into Crown St. passing cathedral on left. Turn left Honey Hill. Shire Hall at foot of hill.

Driving: M11–A11 to Newmarket then A14 to Bury. Follow signs to cathedral precinct. Turn right along Crown St. and left into Honey Hill, Shire Hall at bottom of hill on left.

Parking: Domestic car park.

Eating out:

Angel Hotel	restaurant	Angel Hill

BURY ST. EDMUNDS EMPLOYMENT TRIBUNALS

100 Southgate St., Bury St. Edmunds, Suffolk IP33 2AQ.

Telephone: 01284 762171. Fax: 01284 706064.

Court times: Tribunal sits 10.00 a.m.

Facilities: Waiting room. Drinks machine.

Travel: Call for map.

NR Bury St. Edmunds (30 min. walk).

Parking: Free on site.

Eating out: Town centre is 20 min. walk.

CAMBERWELL GREEN MAGISTRATES' COURT

15 D'Eynsford Rd., Camberwell Green, London SE5 7UP.

Telephone: 0845 601 3600, Fax: (020) 7805 9896

DX: 35305 Camberwell Green.

Court times: 9.30 a.m.–4.30 p.m.

Facilities: Two interview rooms.

INNER LONDON YOUTH COURTS CENTRE 2,
CAMBERWELL GREEN YOUTH COURT (also sits at Greenwich)

4 Kimpton Rd., Camberwell Green, London SE5 7UP.

Inner London Youth Courts Centre dealing with youth cases arising in the boroughs of Southwark and Lewisham.

Camberwell Green Youth Court dealing with youth cases arising in Greenwich, Woolwich, and Belmarsh.

Telephone: (020) 7805 9845. Fax: (020) 7805 9899.

INNER LONDON YOUTH COURTS CENTRE 2—
CONTINUED

Greenwich Magistrates' Court: (020) 8276 1341.

Woolwich Magistrates' Court: (020) 8918 9000.

Belmarsh Magistrates' Court: (020) 8918 9099.

DX: 35305 Camberwell Green.

Court times: Doors open: Mags 9.30 a.m., Y 9.15 a.m. Courts sit: Mags 10.30 a.m., Y 10.00 a.m.

Facilities: Mags: Advocates' room. Interview room. Y: Advocates' room. Interview room.

Travel: Und. Elephant and Castle (Bank 6 min., Baker St. 15 min.) plus 12, 35, 40, 45, 68, 171. Oval (Embankment 6 min., Bank 10 min.) plus 36, 185.

LRT 12, 35–6, 40, 42, 45, 68, 68A, 171, 176, 185, 345, 484.

Courts situated at north-eastern corner of Camberwell Green. Youth Courts to rear of building.

Driving: Court at Camberwell Green, junction of A202 and A215.

Parking: Free parking in side-streets and to rear.

Eating out:

Silver Buckle	bar food	Denmark Hill
Spaghetti Classics	Italian restaurant	Coldharbour Lane

CAMBRIDGE COUNTY COURT

197 East Rd., Cambridge, Cambs. CBI IBA.

Telephone: 01223 224500. Fax: 01223 224590.

DX: 97650 Cambridge 3.

Court times: Court sits 10.00 a.m. Office hours Mon.–Fri. 10.00 a.m.–4.00 p.m. 7.30 a.m.–10.30 a.m. (Bailiffs).

Facilities: Advocates' room and a good supply of consultation rooms.

CAMBRIDGE CROWN COURT

The Court House, 83 East Rd., Cambridge, Cambs. CBI IBT.

Telephone: 01223 48832. Fax: 01223 224654 488333.

DX: 97365 Cambridge 2.

Court times: Doors open 9.00 a.m. Court sits 10.30 a.m. Office hours 10.00 a.m.–4.00 p.m.

Facilities: Robing room. Interview room. On-premises catering.

CAMBRIDGE MAGISTRATES' COURT, CAMBRIDGE YOUTH COURT

The Court House, 43 Hauxton Rd. Trumpington, Cambridge, Cambs. CB2 2EY.

Telephone: 0845 3100575. Fax: 01223 844980.

DX: 131966 Cambridge 6.

Court times: Doors open 9.00 a.m. Court sits 10.00 a.m. Office hours 9.00 a.m.–4.30 p.m. (4.00 p.m. Fri.).

CAMBRIDGE MAGISTRATES' COURT—
CONTINUED

Facilities: Advocates' room. Interview rooms. Baby changing room. Drinks and snacks. Vending machines.

Travel: NR Cambridge (Liverpool St. 50 min.–1 hr. 20 min.) Plus for Cty and Crown Cts. taxi or City Bus 2 or 8 from station (25–30 min. walk). For Mags from station take taxi or City Bus 7 to Trumpington Waitrose and walk (adjacent to court building) or from town centre take Trumpington Park and Ride.

Driving: Take M11 to Junc. 11 and follow signs to city centre. For Mags Ct. follow signs to Park and Ride at Trumpington. Turn left into Park and Ride facility. Court situated immediately behind facility. For Crown and Cty Cts take A10 Trumpington Rd. into city centre. Follow A10 as it turns right into Lensfield Rd. Cross over into Gonville Place and again into East Rd. Courts 800 yds on right. Public car park opposite on left.

Parking: Mags Ct: Use Trumpington Park and Ride. Crown and Cty Ct.: Public car park opposite off East St.

Eating out:
A good selection of sandwich bars and cafes in East St.

CANTERBURY COUNTY COURT,
CANTERBURY CROWN COURT

The Law Courts, Chaucer Rd., Canterbury, Kent CT1 1ZA.

Telephone: 01227 819200. Fax: Crown 01227 819329. Cty 01227 819283.

DX: 99710 Canterbury 3.

Court times: Doors open 9.00 a.m. Court sits 10.00 a.m. Office hours 10.00 a.m.–4.00 p.m.

Facilities: Robing rooms. Interview rooms. Disabled access. Public parking. Restaurant. Telephones.

Travel: From station (see below) take taxi (30 min. walk). Bus: 649 from City Centre to Ct.

Driving: M2/A2 to Canterbury ring road ('Rhodaus Town'). From station continue along inner ring road over two roundabouts into Broad St. Take 2nd exit from next roundabout and bear right into Chaucer Rd. to court complex.

Parking: Car park to the right and behind Court building.

CANTERBURY MAGISTRATES' COURT,
CANTERBURY YOUTH COURT

The Magistrates' Court, Broad St., Canterbury, Kent CT1 2UE. (Admin. at Dover.)

Telephone: 01304 218600. Fax: 01304 213819.

Court times: Doors open 9.00 a.m. Court sits 10.00 a.m.

Facilities: Advocates' room. Interview room. No on-premises catering.

Travel: NR Canterbury East (Victoria 1 hr. 15 min.) plus walking
(10–25 min.).
EK 702.
From station cross bridge over road, turn right, and follow old town
wall to end. Proceed along Upper Bridge St. to roundabout and cross
to Lower Bridge St. Court 100 yds on right (15 min.).
Driving: A2–M2–A2 to Canterbury. A2 becomes inner ring road
passing station. Follow walking directions.
Parking: Public car park opposite.
Eating out:

The Olive Branch	bar food	Burgate
Chaucer Hotel	restaurant	Ivy Lane
Augustine's	restaurant	Longport

CENTRAL CRIMINAL COURT

Old Bailey, London EC4M 7EH.
Telephone: (020) 7248 3277. Fax: (020) 7248 5735.
DX: 46700 Old Bailey.
Court times: Doors open 8.00 a.m. Court sits 10.30 a.m.
Facilities: Male and female robing rooms. Interview rooms. Soli-
citors' room. Bar mess. Public cafeteria.
Travel: NR City Thameslink.
Und. St. Paul's, Blackfriars.
LRT 4, 8, 25, 141, 501, 502.
10 min. walk Inns of Court.
Parking: Meters Smithfield. NCP car parks Smithfield.
Eating out:

The Gallery	wine bar	Newgate St.
La Bastille	restaurant	Newgate St.
Pomeroys	wine bar	Old Bailey

CENTRAL LONDON CIVIL TRIAL CENTRE,

26–29 Park Crescent, London W1B 1HT.

CENTRAL LONDON COUNTY COURT

13–14 Park Crescent, London W1B 1HT.
(All correspondence to either court to be sent to this address.)
Telephone: (020) 7917 5000. Fax: (020) 7917 7940 (Trial Centre).
(020) 7917 5014/5026 (County Court and Listing).
DX: 97325 Regents Park 2.
e-mail: enquiries@centrallondon.countycourt.gsi. gov.uk; e-filing@
centrallondon. countycourt.gsi.gov.uk.
Court times: Doors open 9.30 a.m. Circuit Judge 10.30 a.m. District
Judge 10.00 a.m. Office hours 10.00 a.m.–4.00 p.m.

CENTRAL LONDON CIVIL TRIAL CENTRE—
CONTINUED

Facilities: Consultation rooms. Advocates' suites. Public dining room (at Trial Centre). Vending machine. Court News Service member (e-mail messages to Central London County Court). Public photocopying and fax services (at Trial Centre).

Travel: Und. Regents Park, Gt Portland St.

LRT 74, 18, or 30.

From stations turn left along Marylebone Rd. to Park Crescent.

Parking: Meters: Clipstone St. NCP: Carburton St., Cleveland St. Pay and display meters: Park Crescent.

Eating out:

Albany	bar food	Gt Portland St.
Trends	restaurant	Gt Portland St.
Willows	restaurant	2nd floor, 26 Park Crescent

CHELMSFORD COUNTY COURT

London House, New London Rd., Chelmsford, Essex CM2 0QR.

Telephone: 01245 264670/350718. Fax: 01245 496216.

DX: 97660 Chelmsford 4.

Court times: Doors open 9.30 a.m. Court sits 10.00 a.m. Office hours 10.00 a.m.–4.00 p.m.

Facilities: Robing room. Interview rooms. Drinks vending machines. Childcare suite. Baby changing room.

CHELMSFORD CROWN COURT

PO Box 9, New St., Chelmsford, Essex CM1 1EL.

Telephone: 01245 603000. Fax: 01245 603011/603020.

DX: 97375 Chelmsford 3.

Court times: Doors open 8.00 a.m. Court sits 10.30 a.m. Office hours 9.00 a.m.–5.00 p.m.

Facilities: Advocates' robing room. Advocates' dining room. Interview rooms. Public dining. Children's room. Witness service. Drinks machine. Defendants/defence witness room.

CHELMSFORD (MID-NORTH ESSEX) MAGISTRATES' COURT

The Shire Hall, Tindal Sq., Chelmsford, Essex CM1 1RA.

Telephone: 01245 313300. Admin. at Harlow: 01279 693200. Fax: 01245 373399.

Court times: Doors open 9.00 a.m. Court sits 10.00 a.m. Office hours 9.00 a.m.–4.30 p.m.

Facilities: Interview room. No on-premises catering.

Travel: NR Chelmsford (Liverpool St. 29–40 min.) plus walking 15–25 min.

Crown: From station, left into Victoria Rd. Follow road to junction New St., turn right. Court 50 yds on left.

CHELMSFORD (MID-NORTH ESSEX) MAGISTRATES' COURT—CONTINUED

Cty: From station, proceed left down Duke St. and turn right into Victoria Rd. South. First exit roundabout into Parkway. First right New London Rd. Court 300 yds on left (over bridge).

Mags: From station, proceed south to end of Duke St. Shire Hall on left.

Driving: A12 into town on London and New London Rd. Pass Cty Court on right. Turn left at Parkway and follow to Victoria Rd. South and cross two sets of traffic lights to large car park on right.

Parking: Crown/Mags: as above. Cty: immediately behind court via New Writtle St. and George St.

Eating out:

Cty: The United Brethren	bar food	New Writtle St.
Crown/Mags: Peeler's	wine bar	Waterloo St.
Duke's Hideaway	restaurant	Duke St.
Batton's	coffee bar/bakery	Chelmscroft Centre

CHESHUNT MAGISTRATES' COURT, EAST HERTS MAGISTRATES' COURT (Also sits at Hertford.) (Admin. from Stevenage.)

King Arthur Court, Cheshunt, Herts. EN8 8LD.

(Same-day hearings only.)

Telephone: 01992 411040. Fax: 01992 411047.

(All correspondence to North and East Herts. Area Administration Office, Bayley House, Sish Lane, Stevenage, Herts. SG1 3SS. Office hours 9.00 a.m.–4.00 p.m.)

Telephone: 01438 730412. Fax: 01438 730413.

DX: 122187 Old Stevenage.

Court times: Doors open 9.30 a.m. Court sits 10.00 a.m.

Facilities: Interview room. Witness waiting room. Refreshment facilities.

Travel: NR Cheshunt (Liverpool St. 32 min.) plus 15 min. walk.
LRT 242, 279, 279A.
Ar 310, 316, 324, 334, 360, 390.

Turn left from station, proceed 10 min. up Windmill Lane to Turners Hill. Turn left. Cross roundabout and proceed 500 yds on left. Court situated behind public library.

Driving: Follow signs to Cheshunt town centre from A10. At roundabout turn right, Court 300 yds on left.

Parking: Car park outside.

Eating out:

Rose & Crown	bar food	Turners Hill
Wimpy	restaurant	Turners Hill
Coffee House Express	restaurant	Turners Hill
The Old Pond	bar food	Turners Hill

CHICHESTER COUNTY COURT, CHICHESTER CROWN COURT

The Court House, Southgate, Chichester, West Sussex PO19 1SX.

Telephone: Cty: 01243 520700. Fax: 01243 533756. Crown: 01243 520742. Fax: 01243 538252. Robing room: 01243 777963.

DX: 97460 Chichester 2.

Court times: Doors open 9.00 a.m. Court sits 10.00 a.m. Office hours 9.00 a.m.–4.00 p.m.

Facilities: Robing room. Interview rooms. WRVS coffee. Vending machine. Disabled access. Water dispenser.

CHICHESTER MAGISTRATES' COURT, CHICHESTER YOUTH COURT

6 Market Ave., Chichester, West Sussex PO19 1YE.

Telephone: 01243 817000. Fax: 01243 533655.

Website: www.sussex-magistrates.co.uk.

DX: 97463 Chichester 2.

Court times: Doors open 9.00 a.m. Court sits 10.00 a.m. Office hours 9 a.m.–4.30 p.m.

Facilities: Interview room. Advocates' room. Vending machine for hot/cold drinks, snacks. Public telephone.

Travel: NR Chichester (Victoria 1 hr. 38 min.) plus 5 min. walk.

SD 250–4, 256, 260, 268, 700, 752–3, 900.

From station turn left. Crown Court 100 yds on right at Southgate. Mags Ct. 100 yds further on.

Driving: A3 then A286 to Chichester. Drive into city centre s/p station then follow walking directions.

Parking: Avenue Des Chartres, off Southgate. Car park at The Baffins.

Eating out:

Clinches Salad House		Southgate
Cathedral Tavern	bar food	South St.
The Globe	bar food	South St.

CITY OF LONDON CORONER'S COURT

Milton Court, Moor Lane, London EC2 9BJ.

Telephone: (020) 7332 1598. Fax/phone: (020) 7601 2714.

Court times: As arranged.

Facilities: Advocates' room. Interview room. No on-premises catering.

Travel: NR, Und. Moorgate plus 5 min. walk.

LRT 9, 11, 21, 43, 76, 133, 141, 279A, 502.

From station take Moorfields exit and cross over road. Proceed down Tenter St. to Moor Lane.

Driving: Court in vicinity of junction of Moorgate and London Wall (A1211).

Parking: Barbican complex car parks then walk via Fore St. or Silk St.

Eating out: Various sandwich bars and restaurants in Moorfields and the Barbican complex.

CITY OF LONDON MAGISTRATES' COURT
1 Queen Victoria St., London EC4N 4XY.

Telephone: (020) 7332 1830/1838. Fax: (020) 7332 1493.

DX: 98943 Cheapside 2.

Court times: Doors open 9.15 a.m. Court sits 10.30 a.m.

Facilities: Interview rooms. Hot drinks machine.

Travel: Und. Bank, exit 8.

LRT 6, 8, 9, 11, 15, 21, 22, 25, 43, 76, 133, 501, 513.

Court on corner of Queen Victoria St. by Mansion House.

Parking: Limited meters to rear of Walbrook.

Eating out: Numerous pubs, cafes, and restaurants on Bow Lane and in the Cheapside area.

CLERKENWELL COUNTY COURT
33 Duncan Terrace, Islington, London N1 8AN.

Telephone: (020) 7359 7347. Fax: (020) 7354 1166.

DX: 146640 Islington 4.

Court times: Doors open 9.00 a.m. Court sits 10.30 a.m. Office hours 10.00 a.m.–4.00 p.m.

Facilities: Robing room. No on-premises catering.

Travel: Und. Angel plus 5 min. walk.

LRT 4, 19, 30, 38, 43, 73, 104, 171, 277, 279, 279A.

Proceed ahead 200 yds from station. Duncan St. 1st right. Court 300 yds on left.

Driving: Court near Angel Islington junc. of A1 City Rd., Upper St., and Pentonville Rd.

Parking: Meters in vicinity. NCP car park Duncan St.

Eating out:

The York	bar food	Duncan St.
Grapes	wine bar	Angel Arcade, Camden Passage
Pied Bull	bar food	Liverpool Rd.
Fredericks	restaurant	Camden Passage

CLERKENWELL MAGISTRATES' COURT
(Now merged with Hampstead Magistrates' Court.)

78 King's Cross Rd., London WC1X 9QJ.

Telephone: (020) 7278 6541. Fax: (020) 7837 4526.

DX: 37905 Kings Cross.

Court times: Doors open 9.45 a.m. Court sits 10.30 a.m.

Facilities: No advocates' room. Interview room. No on-premises catering.

Travel: NR, Und. King's Cross, St. Pancras plus 5 min. walk. 30 min. walk from Inns of Court.

LT 18, 45, <u>63</u>, <u>153</u>, 171, <u>172</u>, <u>221</u>, <u>259</u>.

From King's Cross station tube Thameslink exit. Turn right and bear right into King's Cross Road. Court 150 yds on left.

CLERKENWELL MAGISTRATES' COURT—
CONTINUED
Parking: Meters in streets to rear.

Eating out:

Carpenters Arms	bar food	King's Cross Rd.
Prince Albert	bar food	King's Cross Rd.
Royal Scot Hotel	coffee lounge/bar	King's Cross Rd.
Leila's Snacks		King's Cross Rd.
Supertaste	sandwich bar	King's Cross Rd.

COLCHESTER COUNTY COURT
Trial Centre: Norfolk House, 23 Southway, Colchester, Essex CO3 3ES.

Office: Falkland House, 25 Southway, Colchester, Essex CO3 3EG.

Telephone: 01206 717200. Fax: 01206 717250.

DX: 97670 Colchester 2.

Minicom: 0191 478 1476.

Court times: Doors open 9.30 a.m. Court sits 10.00 a.m. Office hours 10.00 a.m.–4.00 p.m.

Facilities: Robing room. Interview room. No on-premises catering. Vending machine.

COLCHESTER MAGISTRATES' COURT,
NORTH-EAST ESSEX MAGISTRATES' COURT
The Town Hall, High St., Colchester, Essex CO1 1FP (See also Court House, 363 Main Rd., Harwich.)

(Clerk's Office: Stanwell House, Stanwell St., Colchester, Essex CO2 7DL.)

NORTH-EAST ESSEX FAMILY PROCEEDINGS COURT
Stanwell House, Stanwell St., Colchester, Essex CO2 7DL.

Telephone: 01245 313300. Fax: 01245 313399.

DX: 140222 Colchester 6.

Facilities: Advocates' room. Interview room. Vending machine. Public telephone.

Court times: Doors open 9.15 a.m. Court sits 10.00 a.m. Office hours 9.30–4.00 p.m.

Travel: NR Colchester North Station (Liverpool St. 46 min.–1 hr.) plus 20 min. walk.

Family: cross roundabout to Southway. Stanwell House 100 yds on right. Cty in Norfolk House, adjacent building.

Mags/Y: turn right up St. Botolph's and proceed up Queen St. Turn left into High St. Town Hall 300 yds on right.

Driving: A12 to Colchester. Park as below and follow walking directions.

Parking: Multi-storey in Nunns Rd., Balkerne Hill, Southway, and Osborne St.

Eating out:

Mags: McDonald's	restaurant	High St.
Sloppy Joe's	restaurant	High St.
Pizza Hut	restaurant	High St.
Burger King	restaurant	High St.
Family: Abbey Arms	bar food	St. John's Green
Cty: King's Arms	bar food	Crouch St.
The Bull	bar food	Crouch St.

CRAWLEY MAGISTRATES' COURT, CRAWLEY YOUTH COURT

Court House, County Buildings, Woodfield Rd., Crawley, W. Suss. RH10 1XF.

(Admin. at Mid-Sussex Magistrates' Court.)

Telephone: 01444 417611. Fax: 01444 472639.

DX: Mid-Sussex Magistrates' Court: 135596 Haywards Heath 6.

Website: www.sussex-magistrates.co.uk.

Court times: Doors open 9.00 a.m. Courts sit 10.00 a.m.

Facilities: Interview room. Vending machine for hot/cold drinks, snacks. Public telephone.

Travel: NR Crawley (Victoria 47–61 min.) plus 10 min. walk. From station turn right to end of Station Way. Cross roundabout into College Rd. and turn right and left behind library at end. Court is opposite police station.

Driving: A23–M23 to Crawley. From Crawley Ave. at roundabout enter town centre via Southgate Ave. At end cross roundabout into College Rd. Turn right and left into Woodfield Rd.

Parking: Multi-storey car parks in Kingsgate and Exchange Rd. (behind Ct.).

Eating out:

The Black Dog	bar food	Woodfield Rd.
Wimpy	restaurant	Queen's Sq. Centre
Littlewoods	restaurant	Queen's Sq. Centre

CROMER (NORTH NORFOLK) MAGISTRATES' COURT, NORTH NORFOLK YOUTH COURT

The Court House, Holt Rd., Cromer, Norfolk NR27 9EB.

Telephone: All admin. from Yarmouth: 01493 849800. Fax: 01493 852169.

DX: 139400 Great Yarmouth.

Court times: Doors open 9.00 a.m. Court sits 10.00 a.m.

Facilities: Advocates' room. Interview rooms. VSS room. No on-premises catering.

Travel: NR Cromer Beach (Liverpool St. 3 hrs. 31 min.). (**NB** No trains from London arrive before court sits.)

CROMER (NORTH NORFOLK) MAGISTRATES'
COURT—CONTINUED

Court opposite station.

Driving: M11–A11 to Norwich then A140/A149 to Cromer.

Parking: Car park at station. Off-street parking.

Eating out:

Buffers Bar   bar food   Holt Rd.

CROYDON COUNTY COURT,
CROYDON CROWN COURT

The Law Courts, Altyre Road, Croydon, Surrey CR9 5AB.

Telephone: (020) 8410 4700. Fax: Crown (020) 8781 1007. Cty (020) 8760 0432. Bailiffs: (020) 8410 4764.

DX: 97473 Croydon (Crown Court). 97470 Croydon (County Court).

Court times: Doors open 9.00 a.m. Courts sit: Cty 10.00 a.m., Crown 10.00 a.m.

Facilities: Male/female robing rooms. Interview room. Witness service. Bar mess. Public cafeteria. Drink machines.

Travel: NR East Croydon (Victoria 15–17 min., Blackfriars 25 min., London Bridge 20 min.) plus 5 min. walk.

From NR East Croydon turn left. Cross tramway and turn left to Altyre Rd. Court 150 yds on right.

Driving: A23 to Croydon, then A235 London Rd. to A213 (s/p Central Croydon) Wellesley Rd. underpass to Fairfield Halls. Turn left into Barclay Rd. and then left into Altyre Rd.

Parking: Public multi-storey car park at rear.

Eating out: As for Magistrates' Court.

CROYDON MAGISTRATES' COURT,
CROYDON CORONER'S COURT,
CROYDON FAMILY PROCEEDINGS COURT,
CROYDON YOUTH COURT

The Magistrates' Court, Barclay Rd., Croydon, Surrey CR9 3NG.

Telephone: Mags (020) 8603 0476. Fax: (020) 8680 9801. Cor. (020) 8681 5019. Fax: (020) 8686 3491.

DX: 97474 Croydon 6.

Court times: Doors open 9.00 a.m. Court sits 10.00 a.m.

Facilities: Interview room. Advocates'/staff cafeteria. Public cafeteria.

Travel: NR East Croydon (Victoria 15–17 min., Charing Cross 27 min., Waterloo East 25 min., London Bridge 20 min.) plus 5 min. walk.

From station proceed to Crown Court in Altyre Rd. Follow to end and turn right into Fairfield Rd. Court on right. Nearest Tramlink stop at East Croydon BR and nearest bus stops Fairfield Halls or East Croydon BR.

CROYDON MAGISTRATES' COURT—
CONTINUED

Driving: A23 to Croydon, then A235 London Rd. to A213 (s/p Central Croydon). Wellesley Rd. underpass to Fairfield Halls. Turn left into Barclay Rd.

Parking: Multi-storey car parks next to court, meters opposite.

EMPLOYMENT TRIBUNALS (LONDON SOUTH)

Montague Court, 101 London Rd., Croydon, Surrey CR0 2RF.

Telephone: (020) 8667 9131. Fax: (020) 8649 9470.

Court times: Doors open 9.00 a.m. Tribunal sits 10.00 a.m.

Facilities: Waiting rooms. Drinks machines. Pay phones. Consultation rooms. Disabled toilets.

Travel: NR East Croydon plus 15 min. walk (Victoria 15–17 min., London Bridge 13–20 min.). West Croydon Station plus 5 min. walk (Victoria 30 min., London Bridge 30 min.).

From East Croydon turn right. Cross over into George St. to end. Turn right along North End. Proceed for 10 min. passing West Croydon Station into London Rd. (A235). Tribunal is opposite Panton Close.

Driving: A23 to Croydon then A235 London Rd.

Parking: Lidl supermarket pay and display car park, and pay and display opposite along roadside.

Eating out:

Palm Beach Cafe	baker/cafe	London Rd.
Greggs	bakery	London Rd.

DARTFORD COUNTY COURT

Home Gardens, Dartford, Kent DA1 1DX.

Telephone: 01322 629820. Fax: 01322 270902.

DX: 98090 Dartford 2.

Court times: Doors open 9.00 a.m. Court sits 10.30 a.m. Office hours 10.00 a.m.–4.00 p.m.

Facilities: Mixed robing rooms. Interview rooms. Vending machine. Disabled facilities.

DARTFORD MAGISTRATES' COURT,
DARTFORD YOUTH COURT (Tues. 10.00 a.m. and 2.15 a.m.)
(Y. Ct. also sits at Chatham (Medway)).

Sessions House, Highfield Rd., Dartford, Kent DA1 2JW.

Telephone: 01634 830232. Fax: 01634 847400.

Enquiries and admin to Medway Magistrates' Court.

Court times: Doors open 9.00 a.m. Court sits 10.00 a.m. and 2.15 p.m.

Facilities: Advocates' room. Interview rooms. Coffee machine.

Travel: NR Dartford (Charing Cross 37 min., Waterloo East 35 min., Cannon St. 45 min., London Bridge 30 min.) plus 5 min. walk (Cty) or 15 min. walk (Mags).

ERRATUM

Andrew Goodman
The Court Guide 2006/2007
978-0-19-929749-8

Page 31

The correct fax number for Dorking Magistrates' Court is as follows:
01306 877447

DARTFORD MAGISTRATES' COURT—
CONTINUED

LRT 96.

Ar 400, 477, 492.

For Cty Ct: from station turn left along Station Approach and left again into Home Gardens (part of ring road A226). Court 400 yds on left.

For Mags Ct: cross main road, walk through Orchard Shopping Centre onto High St. Turn right and proceed along Spital St. West Hill. Mags Ct in Highfield Rd. on left, close to junction with West Hill.

Driving: A207/M25 then A226 into Dartford town centre: A226 becomes West Hill, then Spital St.

Parking: Multi-storey car park Orchard St. (1st left past Cty Ct.).

Eating out:

Royal Oak	bar food	Spital St.
Mason's Arms	bar food	Spital St.
Pizza Parlour	restaurant	Spital St.

DIDCOT (SOUTHERN OXFORDSHIRE) MAGISTRATES' COURT (Mon. and Thur.),
SOUTHERN OXFORDSHIRE YOUTH COURT (Combined with Northern Oxfordshire and Oxford Petty Sessional Divisions. Fri.)
The Court House, Mereland Rd., Didcot, Oxon. OX11 8BG. (Admin. by Oxford Magistrates' Court.)

Telephone: 0870 2412808.

DX: 96452 Oxford 4.

Court times: Mon. and Thurs. Doors open 9.00 a.m. Youth Court Fri. Court sits 10.00 a.m.–1.00 p.m., 2.00 p.m.–4.30 p.m. All enquiries to Oxford Magistrates' Court.

Facilities: Two interview rooms. Probation office. WI refreshments. Public telephone.

Travel: NR Didcot Parkway (Paddington 40 min.–1 hr. 13 min.) plus taxi—1 mile from court.

Local bus: Oxford to Didcot 32A, 32 from St. Aldates.

National Bus: To Oxford, Gloucester Green, then local service.

Driving: From A34 Marcham Interchange next exit to Milton Trading Park, follow signs to Didcot Broadway (B4016). Court near junction of Broadway and Mereland Rd.

Parking: Very limited parking space front of court. Public car park behind Somerfield.

Eating out: Take away only, within 5 min. walk.

DORKING MAGISTRATES' COURT,
SOUTH EAST SURREY MAGISTRATES' COURT (Also sits at Redhill (Reigate).)
The Court House, London Rd., Dorking, Surrey RH4 1SX.

Telephone: 01306 885544. Fax: 01306 877477 (01737 765581 Redhill).

DORKING MAGISTRATES' COURT—
CONTINUED
Court times: Doors open 9.30 a.m. Court sits 10.00 a.m. Admin office at Redhill.

Facilities: Advocates' room. Interview room.

Travel: NR Deepdene (Waterloo 1 hr. 37 min.) plus 10 min. walk or Dorking North (Victoria 45 min.). **NB** Not Dorking Town.

From either station turn left along main road (A24). Cross and take 1st right. Court 100 yds on left.

Driving: Court on A25 (London Rd., Dorking) near junction of A24 and A25.

Parking: Very limited at court. Municipal car park in town.

Eating out: Various eating places in High St.

The Star and Garter	pub food	Dorking Station forecourt

DOVER (CHANNEL) MAGISTRATES' COURT
Pencester Rd., Dover, Kent CT16 1BS.

Telephone: 01304 218600. Fax: 01304 213819.

Court times: Doors open: 9.30 a.m. Court sits 10.00 a.m. Office hours 9.30 a.m.–5.00 p.m.

Facilities: Interview rooms. Vending machine.

Travel: NR Dover Priory (Charing Cross 1 hr. 40 min.) plus 10 min. walk.

From station approach down St. Martin's Hill to roundabout. At roundabout cross by lights and turn left. Proceed as far as Post Office. Cross over at Boots chemists. Turn right then turn left into Pencester Rd. Court next door to bus station.

Driving: A2–M2–A2 to Dover. Stay on A2 and proceed down Jubilee Way into town. Along Marine Parade, into Townwall St. Turn right at roundabout into York St. Cross Priory Place at end into High St. Turn 2nd right Ladywell and park. Then follow walking directions.

Parking: Car park Ladywell.

Eating out:

The Falstaff	bar food	Ladywell
Flicks Diner	restaurant	High St.
Macari's	coffee bar	Pencester Rd.

EALING MAGISTRATES' COURT
Green Man Lane, London W13 0SD.

Telephone: (020) 8579 9311. Fax: (020) 8579 2985. Warrant office: (020) 8567 2401.

DX: 5166 Ealing.

Court times: Doors open 9.00 a.m. Court sits 10.00 a.m. Office hours 9.30 a.m.–4.30 p.m.

Facilities: Interview room. Drinks machine. Witness service.

Travel: NR West Ealing (Paddington 15 min.) plus 5 min. walk.

EALING MAGISTRATES' COURT—
CONTINUED

Und. Ealing Broadway (Embankment 30 min., Oxford Circus 26 min.) and bus along Broadway.

LRT 83, 207, E1, E3.

From NR station turn right along Drayton Green Rd. Turn right into Broadway. Green Man Lane is 4th right. Court 100 yds on right.

Driving: Court off A4020 Uxbridge Rd. beyond junction with B452 Northfield Ave.

Parking: Pay and display car parks behind Marks & Spencer.

Eating out:

Rossis	coffee bar	Leeland Rd.
Halfway House	bar food	Broadway
McDonald's	restaurant	Broadway

EASTBOURNE COUNTY COURT

4 The Avenue, Eastbourne, East Sussex BN21 3SZ.

Telephone: 01323 735195. Fax: 01323 638829.

Court times: Doors open 9.00 a.m. Court sits 10.00 a.m. Office hours 10.00 a.m.–4.00 p.m.

DX: 98110 Eastbourne 2.

Facilities: Advocates' room. Two interview rooms. No on-premises catering.

EASTBOURNE MAGISTRATES' COURT
EASTBOURNE YOUTH COURT

The Law Courts, Old Orchard Rd., Eastbourne, East Sussex BN21 4UN.

Telephone: 01323 727518. Fax: 01323 649372.

Court times: Doors open 9.00 a.m. Court sits 10.00 a.m. Office hours 9.00 a.m.–4.30 p.m.

Facilities: Interview room. Public telephone. Vending machines for hot/cold drinks, snacks.

Travel: NR Eastbourne (Victoria or London Bridge 1 hr. 30 min.) plus 5 min. walk.

Mags: From station bear right and cross five-ways junction into Old Orchard Rd. Court 350 yds on left.

Driving: A22 to Eastbourne becomes Willingdon Rd. on entry into-town. Proceed to railway by station, then park and follow walking directions.

Parking: Car parks in Hyele Gardens and Eastbourne railway station and at Arndale Centre. Off-street parking beyond Saffrons Rd. and Grange Rd.

Eating out:

The Gildredge	bar food	Terminus Rd.
Fiesta Bistro	Meals and snacks	Grove Rd.
Flava Bar	Meals and snacks	Terminus Rd.

EDMONTON COUNTY COURT

59 Fore St., Upper Edmonton, London N18 2TN.

Telephone: 1. (020) 8884 6555. 2. (020) 8884 6560 (Family office).

Fax: (020) 8803 0564 (General office). (020) 8887 0413 (Family Office).

DX: 136686 Edmonton 3.

Court times: Doors open 9.00 a.m. Court sits 10.00 a.m.

Facilities: Male/female robing rooms. Three interview rooms. No on-premises catering.

Travel: NR Silver St. (Liverpool St. 20 min.) plus 10 min. walk.

Und. Seven Sisters (Kings Cross 10 min., Victoria 18 min.) plus 149, 259, 279.

LRT 34, 102, 144, 149, 259, 279.

From Silver St. Station turn left to lights. Turn right at lights into Upper Fore St. Court on corner of Grove St. Third on right.

Driving: Court on A1010 north of Tottenham and 500 yds south of junction with North Circular A406.

Parking: Street parking in Grove St.

Eating out:

McDonald's	restaurant	Fore St.
Greg's Bakery	take-away	Fore St.
Percy Ingles Bakery	take-away	Fore St.

ELY MAGISTRATES' COURT, ELY YOUTH COURT

(All correspondence to Cambridge Magistrates' Court, 43 Hauxton Rd., Trumpington, Cambridge, Cambs. CB2 2EY.)

The Sessions House, Lynn Rd., Ely, Cambs.

Telephone: 0845 3100575 (Cambridge). **Fax:** 01223 355237.

Court times: Doors open 9.30 a.m. Court sits 10.00 a.m. Tues. and Thurs.

DX: 131966 Cambridge 6.

Facilities: Advocates' room. Interview room. Refreshment machines.

Travel: NR Ely (Liverpool St. 1 hr. 22 min.) plus 15 min. walk.

From station turn left. Cross mini-roundabout and proceed up hill. Bear right passing Cathedral precinct. Cross traffic lights by Lamb Hotel. Court 40 yds on right.

Driving: A10 to Ely via Cambridge. Follow main road into town. At traffic lights by Lamb Hotel turn left into Lynn Rd. Court 40 yds on right.

Parking: Free car park Northolt Lane.

Eating out:

Lamb Hotel	bar food	Lynn Rd.
Cloisters	restaurant	St. Mary's St.
King's Arms	bar food	St. Mary's St.

EMPLOYMENT APPEALS TRIBUNAL

Audit House, 58 Victoria Embankment, London EC4Y 0DS.

Telephone: (020) 7273 1041. Fax: (020) 7273 1045/68.

Court times: Doors open 9.00 a.m. Tribunal sits 10.30 a.m.

Facilities: Waiting rooms. Drinks vending machine.

Travel: Und. Blackfriars, Temple plus 5 min. walk from Inns of Court. From junction with Blackfriars Bridge walk along river towards Waterloo. EAT 220 yds on right.

EMPLOYMENT TRIBUNALS (LONDON CENTRAL*)

Victory House, 30–34 Kingsway, London WC2B 6EX.

Telephone: (020) 7273 8640. Fax: (020) 7273 8686.

DX: 141420 Bloomsbury 7.

Court times: Tribunal sits 10.00 a.m.

Facilities: Waiting rooms. Tribunal room with induction loops.

Travel: Und. Holborn plus 5 min. walk.

LRT 68, 77, 170, 188, 196, 239.

From Holborn Station turn left down Kingsway.

Eating out:

Cafes and pubs within walking distance.

*For London South see separate entry (Croydon).

ENFIELD MAGISTRATES' COURT,
ENFIELD FAMILY PROCEEDINGS COURT (Wed. 10.00 a.m.),
ENFIELD YOUTH COURT (Wed. 10.00 a.m.),
HARINGEY MAGISTRATES' COURT (See also sittings at Haringey.)

The Court House, Lordship Lane, Tottenham, London N17 6RT.

Telephone: (020) 8808 5411. Fax: (020) 8885 4343.

DX: 134490 Tottenham 3.

Court times: Doors open 9.00 a.m. Court sits 10.00 a.m and 2.00 p.m.

Facilities: Advocates' room. Drinks machine.

Travel: NR Bruce Grove (Liverpool St. 15–19 min.) plus 10 min. walk.

Und. Seven Sisters (King's Cross 10 min., Victoria 18 min.) plus 76, 123, 149, 243, 259, 318, 341.

Wood Green (King's Cross 13 min., Piccadilly Circus 21 min.) plus 123.

LRT 76, 149, 171A, 243, 259, 279, 279A.

From Bruce Grove Station turn left up Bruce Grove and right at junction with Lordship Lane. Court 150 yds on right.

Driving: Court on A109 near junction with A1010 Tottenham High Rd.

Parking: Lordship Lane and side-streets. Small domestic car park.

ENFIELD MAGISTRATES' COURT—
CONTINUED

Eating out:

The Elmhurst	bar food	Lordship Lane (West)
Red Lion	bar food	High Rd.

EPPING (NORTH WEST ESSEX) MAGISTRATES' COURT, NORTH WEST ESSEX MAGISTRATES' COURT (also sits at Harlow)

The Court House, Epping, Essex CM16 4LJ.

Telephone: 01245 313300. Fax: 01245 313399. Admin. from Harlow: 01279 693200. Fax: 01279 693298.

DX: 140080 Harlow 5.

Court times: Doors open 9.00 a.m. Court sits 10.00 a.m.

Facilities: No advocates' room. Two interview rooms. Cold drinks machine.

Travel: Und. Epping (Liverpool St. 38 min., Oxford Circus 49 min.) plus 10 min. walk.

From station up Station Rd. to High St. Turn right along High St. 400 yds on right. Court situated immediately to rear of police station.

Driving: A104 then B1393 to Epping High St. Alternatively M11 to Junc. 7 then B1393.

Parking: High St. bays opposite. Two large pay and display car parks to rear of High St. (West) via St. John's Rd.

Eating out:

Cousins	wine bar	High St.
Black Lion	bar food	High St.
Poppy's	coffee shop	High St.
Italian restaurant		High St.

EPSOM COUNTY COURT

The Parade, Epsom, Surrey KT18 5DN.

Telephone: 01372 721801. Fax: 01372 726588.

DX: 97850 Epsom 3.

Court times: Doors open 9.00 a.m. Court sits 10.00 a.m. Office hours 10.00 a.m.–4.00 p.m.

Facilities: Robing rooms. Two interview rooms. Drinks machine.

Travel: NR Epsom (Waterloo 31 min., Victoria 36 min.) plus 5 min. walk.

LRT 293.

From station turn left along Station Approach. Turn right into Waterloo Rd. and proceed across High St. into Ashley Rd. County Ct. 1st left, 50 yds on right.

Driving: A24 to Epsom town centre. From High St. bear left into Ashley Rd. onto one-way system. Follow walking directions.

Parking: Pay and display, Hook Rd. Multi-storey, Ashley Centre via one-way system.

EPSOM COUNTY COURT—
CONTINUED
Eating out:

McDonald's	restaurant	High St.
Coffee bars		The Mall

FELTHAM MAGISTRATES' COURT,
HOUNSLOW MAGISTRATES' COURT (Also sits at
Brentford.)

Hanworth Rd., Feltham, Middx. TW13 5AF.

Telephone: (020) 8917 3400. Fax: (020) 8917 3527.

DX: 133821 Feltham 3.

Court times: Doors open 9.00 a.m.–4.00 p.m. Court sits 10.00 a.m. and 2.15 p.m. daily. Block booking/appointment system in operation—contact Scheduling Office for timing detail if in doubt at Brentford ((020) 8917 3400). Office hours 9.00 a.m.–4.00 p.m. Telephone contact 8.45 a.m.–5.00 p.m.

Facilities: Advocates' room. Witness waiting room. Interview rooms. Stair lift. Drinks machine.

Travel: NR Feltham (Waterloo 22–7 min.) plus 5 min. walk.

LRT 117, 235, 285, 490.

From station cross road into Hanworth Rd. Court 350 yds on left.

Driving: A315 Staines Rd. to A244 Hounslow Rd. to Feltham. Turn left opposite Feltham Station into Hanworth Rd.

Parking: Side-streets.

Eating out:

Moon on the Square	bar food	High St.
Jenny's	restaurant	High St.
The Airman	bar food	Hanworth Rd.
The Baker's Oven	take-away	High St.
McDonald's	restaurant/take-away	High St.
Tennessee Fried Chicken	restaurant/take-away	High St.
Seaworld	restaurant/take-away	High St.

FOLKESTONE COUNTY COURT
(Admin. from Ashford Cty Ct.),
FOLKESTONE (CHANNEL) MAGISTRATES' COURT,
FOLKESTONE YOUTH COURT

The Law Courts, Castle Hill Ave., Folkestone, Kent CT20 2DH.

Telephone: Mags: 01303 221762. Fax: 01303 220512. Cty: 0410 009127 (Fri. only).

DX: 135130 Dover 2.

Court times: Doors open 9.30 a.m. Court sits 10.00 a.m. Office hours 9.30 a.m.–12.30 p.m., 2.00 p.m.–4.00 p.m. Cty Ct. sits 10.00 a.m. Office hours 10.00 a.m.–4.00 p.m.

Facilities: Robing room. Advocates' room. Interview room. Public cafeteria. Vending machine.

FOLKESTONE COUNTY COURT—
CONTINUED

Travel: NR Folkestone Central (Charing Cross 1 hr. 15 min.–1 hr. 25 min.) plus 7 min. walk.

From Central Station bear right across Shorncliffe Rd. to Castle Hill Ave. opposite. Walk up hill. Law Cts. 400 yds on right. County Ct. immediately behind.

Driving: Follow M20 to Junc. 13. Turn right into Cherry Garden Ave. Cross Cheriton Rd./High St. at traffic lights, into Benchborough Rd. Follow road, which turns into Shorncliffe Rd., until roundabout. Turn right into Castle Hill Ave.

Parking: Side-streets by Ct. building.

Eating out:

The Central Hotel	bar food	Broadmead Rd.
The Happy Frenchman	bar food	Christchurch Rd.
USA Hamburger Bar	restaurant	Bouverie Rd. West

GRAVESEND COUNTY COURT,
KENT IMMIGRATION TRIBUNALS

26 King St., Gravesend, Kent DA12 2DU.

Telephone: 01474 321771. Fax: 01474 534811.

DX: 98140 Gravesend 2.

Court times: Doors open 9.00 a.m. Court sits 10.00 a.m. and 2.15 p.m.

Facilities: None.

Travel: NR Gravesend (Charing Cross, Cannon St., London Bridge 47 min.) plus 10 min. walk.

From station turn right into Clive Rd. First left Stoke St. Right into King St. Court on right.

Driving: A2 to junction with A227 11 miles east of Dartford. Take A227 north then A226 to Gravesend.

Parking: Multi-storey car parks for Anglesea and St. George's shopping centres.

Eating out:

The Albion	bar food	High St.
McDonald's	restaurant	New St.
Caesar's American Restaurant		King St.
King's Head	bar food and restaurant	King St.

GRAYS MAGISTRATES' COURT,
SOUTH WEST ESSEX MAGISTRATES' COURT

The Court House, Orsett Rd., Grays, Essex RM17 5DA.

Telephone: 01268 363400. Fax: 01268 363497 (Admin. Centre).

DX: 140100 Basildon 10.

Court times: Doors open 9.30 a.m. Court sits 10.00 a.m.

GRAYS MAGISTRATES' COURT—
CONTINUED

Facilities: Advocates' room. Interview room. No on-premises catering.

Travel: NR Grays (Fenchurch St. 33 min.) plus 5 min. walk.

From station/bus station: Mags Ct.: Proceed into High St. down hill to end. Court opposite.

Driving: A13 to Grays then A126 into town centre. Mags Ct. on one-way system at London Rd. A2013.

Parking: Free multi-storey behind shopping centre in High St.

Eating out:

McDonald's	restaurant	High St.
Seafarer	restaurant	High St.
The Pullman	bar food	Station

GREAT YARMOUTH AND NORTH NORFOLK MAGISTRATES' COURT, GREAT YARMOUTH YOUTH COURT

The Court House, North Quay, Great Yarmouth, Norfolk NR30 1PW.

Telephone: 01493 849800. Fax: 01493 852169.

DX: 139400 Great Yarmouth 3.

Court times: Doors open 9.00 a.m. Court sits 10.00 a.m.

Facilities: Waiting room. Interview room. Advocates' room. Canteen.

Travel: NR Great Yarmouth (Liverpool St. 3 hrs. 5 min. via Norwich) plus 10 min. walk.

From station cross footbridge over river and bear left. Mags Ct. is cream brick building on riverside. County Ct. is located in Mags Ct.

Driving: M11–A11–Norwich–A47 Great Yarmouth then signs to Quay.

Parking: Pay and display 200 yds from Court House.

Eating out:

The Star Hotel	bar food	North Quay
The White Swan		North Quay
Fatso's		King St.
Zak's		King St.

GREENWICH MAGISTRATES' COURT, INNER LONDON YOUTH COURTS CENTRE 2 (Also sits at Camberwell.)
(LEWISHAM, SOUTHWARK, GREENWICH YOUTH COURTS)

7–9 Blackheath Rd., Greenwich, London SE10 8PG.

Telephone: Mags: (020) 8276 1341. Fax: (020) 8276 1399.

DX: 35203 Greenwich West.

Court times: Doors open 9.15 a.m. Courts sit: Mags 10.15 a.m., Y. 10.00 a.m.

GREENWICH MAGISTRATES' COURT—
CONTINUED

Facilities: Interview rooms. Vending machines.

Travel: NR, Und. New Cross (London Bridge 6 min., Charing Cross 13 min., Whitechapel 11 min.) plus 15 min. walk or 53.

NR DLR Greenwich (Cannon St. 11 min., London Bridge 8 min.) plus 10 min. walk.

LRT 47, 53, 177.

From New Cross Station turn left along New Cross Rd. and proceed approx. 1 mile. Court on left at junction of Blackheath Rd. and Greenwich High Rd.

From Greenwich Station turn right into High Rd. Court 600 yds on left, around corner of main road.

Driving: Courts situated on A2 at junction with A206 Greenwich High Rd.

Parking: Very limited in side-streets to rear.

Eating out:

Cafe	snacks	Blackheath Rd.
Cafe	snacks	Greenwich High Rd.
Greenwich Inn	bar food	Greenwich High Rd.

GUILDFORD CROWN COURT

Bedford Road, Guildford, Surrey GU1 4ST.

Telephone: 01483 468500. Fax: 01483 579545.

DX: 97862 Guildford 5.

Court times: Doors open 9.00 a.m. Court sits 10.15 a.m. Office hours 9.00 a.m.–5.00 p.m.

Facilities: Robing room. Interview rooms. Bar mess. Public canteen.

GUILDFORD COUNTY COURT,
GUILDFORD (SOUTH WEST SURREY) MAGISTRATES' COURT,
GUILDFORD YOUTH COURT,
GUILDFORD CORONER'S COURT

The Law Courts, Mary Rd., Guildford, Surrey GU1 4AS.

Telephone: Cty: 01483 595200. Fax: 01483 300031. Mags: 01483 534811. Fax: 01483 449208. Robing room: 01483 64499.

DX: (Cty) 97860 Guildford 5. (Mags) 97865 Guildford 5.

Court times: Doors open 9.00 a.m. Courts sit: Mags/Y 10.00 a.m., District Judges' Lists 10.00 a.m. Cty 10.00 a.m. Office hours: Cty: 10.00 a.m.–4.00 p.m. Mags: 9.00 a.m.–4.30 p.m.

Facilities: Cty: Robing room. Interview room. Drinks machine. Mags: WRVS coffee a.m.

Travel: NR Guildford (Waterloo 35–58 min.) plus 10 min. walk. Through station car park. Turn left to Bridge St. and cross river. Turn left Onslow St. and proceed 300 yds along main road. Court 100 yds on left before police station. Crown Court is directly behind across the public car park.

GUILDFORD COUNTY COURT—
CONTINUED

Driving: A3 s/p Guildford. At traffic lights turn right. At 500 yds traffic lights turn left into Woodbridge Rd. Under bridge take 2nd right s/p Law Courts.

Parking: Pay and display Bedford Rd. immediately at rear of courts and in front of Crown Court.

Eating out:

The Food Court	restaurant	top floor, Friary Centre

HAMPSTEAD (CLERKENWELL) MAGISTRATES' COURT

55 Downshire Hill, Hampstead, London NW3 1PB.

Telephone: (020) 7435 1436. Fax: (020) 7794 1803.

Court times: Doors open 9.15 a.m. Court sits 10.00 a.m. Office hours 8.30 a.m.–4.30 p.m.

Facilities: Cold drinks. Public telephone. Advocates' room.

Travel: Und. Hampstead plus 5 min. walk.

NR Hampstead Heath (North London Line) plus 10 min. walk.

LT 268, 46.

From Und. station turn left down Rosslyn Hill (High St). Downshire Hill fifth on left. Court 25 yds on right.

From NR station turn right up South End Rd. Left into Keats Grove and left into Downshire Hill. Court 150 yds on left.

Driving: Court on corner of A502 High St. (Rosslyn Hill).

Parking: In Downshire Hill and side-streets. Restricted parking on vouchers. Car park in East Heath Rd.

Eating out:

Beths	English restaurant	Downshire Hill
House on the Hill	wine bar	Rosslyn Hill
Rosslyn Arms	bar food	Rosslyn Hill
Dome	cafe/restaurant	Rosslyn Hill
Cafe Rouge	cafe/restaurant	Rosslyn Hill

HARINGEY MAGISTRATES' COURT (See also Enfield),
HARINGEY YOUTH COURT (Thurs. 10.00 a.m.),
HARINGEY FAMILY PROCEEDINGS COURT (Mon.,
Tues., and Fri. 10.00 a.m.)

Highgate Court House, Bishops Rd., Highgate, London N6 4HS.

Telephone: (020) 8340 3472. Warrant office: (020) 8340 8055. Fax: (020) 8348 3343.

DX: 123550/1/2 Highgate 3.

Court times: Doors open 8.00 a.m. Court sits 10.00 a.m. and 2.00 p.m.

Facilities: Advocates' room. Drinks machine. CPS room.

Travel: Und. Highgate (Embankment 20 min.) plus 5 min. walk.

LRT 43, 134, 143, 263.

HARINGEY MAGISTRATES' COURT— CONTINUED

From station turn right up hill. Over traffic lights. Bishops Rd. first left. Court opposite.

Driving: Court on A1 south of junction with B550 (at The Woodman).

Parking: In front and side-streets.

Eating out:

The Woodman	bar food	Archway Rd.
The Black Rose	bar food	Archway Rd.
Cooks on the Hill	sandwich bar	Archway Rd.

HARLOW COUNTY COURT

Gate House, The High, Harlow, Essex CM20 1UW.
Telephone: 01279 443291, 01279 635628. Fax: 01279 451110.
DX: 97700 Harlow 2.
Court times: Doors open 9.00 a.m. Court sits 10.00 a.m. (District Judge). Office hours 10.00 a.m.–4.00 p.m.
Facilities: Male/female robing rooms. Interview rooms. Drinks machine. Lift. Nearby parking facilities.

HARLOW (NORTH WEST ESSEX) MAGISTRATES' COURT (see also Epping),
HARLOW YOUTH COURT

The Court House, South Gate, The High, Harlow, Essex CM20 1HH.
Telephone: 01279 693200. Fax: 01279 693298.
DX: 140080 Harlow 5.
Court times: Doors open 9.00 a.m. Court sits 10.00 a.m. Office hours 9.00 a.m.–4.30 p.m.
Facilities: Advocates' room. Vending machines. Video link Remand/Conference. Loop system.
Travel: NR Harlow Town (Liverpool St. 35 min.) plus Town buses or taxis.

From bus station Mags Ct. by Civic Sq. South Gate next to police station. County Ct. through Harvey Centre, exit by Tesco. Court in building above HSBC Bank.

Driving: M11 Junc. 7 then A414/A1075 to town centre. Proceed to inner ring road, Hayden's Rd. For Cty Ct. park in multi-storey car park by Tesco or Playhouse Theatre.

For Mags Ct. continue past Harlow Technical College. Turn left at roundabout onto Third Avenue, over roundabout to Velizy Avenue and 1st exit on left s/p Police Station.

Parking: Cty: as above. Mags: pay and display on ring road.

Eating out:

McDonald's	restaurant	Harvey Centre
Littlewoods	restaurant	Harvey Centre
Burger King	restaurant	Harvey Centre

HARROW CROWN COURT

Hailsham Drive, off Headstone Drive, Harrow, Middx. HA1 4TU.
Telephone: (020) 8424 2294. Fax: (020) 8424 2209.
DX: 97335 Harrow 5.
Court times: Doors open 9.00 a.m. Court sits 10.00 a.m. Office hours 9.00 a.m.–5.00 p.m.
Facilities: Robing room. Interview rooms. Public dining room.

HARROW MAGISTRATES' COURT,
HARROW YOUTH COURT (Tues. 10.00 a.m. and 2.00 p.m.)

Rosslyn Crescent, Wealdstone, Harrow, Middx. HA1 2JY.
Telephone: (020) 8427 5146. Gaoler: (020) 8427 2711. Fax: (020) 8863 9518.
DX: 30451 Harrow 3.
Court times: Doors open 9.00 a.m. Court sits 10.00 a.m. Office hours 9.15 a.m.–4.00 p.m.
Facilities: Advocates' room. Hot drinks machine.
Travel: NR, Und. Harrow and Wealdstone (Euston 27 min.) plus 5 min. walk.
LRT 140, 182, 186, 258.
From Wealdstone exit of station for Mags Ct. turn right over the bridge. Rosslyn Crescent 2nd left. Court 50 yds on left. For Crown Ct. turn left out of station along High St. Turn left at Headstone Drive. Court on right under bridge.
Driving: Take A405 or A4006 to Harrow-on-the-Hill then A409 s/p Wealdstone. Mags Ct. in road opposite Harrow Civic Centre. For Crown Ct. continue over bridge to Wealdstone High St. Turn left into Headstone Drive.
Parking: Rosslyn Crescent and side-streets.
Eating out:

| New Taj Mahal | Indian restaurant | Station Rd. |
| McDonald's | restaurant | Wealdstone High St. |

HARWICH (NORTH EAST ESSEX) MAGISTRATES' COURT,
NORTH EAST ESSEX YOUTH COURT

363 Main Road, Dovercourt, Harwich, Essex CO12 4DN.
Telephone: All admin. from Chelmsford: 01245 313300. Fax: 01245 313399.
Court times: Doors open 9.30 a.m. Court sits 10.00 a.m.
Facilities: Advocates' room. Interview room. No on-premises catering. Vending machine.
Travel: NR Harwich Parkeston Quay or Dovercourt (Liverpool St. 1 hr. 25 min.–1 hr. 35 min.) plus taxi (*NB* taxis easier to find at Dovercourt).

HARWICH (NORTH EAST ESSEX) MAGISTRATES' COURT—CONTINUED

Driving: A12 to Colchester then A120 to Harwich. Proceed along Main Rd. A604 s/p Parkeston. At large roundabout exit s/p Dovercourt. At top of Parkeston Hill turn left into Main Rd. Court past hospital opposite Dolphin Sails.

Parking: Car park.

Eating out:

Manor Road Stores	coffee shop	Main Rd.

HASTINGS COUNTY COURT,
HASTINGS MAGISTRATES' COURT,
HASTINGS YOUTH COURT

The Law Courts, Horntye Park, Bohemia Rd., Hastings, East Sussex TN34 1ND (1QX for CC).

Telephone: Cty: 01424 435128. Fax: 01424 421585. Mags: 01424 437644. Fax: 01424 429878.

DX: 98150 Hastings 2 (Cty only).

Website: www.sussex-magistrates.co.uk.

Court times: Doors open 9.00 a.m. Mags Ct. sits 10.00 a.m. and 2.15 p.m. Office hours 9.00 a.m.–4.30 p.m. County Ct. sits 10.00 a.m. Office hours 10.00 a.m.–4.00 p.m.

Facilities: Robing room. Interview rooms. Public cafeteria. Public telephone.

Travel: NR Hastings (Charing Cross 1 hr. 50 min.) plus 20 min. walk or taxi.

SD 15, 799 plus local Hastings & District buses.

From station approach cross into and proceed to end of Havelock Rd. Turn right into Cambridge Rd. which becomes Bohemia Rd. Court 500 yds on right by police station.

Driving: A21 to Hastings. Court actually on A21 Bohemia Rd.

Eating out:

Horntye Park Sports Complex	Bohemia Rd.
The Cinque Ports	Bohemia Rd.
Cafes in town and at Warrior Sq.	

HAYWARDS HEATH COUNTY COURT

Milton House, Milton Rd., Haywards Heath, West Sussex RH16 1YZ.

Telephone: 01444 447970. Fax: 01444 415282.

DX: 98160 Haywards Heath 3.

Court times: Doors open 9.30 a.m. Court sits: 10.00 a.m. Office hours 9.00 a.m.–5.00 p.m.

Facilities: Interview room. Drinks machine.

Travel: NR Haywards Heath (Victoria 50 min.) plus 5 min. walk.

SD 161–2, 164, 173, 175, 189, 715, 762, 770.

From station front entrance turn left under bridge and up hill. Turn right at Caffyn's garage into Milton Rd. Court on central island in one-way system.

Driving: M23–A23, from Bolney A273 to Haywards Heath, left at The Dolphin, quarter mile down Paddockhall Rd. on one-way system.

Parking: Court car park, otherwise NCP nearby.

Eating out:

Burrell Arms	bar food	Boltro Rd.
The Green Room	snack bar	Boltro Rd.
Hong Kong	Chinese restaurant	Perrymount Rd. (Nr NR)

MID-SUSSEX (HAYWARDS HEATH) MAGISTRATES' COURT,
MID-SUSSEX YOUTH COURT

The Court House, Bolnore Rd., Haywards Heath, West Sussex RH16 4BA.

Telephone: 01444 417611. Fax: 01444 472639.

DX: 135596 Haywards Heath 6.

Website: www.sussex-magistrates.co.uk.

Court times: Doors open 9.00 a.m. Courts sit 10.00 a.m. Office hours 9.00 a.m.–4.30 p.m.

Facilities: Advocates' room. Duty solicitor's room. Two interview rooms. Vending machines for hot/cold drinks, snacks. Public telephones.

Travel: NR Haywards Heath (Victoria 50 min.) plus 20 min. walk. From station, turn left and under tunnel. Cross over to old police station and proceed up Boltro Rd. Ten min. walk to The Dolphin public house. Court opposite, by new police station.

SD Buses stop at Beech Hurst Gardens or the Broadway, 5 min. walk from Ct. building.

Driving: M23–A23 from Bolney A272 to Haywards Heath. Mags Ct. 50 yds from new police station, opposite The Dolphin.

Parking: Limited public car park at Court House. It is essential to avoid congestion in nearby roads.

Eating out:

The Dolphin	bar food	opposite Court House

Restaurants and sandwich bars in town centre, 15–20 min. walk away.

HEMEL HEMPSTEAD COUNTY COURT

First Floor, Lord Alexander House, Waterhouse St., Hemel Hempstead, Herts. HP1 1FT.

Telephone: 01442 265593. Fax: 01442 219359.

Court times: Doors open 10 a.m. (9.30 a.m. on sitting days.) Court sits 10.00 a.m. and 2.00 p.m.

Facilities: Interview room. Robing rooms. No on-premises catering.

HEMEL HEMPSTEAD (DACORUM) MAGISTRATES' COURT,
HEMEL HEMPSTEAD YOUTH COURT

The Court House, Dacorum Way, Hemel Hempstead, Herts. HP1 1HF.

Telephone: 01923 297500. Fax: 01923 297528.

DX: 51509 Watford 2.

Court times: Doors open 9.00 a.m. Court sits 10.00 a.m. and 2.00 p.m.

Facilities: Advocates' room. Interview room.

Travel: NR Hemel Hempstead (Euston 28–33 min.) plus Rover bus or 301, 307 to bus station.

From bus station: Turn right, facing pond. Cross over into Dacorum Way. Mags Ct. 150 yds on right.

Driving: From M1 Junc. 8 or A41 and A4147 into town. At octagonal roundabout turn into High St. (marked Town Centre). Turn left after Pavilion Theatre into Civic Centre area. Mags Ct. at end of unmarked road, on right. For Cty Ct., from multi-roundabout take 2nd mini-roundabout and turn right along High St. Turn left into Water Gardens.

Parking: Large municipal car park to left, near bus station. Cty: Water Gardens car park.

Eating out:

Sea Pride	fish restaurant	High St.
KFC	restaurant	High St.
Snack Bar		Market Square
Great Harry	bar food	Market Square

HENDON MAGISTRATES' COURT

The Hyde, Hendon, London NW9 7BY.

Telephone: (020) 8441 9042. Warrant Office: (020) 8440 5106. Securicor: (020) 8205 0584. Fax: (020) 8205 4595.

DX: 8626 Barnet.

Court times: Doors open 9.30 a.m. Court sits 10.00 a.m.

Facilities: Interview room. Drinks machine.

Travel: NR Hendon (St. Pancras 16 min., King's Cross Thameslink) plus 15 min. walk or 83, 183.

Und. Hendon Central (Embankment 25 min.) plus 83.

LRT 32, 83, 142, 183.

From NR station turn right across bridge. Proceed down to West Hendon Broadway. Turn right. Cross lights. Court 800 yds on left.

HENDON MAGISTRATES' COURT—
CONTINUED

Driving: Court situated on A5 Edgware Rd. one mile north of Staples Corner flyover, opposite Sainsbury's.

Parking: Domestic car park. Side-streets.

Eating out:

Surrey Arms	bar food	The Hyde (North)
Wimpy	restaurant	The Hyde (Colindale)
Sainsbury's	cafeteria	The Hyde

HERTFORD MAGISTRATES' COURT,
EAST HERTS MAGISTRATES' COURT (Also sits at Cheshunt.)
EAST HERTS YOUTH COURT

Shire Hall, Fore St., Hertford, Herts. SG13 1DF. (The office for both North and East Herts is now at Bayley House, Sish Lane, Stevenage, SG1 3SS.)

Telephone: 01992 588988. Office 01438 730412. Fax: 01438 730413.

DX: 122187 Old Stevenage.

Court times: Doors open 9.00 a.m. Court sits 10.00 a.m. Office hours 9.00 a.m.–4.00 p.m.

Facilities: Advocates' room. Interview rooms. Refreshments.

Travel: NR Hertford North (Moorgate 35 min.) plus bus 390 or 25 min. walk. Hertford East (Liverpool St. 48 min.) plus 15 min. walk. From Hertford North turn right onto North Rd. and left into St. Andrews St. Cross Mill Bridge to roundabout and turn left into Fore St. Court on left beyond Market Sq.

From Hertford East turn right into Railway St. Bear left into South St. and turn right into Fore St. Court 250 yds on right, corner of Salisbury Sq.

HERTFORD COUNTY COURT

4th Floor, Sovereign House, Hale Rd., Hertford, Herts. SG13 8DY.

Telephone: 01992 503954. Fax: 01992 501274.

DX: 97710 Hertford 2.

Court times: Doors open 9.30 a.m. Court sits 10.00 a.m. Office hours 10.00 a.m.–4.00 p.m.

Facilities: Two interview rooms.

Travel: NR Hertford North (see above).

From Hertford North turn right out of station. Follow road over mini-roundabout into St. Andrew St. After Waters Garage take subway on right. At end of subway turn left into Gascoyne Way. Follow road over West St., passing garage on right. Sovereign House is next office block. From Hertford East turn right at mini-roundabout into Railway St. At next mini-roundabout turn right (still following Railway St). Cross road leading to bus depot and continue through shopping centre.

Cross at pelican crossing and turn left. Follow road past memorial in Parliament Sq. Turn right into Castle St. Take underpass on left. Sovereign House is at end of underpass.

Driving: A10 then A414 s/p Hertford Town Centre. For Mags Ct.: park at multi-storey on inner ring road (Gascoyne Way). Walk through passage by main post office. Turn left into Fore St. Shire Hall is large building on island in market place 200 yds on right. For Cty Ct. follow ring road to County Hall and park.

Parking: As above.

Eating out: Mags:

Salisbury Arms Hotel	bar food	Market Place
Pizza Town	restaurant	Fore St.
Dinsdale Arms	bar food	Fore St.
Cty:		
The Gaunt	bar food	Hale Rd.

HIGHBURY CORNER MAGISTRATES' COURT

51 Holloway Rd., London N7 8JA.

Telephone: (020) 7506 3147. Fax: (020) 7506 3191.

Inner London Magistrates' Court Service central switchboard 0845 600 8889.

DX: 51855 Highbury.

Court times: Doors open 9.30 a.m. Court sits 10.30 a.m.

Facilities: Advocates' room. Interview rooms. No on-premises catering. No childcare. Disabled access.

Travel: NR Highbury and Islington (Moorgate 6 min., Liverpool St. 9 min.).

Und. Highbury and Islington (Victoria 11 min.).

LRT 4, 19, 30, 43, 271.

From station turn left. Court 150 yds on left.

Driving: Court on A1 at Holloway Rd.

Parking: No easy parking in vicinity.

Eating out:

Trattoria Trevi	Italian restaurant	Holloway Rd.
The White Swan	bar food	Highbury Corner

Sandwich bars at Holloway Rd. and Upper St.

HIGH WYCOMBE COUNTY COURT
(Now incorporates Amersham County Court),
WYCOMBE MAGISTRATES' COURT,
WYCOMBE FAMILY PROCEEDINGS COURT (Thurs.),
WYCOMBE YOUTH COURT (Tues.)

The Law Courts, Easton St., High Wycombe, Bucks. HP11 1LR.

HIGH WYCOMBE COUNTY COURT—
CONTINUED

Telephone: Cty: 01494 436374. Fax: 01494 459430. Mags/Y: 01494 651035. FP: 01494 651028. Fax: 01494 651030. Accounts: 01908 684902.

DX: (Mags/Y/FP) 4437 High Wycombe 1. (Cty) 97880 High Wycombe 3.

e-mail: wycombe.magistrates@tv.mcs.gsi.gov.uk.

Court times: Doors open 9.00 a.m. Courts sit 10.00 a.m. Office hours: Cty 10.00 a.m.–4.00 p.m. Mags/FP 9.30 a.m.–4.30 p.m.

Facilities: Robing room. Interview rooms. Witness rooms. Duty solicitor (Mon.–Fri.). Tea bar. Mother and baby room.

Travel: NR High Wycombe (Marylebone 42–57 min.) plus 10 min. walk. From station turn left down hill. First left into Easton St. at lights. Courts 200 yds on right.

Driving: A404–M40 Junc. 4 into town. Follow one-way system to Easton St. Courts on right.

Parking: Multi-storey 100 yds from court in Easton St. Pay and display on left beyond court.

Eating out: In Easton St., High St., Crendon St., and Castle St.

HITCHIN COUNTY COURT

Park House, 1–12 Old Park Rd., Hitchin, Herts. SG5 1LX.

Telephone: 01462 443750. Fax: 01462 443758.

DX: 97720 Hitchin 2.

Court times: Doors open 9.00 a.m. Court sits: Circuit Judge 10.30 a.m. District Judge 10.00 a.m. Office hours 10.00 a.m.–4.00 p.m.

Facilities: Robing room. Interview room. Water dispensing machine. Disabled access.

Travel: NR Hitchin (King's Cross 33–41 min., Moorgate 53 min.) plus taxi LC <u>83</u>, <u>84</u>, or Town <u>182</u>, or 30 min. walk.

Ar 300, 303–4, 314, 323, 386.

Cty Ct.: From main town shops proceed through Woolworth's to rear exit. Cross over to library. Court in office block on opposite corner by roundabout.

Driving: Take A1(M) to turn off s/p Hitchin Stevenage. A602 into Hitchin town centre. On entry into town take 4th exit at roundabout into London Rd. At foot of hill for Cty Ct. turn left. Court half a mile on left.

Parking: Small domestic car park. Public car park off Bancroft and at St. Mary's Sq.

Eating out: in main square.

HORNSEY CORONER'S COURT

Myddelton Road, Hornsey, London N8 7PY.

Telephone: (020) 8348 4411. Fax: (020) 8347 5229.

Court times: Doors open 8:00 a.m. Court sits 9.30 a.m.

HORNSEY CORONER'S COURT—
CONTINUED

Facilities: Waiting room. No on-premises catering.

Travel: NR Hornsey (Moorgate 15 min.) plus 5 min. walk.

Und. Turnpike Lane (King's Cross 12 min., Piccadilly Circus 20 min.) plus 15 min. walk.

LRT 41, 144, 144A, W2.

From Hornsey Station exit left on bridge and turn right into Tottenham Lane. Turn left into High St. Myddleton Rd. is 2nd on right. Court 200 yds.

From Turnpike Lane Station exit into and proceed up Turnpike Lane (which becomes Hornsey High St.) for 1,000 yds. Myddleton Rd. is 8th turning on right.

Driving: From central London via Green Lanes A105 to Turnpike Lane A504 and turn left. At 3rd set traffic lights bear right into High St. Court 2nd turning on right. Via Campsbourne Rd.

Parking: Side-streets to front.

Eating out: Pubs and restaurants within 5 min. walk.

HORSEFERRY ROAD MAGISTRATES' COURT

70 Horseferry Rd., London SW1P 2AX.

Telephone: (020) 7805 1159. Fax: (020) 7805 1193.

Magistrates' Court Service central switchboard 0845 600 8889.

DX: 120551 Victoria 6.

Court times: Doors open 9.15 a.m. Court sits 10.30 a.m.

Facilities: Advocates' room. Interview room. Witness waiting room. Disabled facilities.

Travel: Und. Pimlico, St. James' Park, Victoria, and Westminster plus 15 min. walk each.

LRT 3, 77, 77A, 88, 149, 159, 507.

From Westminster station cross Parliament Sq. Along Millbank. Horseferry Rd. on right at roundabout. Court 200 yds on right at corner of Tufton St.

Parking: Limited meters in vicinity. NCP car park nearby.

Eating out:

Marquis of Granby	bar food	Dean Bradley St.
The Millbank	snack bar	Horseferry Rd.
The Grosvenor	snack bar	Horseferry Rd.
The Barley Mow	bar food	Horseferry Rd.
White Horse and Bower	bar food	Horseferry Rd.
Selmo's	snack bar	Horseferry Rd.
The Crypt	restaurant	Smith Sq.
Smith's Square	café bar	Smith Sq.

HORSHAM COUNTY COURT,
HORSHAM MAGISTRATES' COURT (admin. from Mid-Sussex Magistrates' Court),

HORSHAM COUNTY COURT—
CONTINUED
HORSHAM YOUTH COURT
The Law Courts, Hurst Rd., Horsham, West Sussex RH12 2EU (Mags: RH12 2ET).
Telephone: Cty: 01403 252474. Fax: 01403 258844. Mags: 01444 417611. Fax: 01444 472639.
DX: (Cty) 98170 Horsham 2. (Mags) 135596 Haywards Heath 6.
Website www.sussex-magistrates.co.uk.
Court times: Doors open: Cty: 9.30 a.m. Mags: 9.00 a.m. Courts sit: Cty: 10.00 a.m. Mags: 10.00 a.m. Office hours: Cty 10.00 a.m.–4.00 p.m.
Facilities: Male/female robing rooms. Interview rooms. Public telephone. Vending machine for hot/cold drinks, snacks.
Travel: NR Horsham (Victoria 1 hr. 15 min.) plus 5 min. walk. From station cross roundabout to Hurst Rd. Courts 300 yds on left.
Driving: M23 to Crawley then A264 to Horsham. Follow road into town and take directions as from station.
Parking: Car park for Law Courts visitors.
Eating out:

Station Hotel	restaurant	Hurst Rd.
Maltshovel		Springfield Rd.
The Station	restaurant	Hurst Rd.

HOVE TRIAL CENTRE
The Court House, Lansdowne Rd., Hove, East Sussex BN3 3BN. (For hearings only. Admin. by Lewes Combined Crown and County Court.)
Telephone: 01273 229200. Fax: 01273 229229.
DX: 99402 Hove 3.
Court times: Doors open 9.30 a.m. Court sits 10.30 a.m.
Facilities: Advocates' room. Interview room. Tea bar. Robing room.
Travel: NR Hove (Victoria 1 hr. 5 min.) plus 15 min. walk or NR Brighton plus No. 6 bus (Town).
SD 230, 700, 736, 738, 799.
From station proceed down Goldstone Villas. Take second left Blatchington Rd. Cross to Eaton Rd. and cross The Drive. At end of Eaton Rd. court is diagonally opposite to right.
Driving: M23–A23 to Brighton. At Preston Circus turn right into New England Rd. Over Seven Dials into Vernon Terrace. Take 4th right Western Rd., 5th right Holland Rd. Court on corner of Lansdowne Rd. next left.
Parking: Car park adjoining.
Eating out:

The Wick	bar food	Western Rd.
Grubbs	cafe	Western Rd.
Twizzles	cafe	Western Rd.

HUNTINGDON COUNTY COURT

Grd Floor Godwin House, George St., Huntingdon, Cambs. PE28 3BD.
Telephone: 01480 450932. Fax: 01480 435397.
DX: 96650. Huntingdon 2.
Court times: Court sits 10.00 a.m.–4.00 p.m.
Facilities: Consulting room (one). Solicitors' room (one).

HUNTINGDON MAGISTRATES' COURT (Mon., Wed., Thur., Fri.),
HUNTINGDON YOUTH COURT (Tue.)

The Town Hall, Market Hill, Huntingdon, Cambs. PE29 3PJ.
Telephone: 01733 763971. Fax: 01733 313749.
Court times: Doors open 9.00 a.m. Court sits 10.00 a.m.
Facilities: Advocates' room. Interview room.
Travel: NR Huntingdon (Kings Cross 1 hr.) plus 5–10 min. walk.
For Cty Ct.: from station turn right into George St. For Mags Ct.:
from station turn right along high street to T junction. Turn right.
Town Hall 300 yds ahead.
Driving: From A14 turn off onto Brampton Rd. which leads onto
George St. George St. also comes off the High St.
Parking: At rear of court for disabled users only. At railway station
400 yds away.
Eating out: George Hotel 200 yds.

ILFORD COUNTY COURT

Buckingham Rd., Ilford, Essex IG1 1BR.
Telephone: (020) 8478 1132. Fax: (020) 8553 2824.
DX: 97510 Ilford 3 (receive only).
Court times: Doors open 8.00 a.m. Court sits 10.00 a.m. Office
hours 10.00 a.m.–4.00 p.m.
Facilities: Robing rooms. No on-premises catering. Hot/cold drinks
machine.
Travel: NR Ilford/Seven Kings (Liverpool St. 15–18 min.) plus
20 min. walk.
LRT 25, 86, 145, 148, 150, 167, 247.
From Ilford Station turn right and left into Ilford Shopping Precinct
towards Seven Kings s/p Romford. Court mile on right.
From Seven Kings Station turn right into High Rd. Court 600 yds on
left.
Driving: Court on A118 High Rd., Ilford. From Ilford town centre
follow new one-way system at rear of High Rd. s/p Seven Kings,
Romford. Court 4th right on corner of High Rd. at Buckingham Rd.
Parking: Meters and side-streets to rear.

ILFORD COUNTY COURT—
CONTINUED

Eating out:

McDonald's	restaurant	High Rd.[*]
El Greco	Greek restaurant	High Rd.[*]
The Cauliflower	St. George's Tavern bar food	High Rd.[†]
The Cabin	snack bar	High Rd.[†]

[*]to Ilford †to Seven Kings

IMMIGRATION APPEALS TRIBUNALS

1. Taylor House, 88 Rosebery Ave., London EC1R 4QU.

Telephone: (020) 7862 4400. Fax: Tribunal listing section (020) 7862 4598. Courts section: (020) 7862 4280.

Court times: Doors open 9.00 a.m. Court sits 10.00 a.m. Office hours 9.00 a.m.–5.00 p.m.

Facilities: Waiting room. Consultation rooms. Disabled facilities. Baby changing facilities. Vending machines.

Travel: NR Kings Cross plus 15 min. walk from Grays Inn, 25 min. walk from Temple.

Und. Angel plus 10 min. walk. From station turn left along Upper St. and across traffic lights onto St. Johns St., 2nd right into Rosebery Ave.

2. York House, 2–3 Dukes Green Ave., Faggs Rd., Feltham, Middx TW14 0LS.

Telephone: (020) 8831 3567. Fax: (020) 8831 3500.

Court times: Doors open 9.00 a.m. Court sits 10.00 a.m. Office hours 9.00 a.m.–5.00 p.m.

Facilities: Waiting room. Consultation rooms. Vending machines. Disabled facilities. Baby changing facilities.

Travel: NR Feltham plus 15 min. walk or taxi.

Und. Hatton Cross (Holborn 25 min.) plus 10 min. walk. From Feltham station turn left along Hounslow Rd. and left into Harlington Rd. West. Cross over Staines Rd. into Faggs Rd. Dukes Green Ave. on left beyond Fire Station.

From Hatton Cross cross over Great South West Rd. into Hatton Rd. which becomes Faggs Rd. (A312). Dukes Green Ave. on right.

Driving: From central London take Great West Rd. A4 to Heston. At Cranford Roundabout take A30 Great South West Rd. At first traffic lights turn left onto A312 The Causeway which becomes Faggs Rd. Follow road round to left. Dukes Green Ave. on right.

Parking: Large car park.

Eating out:

Crown and Sceptre	bar food	Staines Rd.

INNER LONDON AND CITY FAMILY PROCEEDINGS COURT

59–65 Wells St., London W1A 3AE.

Telephone: (020) 7805 3400. Fax: (020) 7805 3490.

DX: 89268 Soho Square.

Court times: Doors open 9.00 a.m. Court sits 10.30 a.m. Office hours 9.00 a.m.–4.30 p.m. Switchboard open for enquiries until 5.00 p.m.

Facilities: Vending machines for hot/cold drinks, snacks. Facilities for the disabled: toilets, lifts to all floors, and ramp access. Baby changing rooms. Unsupervised playroom for toddlers. Public telephones on each floor.

Travel: Und. Oxford Circus, Tottenham Court Rd., Goodge St.

LRT 7, 8, 10, 25, 55, 73, 98, 176 pass at the end of Wells St.

From first two stations along Oxford St. to Wells St. Court 250 yds on left.

From Goodge St., along Goodge St. to Wells St. Court 50 yds on right.

Eating out:

Johnnies	fish restaurant/wine bar	Wells St.
The Champion	bar food	Wells St.
The Holyrood	bar food	Wells St.
West One	sandwich bar	Wells St.
The One Tun	bar food	Goodge St.

Many first-class restaurants in Charlotte St.

INNER LONDON CROWN COURT

Sessions House, Newington Causeway, London SE1 6AZ.

Telephone: (020) 7234 3100. Fax: (020) 7234 3222.

DX: 97345 Southwark 3.

Court times: Doors open 8.00 a.m. Court sits: from 10.00 a.m.

Facilities: Non-smoking building. Disabled access. Two male robing rooms. Female robing room. Consultation rooms. Bar mess. Public cafeteria (breakfast from 9.00 a.m.). Vending machines.

Travel: NR Elephant and Castle plus 5 min. walk.

Und. Elephant and Castle (Bank 6 min., Baker St. 15 min.) plus 10 min. walk. Borough (Bank 4 min.) plus 5 min. walk.

LRT 35, 40, 95, 133, P3.

From Elephant and Castle Station (Bakerloo exit) turn left along Newington Causeway. From Borough Station turn right along Borough High St.

Driving: A3/A3202 to Elephant and Castle roundabout. Follow walking directions.

Parking: Meters in side-streets. Limited parking at the Court. Public car parks nearby.

INNER LONDON CROWN COURT—
CONTINUED

Eating out:

The Ship	bar food	Borough Rd.
Trinity Arms	bar food	Trinity St.

Local sandwich bars.

INNER LONDON YOUTH COURTS
185 Marylebone Road, London NW1 5QG.

Telephone: FP (020) 7262 3211. Fax: (020) 7724 9685. Y (020) 7724 2305.

DX: 41741 Marylebone 2.

Court times: Doors open 9.15 a.m. Court sits 10.00 a.m. Office hours 9.15 a.m.–4.00 p.m.

Facilities: Advocates' room. Drinks machine.

Travel: Und. Edgware Road, Marylebone, Baker St.

NR Marylebone.

Courts on Marylebone Rd. just beyond junction with Seymour Place, adjacent to Magistrates' Court.

Driving: Court is on A40 where it becomes A501 Marylebone Rd.

Parking: Limited meter parking in vicinity.

Eating out: see entry for Marylebone Magistrates' Court.

*Other individual Family Proceedings and Youth Courts that may be contacted on the day of sitting in relation to that day's cases only are listed by separate entry as follows:

For ISLINGTON, CAMDEN, HACKNEY, and TOWER HAMLETS see separate entry under THAMES MAGISTRATES' COURT, INNER LONDON YOUTH COURTS CENTRE 1.

For LEWISHAM, SOUTHWARK, and GREENWICH YOUTH COURTS see entry under INNER LONDON YOUTH COURTS CENTRE 2.

For LAMBETH and WANDSWORTH see entry under BALHAM YOUTH COURT.

For HAMMERSMITH AND FULHAM, KENSINGTON AND CHELSEA, and WESTMINSTER YOUTH COURTS see entry under WEST LONDON MAGISTRATES' COURT.

IPSWICH COUNTY COURT
8 Arcade St., Ipswich, Suffolk IP1 1EJ.

Telephone: 01473 214256. Fax: 01473 251797.

DX: 97730 Ipswich 3.

Court times: Doors open 9.00 a.m. Court sits 10.00 a.m. Office hours 10.00 a.m.–4.00 p.m.

Facilities: Robing room. Interview rooms. Drinks machine. Children's room.

IPSWICH CROWN COURT

The Court House, 1 Russel Rd., Ipswich, Suffolk IP1 2AG.
Telephone: 01473 228585. Fax: 01473 228560.
DX: 729480 Ipswich 19.
Court times: Doors open 8.30 a.m. Court sits 10.30 a.m. Office hours 9.00 a.m.–5.00 p.m.
Facilities: Robing room. Interview room. Everest caterers refreshments.

SOUTH EAST SUFFOLK MAGISTRATES' COURT, SOUTH EAST SUFFOLK YOUTH COURT

Elm St., Ipswich, Suffolk IP1 2AP.
Telephone: 01473 217261. Fax: 01473 231249.
DX: 3232 Ipswich.
Court times: Doors open 9.00 a.m. Court sits 10.00 a.m. Office hours 8.30 a.m.–5.00 p.m. (Fri. 4.30 p.m.)
Facilities: Advocates' room. Interview room. Vending machine for drinks/snacks.
Travel: NR Ipswich (Liverpool St. 1 hr. 8 min.) plus 10–20 min. walk. From station cross to and proceed up Princes St. For Crown: At A137 Commercial Rd. (one-way system) turn left, cross over Chancey Rd. and turn left into Russell Rd. Count 150 yds on left. For Mags and Cty proceed up Princes St. to junction with Civic Drive. For Mags Courts turn left along Civic Drive. Court on right 250 yds. For Cty Ct. proceed across Civic Drive. Turn left into Museum St. and first right Arcade St. Court 200 yds on left.
Driving: A12 to Ipswich. For Crown: Follow inner ring road A137 west, Grafton Way. On Commercial Rd. (one-way system) take first exit to car park. Follow walking directions as from Commercial Rd. For Cty and Mags: Follow signs to station then as per walking directions on reaching Civic Drive; or from main interchange on entering Ipswich cross roundabout s/p Ipswich west and proceed across two more roundabouts into Civic Drive.
Parking: Crown/Mags: Multi-storey Civic Drive. Cty: Underground car park Civic Centre. Park and Ride Bury Rd. (Asda) London Rd.
Eating out: Crown/Mags:

The Black Horse	bar food	Blackhorse Lane
Queen's Head	bar food	Civic Drive
St. Mathew's Crusts	sandwich bar	St. Mathews Rd.
Cty:		
The Swan	bar food	by Town Hall
The Hawley	bar food	by Town Hall

ISLEWORTH CROWN COURT

36 Ridgeway Rd., Isleworth, London TW7 5LP.
Telephone: (020) 8380 4500 Fax: (020) 8568 5368.
DX: 97420 Isleworth 1.

ISLEWORTH CROWN COURT—
CONTINUED

Court times: Doors open 9.00 a.m. Court sits 10.15 a.m. Office hours 9.00 a.m.–5.00 p.m.

Facilities: Robing rooms. Conference rooms. Public canteen. Witness waiting rooms.

Travel: NR Isleworth (Waterloo 29 min.) plus 10 min. walk.

Und. Osterley (Piccadilly line) (Piccadilly Circus 22 min.) plus 15 min. walk.

LRT From Hounslow and Chiswick 237, 235. From Hounslow only H37. All go to Isleworth Station.

From Isleworth Station cross London Rd. and proceed up College Rd. Bear left into Ridgeway Rd. Court 250 yds on left in former hospital.

From Osterley Station turn left and proceed along Great West Rd. Ridgeway Rd. is 3rd right. Court 300 yds on right.

Driving: Great West Rd. A40 through Brentford. Ridgeway Rd. is 5th left past the Gillette Tower at Syon Lane (court s/p from Gt. West Rd.). Alternatively A315 passing Brentford Mags Court to Isleworth Station. Turn right and follow walking directions.

Parking: Car park in Osterley Rd.

Eating out:

The Bridge Inn	Thai	London Rd.
The Osterley Motel	bar meals	Great West Rd.

KING'S LYNN COUNTY COURT

Chequer House, 12 King St., King's Lynn, Norfolk PE30 1ES.

Telephone: 01553 772067. Fax: 01553 769824.

DX: 97740 King's Lynn 2.

Court times: Doors open 9.30 a.m. when court sits, 10.00 a.m. when it doesn't. Office hours 10.00 a.m.–4.00 p.m.

Facilities: Robing/advocates'/interview rooms. Drinks machine.

KING'S LYNN (NORWICH) CROWN COURT,
WEST NORFOLK MAGISTRATES' COURT,
WEST NORFOLK YOUTH COURT

The Court House, College Lane, King's Lynn, Norfolk PE30 1PQ.

Telephone: Crown: 01553 760847. Mags: 01553 770120. Fax: 01553 775098.

Court times: Doors open 9.00 a.m. Courts sit: Mags / Y. 10.00 a.m., Crown 10.30 a.m. Office hours 8.15 a.m.–4.45 p.m. (Fri. 4.00 p.m.).

Facilities: Robing/advocates' room. Interview room. NCS snack bar 9.30 a.m.–2.00 p.m.

Travel: NR King's Lynn (Liverpool St. 2 hrs. 5 min. King's Cross 1 hr. 40 min.) plus 20 min. walk/taxi.

Cty Ct.: From station turn left into St. Johns Terrace and follow into Blackfriars Rd. Proceed up New Conduit St. and into Purfleet St. Turn right into King St. at the end of Purfleet St.

Crown/Mags Cts.: As for Cty Ct. At the end of Conduit St. turn left down High St. to reach St. James St. Turn right and follow on to College Lane. The court is opposite the Town Hall.

Driving: A10 to King's Lynn via Cambridge, Ely, Downham Market, becomes London Rd. For Crown/Mags pass under stone arch (South Gates). At fifth set of traffic lights (including pedestrian crossings) turn left into Millfleet. At small roundabout turn right and park in NCP car park in Church St. or in Saturday Market Place (turn left at end of Church St.).

Parking: Cty: Tuesday Market Place. Mags: On the Quay. Car parks off Saturday Market Place.

Eating out:

Cty Ct.: Wenn's	wine bar	Saturday Market Place
Mags Ct.: Wenn's	wine bar	Saturday Market Place
Littlewoods	restaurant	High St.
Debenhams	restaurant	High St.

KINGSTON-UPON-THAMES COUNTY COURT

St. James' Rd., Kingston-upon-Thames, Surrey KT1 2AD.
Telephone: (020) 8546 8843. Fax: (020) 8547 1426.
DX: 97890 Kingston-upon-Thames 2.
Court times: Doors open 9.30 a.m. Court sits 10.30 a.m. Office hours 10.00 a.m.–4.00 p.m.
Facilities: Robing room. Interview room. No on-premises catering. Disabled access.
Travel: As to Crown Ct.: Station plus 15 min. walk.
LRT 281, 216, K1, K2.
From station cross over main road and proceed along Fife Rd. At T junction with pedestrian precinct turn right and then left. Proceed straight forward, taking left-hand fork. Court is 300 yds on the right.
Driving: A308/A307 to Kingston. Onto one-way system then directions as per walking.
Parking: NCP multi-storey car park opposite court. Limited meters.
Eating out:

The Coffee Cup	bakery	St. James' Rd. precinct
Apple Market Inn	bar food	Eden St.
Burger King	restaurant	Eden St.

KINGSTON-UPON-THAMES CROWN COURT

6–8 Penrhyn Rd., Kingston-upon-Thames, Surrey KT1 2BB.
Telephone: (020) 8240 2500. Fax: (020) 8240 2675.
DX: 97430 Kingston 2.
Court times: Doors open 9.00 a.m. Court sits 10.30 a.m.
Facilities: Male/female robing rooms. Interview rooms. Witness waiting rooms. Public cafeteria 9.00 a.m.–2.30 p.m.
Travel: NR Kingston (Waterloo 23–30 min.) plus 15 min. walk.
LRT 71, 281, 406, 418, 465, 514, 515, 515A, 965, 671, K2 & K3.
From station cross over main road towards town centre following street signs, proceed along Fife Rd., Castle St. into Eden St. Bear left into Brook St. and continue over College roundabout into Penrhyn Rd. The Court entrance is on the right between Kingston Hall Rd. and The Bittoms.
Driving: As per Cty Ct.
Parking: As Cty Ct. and Mags Ct. plus The Bittoms public car park.

KINGSTON-UPON-THAMES MAGISTRATES' COURT, KINGSTON YOUTH COURT (Tues. and Wed. 10.00 a.m.)

The Guildhall, 19 High St., Kingston-upon-Thames, Surrey KT1 1JW. Court Offices at 19 High St. Courtrooms at the Guildhall.
Telephone: (020) 8546 5603. Fax: (020) 8481 4848.
DX: 119975 Kingston-upon-Thames 6.
Court times: Doors open 9.00 a.m. Court sits 10.00 a.m.
Facilities: Advocates'room. Interview room.
Travel: as to Crown/Cty Ct. (Station) plus 15 min. walk.
LRT as Cty Ct.
From station follow Eden St. (as per Cty Ct.) to High St. Road bears around to the left. Guildhall on left 250 yds.
Driving: As per Cty Ct.
Parking: Drapers car park first left after court (Kingston Hall Rd.).
Eating out:

The Ram	bar food	High St.
Druid's Head	bar food	Market Place
Pizza Piazza	restaurant	High St.
Bella Pasta	restaurant	Market Place
Need the Dough	restaurant	Market Place

LAMBETH COUNTY COURT

Court House, Cleaver St., Kennington Rd., London SE11 4DZ.
Telephone: (020) 7735 4425. Fax: (020) 7735 8147.
DX: 33254 Kennington.
Court times: Doors open 9.00 a.m. Court sits 10.00 a.m. Office hours 9.30 a.m.–4.00 p.m.

LAMBETH COUNTY COURT—
CONTINUED

Facilities: Male/female robing rooms. Interview rooms. Hot drinks vending machine. Disabled access. Baby changing room.

Travel: Und. Kennington (Embankment 4 min., Bank 8 min.) plus 5 min. walk.

LRT 3, 59, 95, 133, 155, 355, 322.

From station cross over Kennington Park Rd. and turn left. Turn right at barrier into Cleaver Sq. Cleaver St. in north-west corner. Court 50 yds on right.

Driving: Court by junction of A23 and A3204 at Kennington.

Parking: Cleaver Sq. **NB** If driving, approach from north. No access through Cleaver Sq. from Kennington Park Rd. Cleaver St. unmarked but Spanish restaurant on corner. Parking for residents only or by meter.

Eating out:

The Dog House	bar food	Kennington Lane
Tapas Bar	Spanish restaurant	Kennington Lane
Station Grill	restaurant (12–2 p.m.)	Braganza St.
Prince of Wales	bar food	Cleaver Sq.
Pizza Express	Italian food	Kennington Lane
Sados	café	Kennington Lane

LANDS TRIBUNAL

Procession House, 55 Ludgate Hill, London, EC4M 7JW.
Telephone: (020) 7029 9780. Fax: (020) 7029 9781.
DX: 149065 Ludgate Hill 2.

LEASEHOLD VALUATION TRIBUNAL

10 Alfred Place, London WC1E 7LR.
Telephone: (020) 7446 7700.
Court times: Doors open 9.00 a.m. Hearing times by appointment.
Facilities: Waiting area. Drinks vending machine.
Travel: Und. Goodge St. plus 5 min. walk.
From station cross over Tottenham Court Rd. into Chenies St. First right is Alfred Place.

LEWES COMBINED CROWN AND COUNTY COURT

The Law Courts, High St., Lewes, East Sussex BN7 1YB.
Telephone: 01273 480400. Fax: Crown: 01273 485269. Cty: 01273 485270.
DX: 97395 Lewes 4.
Court times: Doors open 9.00 a.m. Court sits 10.30 a.m.
Facilities: Advocates' rooms. Interview rooms. Robing room. Refreshments.
Travel: NR Lewes (Victoria), see below.

LEWES COMBINED CROWN AND COUNTY COURT—
CONTINUED

From station turn right. Proceed up Station St. to High St. Court is opposite.

Driving: A26/A27 to Lewes. Follow signs to town centre.

Parking: Nearest car park is at NR station.

Eating out:

| White Hart | lunch | High St. |
| Fillers | cafe | Fisher St. |

LEWES MAGISTRATES' COURT,
LEWES YOUTH COURT

The Court House, Friar's Walk, Lewes, East Sussex BN7 2PG.

Telephone: 01273 670888. Fax: 01273 811770.

Website: www.sussex-magistrates.co.uk.

Court times: Doors open 9.00 a.m. Courts sit: (inc. Y) 10.00 a.m. Narey court 9.00 a.m. (Wed.). Office hours: 9.00 a.m.–4.30 p.m.

Facilities: Advocates' room. Interview room. Vending machines for hot/cold drinks, snacks. Public telephone.

Travel: NR Lewes (Victoria 1 hr. 3 min.–1 hr. 24 min.) plus 10 min. walk. From station turn right, then right again to Lansdown Place, proceed to Friars Walk. Court is on right.

Driving: From London A22 via Croydon to Uckfield then A26. From Brighton A27 then A275 into town.

Parking: Car park at rear of building via Court Rd.

Eating out:

| The Volunteer | bar food | Eastgate St. |

LOWESTOFT COUNTY COURT

28 Gordon Rd., Lowestoft, Suffolk NR32 1NL.

Telephone: 01502 586047. Fax: 01502 569319.

DX: 97750 Lowestoft 2.

Court times: Doors open 10.00 a.m. Court sits 10.00 a.m. Office hours 10.00 a.m.–4.00 p.m.

Facilities: Robing room. Interview rooms. Drinks vending machine.

NORTH-EAST SUFFOLK MAGISTRATES' COURTS,
NORTH-EAST SUFFOLK YOUTH COURT

The Court House, Old Nelson St., Lowestoft, Suffolk NR32 1HJ.

Telephone: 01502 501060. Fax: 01502 513875.

DX: 41219 Lowestoft.

Court times: Doors open 9.30 a.m. Court sits 10.00 a.m. and 2.15 p.m.

Office hours/payment enquiries 9.00 a.m.–4. p.m.

Facilities: Non-smoking waiting room. Interview room. Vending machines.

Travel: NR Lowestoft (Liverpool St. 3 hrs.) plus 10 min. walk.

Mags Ct.: From station proceed up London Rd. North to High St. Turn right along Old Nelson St. Mags Ct. on left.

Cty Ct.: Directly opposite bus station in town centre.

Driving: A12 via Ipswich to Lowestoft. Proceed to High St. at centre of town and bus station.

Parking: Cty: Public car park next to court. Mags: Car park to rear of Court in Whapload Rd.

Eating out:

Cty: Hearts of Oak	bar food	Raglan St.
Mags: The Volunteer	bar food	High St.
The Wheatsheaf	bar food	High St.
The Crown	bar food	High St.

LUTON CROWN COURT

7 George St., Luton, Beds. LU1 2AA.

Telephone: 01582 522000. Fax: 01582 522001.

DX: 120500 Luton 6.

Court times: Doors open 8.15 a.m. Court sits 10.30 a.m.

Facilities: Robing room. Interview room. Bar mess. Public canteen. Drinks machine.

Travel: NR Luton (St. Pancras/King's Cross Thameslink 30 min., Blackfriars Thameslink 40 min., Moorgate 50 min.) plus 10 min. walk. From the station walk through covered ramp. Cross and proceed to Arndale Centre. Go through Arndale Centre onto George St. Turn left along frontage of Centre, bear right at Debenhams and cross one-way system. Court is 50 yds on left.

Driving: From M1 Junc. 10 s/p Luton Airport. At next roundabout turn left into London Rd. Proceed down hill to traffic lights, carry on to large roundabout, and turn right. Go down sliproad, pass Courts Furnishers, follow road past traffic lights, turn left at end. Follow road through to Arndale Centre car park.

Parking: No car parking facilities at the Court. Multi-storey car park in the Arndale Centre. Entrance via John St.

Eating out: In and around Arndale Centre. Various wine bars and pubs near court.

LUTON COUNTY COURT

2nd Floor, Cresta House, Alma St., Luton, Beds. LU1 2PU.

Telephone: 01582 506700. Fax: 01582 506701.

DX: 97760 Luton 4.

Court times: Doors open 9.00 a.m. Court sits 10.00 a.m. Office (on 5th floor) hours: 9.30 a.m.–4.00 p.m.

Facilities: Robing room. Interview room. Drinks machines. Lift.

LUTON AND SOUTH BEDFORDSHIRE MAGISTRATES' COURT,
LUTON AND SOUTH BEDFORDSHIRE YOUTH COURT

Stuart St., Luton, Beds. LU1 5BL.

Telephone: 01582 524200. Fax: 01582 524252.

DX: 5963 Luton 1.

Court times: Doors open 9.00 a.m. Court sits 10.00 a.m. Office hours 9.30 a.m.–4.00 p.m.

Facilities: Advocates' room. Interview room. WRVS facility.

Travel: NR Luton (St. Pancras 30 min., King's Cross Thameslink 30 min., Blackfriars Thameslink 40 min., Moorgate 50 min.) plus local bus 'Shires' or 15 min. walk.

From station through covered ramp. Cross and proceed to Arndale Centre. Through centre, turn right for Cty Ct. Alma St. 2nd turning on left. For Mags Ct. turn right on emerging from Arndale Centre into Wellington St. At the top of Wellington St. go through the underpass and up the steps. Mags Ct. on the left (approx. 50 yds).

Driving: M1 Junc. 10 s/p Luton Airport. At next roundabout turn left and proceed downhill into town. At roundabout turn left into Stuart St. (dual carriageway). Mags Ct. approx. half a mile on the left. Cty Ct. two streets behind Crown Ct.

Parking: Multi-storey by Arndale Centre at John St.

MAIDENHEAD (EAST BERKSHIRE) MAGISTRATES' COURT (Tues. and Fri.),
EAST BERKSHIRE YOUTH COURT (Mon. and Thurs.),
EAST BERKSHIRE FAMILY PROCEEDINGS COURT (Fri.)

Court House, Bridge St., Maidenhead, Berks. SL6 8PB. (All enquiries to Slough Magistrates' Court.)

Telephone: 0870 2412820. Fax: 01753 232190.

DX: 98033 Slough 3.

Court times: Doors open 9.00 a.m. only on days Court is sitting. Court sits 10.00 a.m. No court office.

Facilities: Advocates' room. Interview room. WRVS coffee.

Travel: NR Maidenhead (Paddington 38–52 min.) plus 10 min. walk. From station into Queen's St. Cross over High St. and proceed to end of road opposite. Turn right and walk to next roundabout. Court by police station.

Driving: M4 Junc. 8/9 then A308(M) Maidenhead onto A308 and A4 s/p Slough, then into town. Court on ring road by police station.

Parking: Police station car park. Multi-storey car park by Sainsbury's.

Eating out:

The Crown	bar food	Bridge St.
Antonia's	bar food	Bridge St.
Rumpole's	wine bar	St. Mary's Walk
The Bear	bar food	High St.

MAIDSTONE COUNTY COURT, MAIDSTONE CROWN COURT

The Law Courts, Barker Rd., Maidstone, Kent ME16 8EQ.
Telephone: 01622 202000. Crown Fax: 01622 202001. Cty Fax: 01622 202002.
DX: 130065 Maidstone 7.
Court times: Doors open 8.00 a.m. Courts sit 10.00 a.m. Office hours for Cty Ct. 10.00 a.m.–4.00 p.m.
Facilities: Male/female robing rooms. Advocates' suite, lounge, and library. Interview rooms. Bar mess. Public dining room.
Travel: NR Maidstone East (Victoria 50 min.) plus 10 min. walk. Maidstone West (Charing Cross 1 hr. 25 min.) plus 5 min. walk. From East station proceed down hill through town to river and cross bridge. Court is large white building on riverside. From West station turn right. Court on right.
Driving: M20 to Maidstone (exit 6) follow A229 to bridge, cross bridge. Court first left.
Parking: Pay and display in Palace Ave.
Eating out:

Ferryman Tavern	bar food	Barker Rd.
Sandwich Shop	sandwich bar	Maidstone Bridge North
Pizza Hut	restaurant	High St.
The Victoria	bar food	Week St.
McDonald's	restaurant	Week St.
Mr Jones' Pie Shop	snacks	Week St.
Eat n' Time	snacks	Week St.

MAIDSTONE MAGISTRATES' COURT, MAIDSTONE YOUTH COURT

Court House, Palace Ave., Maidstone, Kent ME15 6LL.
Telephone: 01622 671041. Fax: 01622 691800.
DX: 51951 Maidstone 2
Court times: Doors open 9.00 a.m. Court sits 10.00 a.m.
Facilities: Disabled access. Baby changing facilities. Drinks machines. Separate witness rooms. Advocates' room.
Travel: NR Maidstone East (Victoria 50 min.) plus 10 min. walking. Maidstone West (Charing Cross 1 hr. 25 min.) plus 5 min. walking. From West cross courtyard on left. From East cross River Medway into High St. Palace Ave. is courtyard on right.
Driving: M20 to Maidstone. Down hill to town centre. Cross bridge and follow A229 on one-way system.
Parking: Multi-storey car park in shopping centre.
Eating out:
See Maidstone Crown Court.

MARYLEBONE MAGISTRATES' COURT

181 Marylebone Rd., London NW1 5QJ.

Telephone: (020) 7506 3761. Fax: (020) 7724 9884.

DX: 145363 Marylebone 6.

Court times: Doors open 9.30 a.m. Applications and Administration 10.00 a.m. Court sits 10.30 a.m.

Facilities: Interview rooms. Hot drinks machine. Wheelchair access. Toilet facilities for disabled.

Travel: Und. Marylebone, Edgware Rd., Baker St.

LRT 6, 7, 16, 18, 23, 27, 36, 98.

Mags Ct. on corner of Marylebone Rd. and Seymour Place.

Driving: Court on A40 where it becomes A501 Marylebone Rd.

Parking: Limited meters in vicinity.

Eating out:

The Beehive	bar food	Homer St.
The Chapel	bar food	Chapel St.
Harcourt Arms	bar food	Harcourt St.
Windsor Castle	Thai food	Crawford St.

THE MAYOR'S AND CITY OF LONDON COURT

Guildhall Buildings, Basinghall St., London EC2V 5AR.

Telephone: (020) 7796 5400. Fax: (020) 7796 5424.

DX: 97520 Moorgate EC2.

Court times: Doors open 9.30 a.m. Court sits 10.30 a.m. Office hours 10.00 a.m.–4.00 p.m.

Facilities: Robing room. Interview rooms. No on-premises catering.

Travel: NR, Und. Moorgate plus 5 min. walk. **Und**. Bank plus 5 min. walk.

LRT 6, 8, 9, 11, 15, 21, 25, 43, 76, 133, 141, 149, 501–2.

From Moorgate Station turn south into Moorgate, turn right into London Wall, Basinghall St. second on left. Court 250 yds on right following road around.

From Bank Station, up Cheapside, turn right into Old Jewry. Left and right across Gresham St. into Basinghall St. Court 50 yds on left.

Parking: Disabled parking available by arrangement with the court. For a disabled badge holder parking bays within 5 min. walk. Parking meters within 5 min. walk.

Eating out:

Figaro Two	sandwich bar	Basinghall St.
Olde Gresham	restaurant	Gresham St.
Vita's	sandwich bar	Basinghall St.

MEDWAY (CHATHAM) COUNTY COURT

Anchorage House, High St., Chatham, Kent ME4 4DW.

Telephone: 01634 402881. Fax: 01634 811332.

DX: 98180 Chatham 4.

MEDWAY (CHATHAM) COUNTY COURT—
CONTINUED

Court times: Doors open 9.30 a.m. Court sits: District Judge 10.00 a.m.

Circuit Judge 10.00 a.m. Office hours 10.00 a.m.–4.00 p.m. Weds.–Fri. 8.30 a.m.–4.00 p.m.

Facilities: Robing room. Advocates' room. Interview room. No on-premises catering. Drinks vending machine.

MEDWAY (CHATHAM) MAGISTRATES' COURT, MEDWAY FAMILY PROCEEDINGS COURT

(Wed., Thurs., Fri. 10.00 a.m. and 2.15 p.m.),
MEDWAY YOUTH COURT (Mon and Tues. 10.00 a.m. and 2.15 p.m.)

The Court House, The Brook, Chatham, Kent ME4 4JZ.
Telephone: 01634 830232. Fax: 01634 847400.

Court times: Doors open 9.00 a.m. Court sits 10.00 a.m. and 2.15 p.m.

Office hours Mon.–Fri. 9.00 a.m.–5.00 p.m.

Facilities: Advocates' room. Interview room. Tea and coffee available a.m. Drinks machine in Y and F courts. Refreshments provided by Charity.

Travel: NR Chatham (Victoria 43–58 min., Charing Cross 1 hr. 6 min.) plus 15 min. walk both.

Cty: From station turn down Railway St. and proceed down hill to junction with High St. Turn left. Court 600 yds on right by office block.

Mags: From station as for Cty Ct. Proceed across junction with High St. into Military Rd. and turn right beyond Pentagon shopping centre into The Brook. Proceed up Wiffens Ave. and turn right into Rope Walk. Court 200 yds on right.

Driving: A2/M2 to Chatham. Follow walking directions from station.

Parking: Cty: Small domestic car park. Car park at Ship Lane pier. Mags: Multi-storey for Pentagon Centre.

Eating out: Cty:

Simpson's	wine bar	High St.
Clarke's	bakery/coffee bar	High St.
Fetherstone's	cafe/wine bar	High St.
Mags:		
Juddy's	bar food	Rope Walk
Lite Bite	cafe	Pentagon
Blueberry Park	cafe	Military Rd.

MIDDLESEX GUILDHALL CROWN COURT

Middlesex Guildhall, Little George St., Westminster, London SW1P 3BB.

Telephone: (020) 7202 0370. Fax: (020) 7202 0392.

DX: 122920 Parliament Square.

Court times: Doors open 9.00 a.m. Court sits 10.00/10.30 a.m. Office hours 9.00 a.m.–5.00 p.m.

Facilities: Male/female robing rooms. Interview rooms. Advocates' mess. Public cafeteria. Disabled access.

Travel: Und. Westminster plus 5 min. walk.

LRT 3, 11, 24, 29, 39, 77, 77A, 159, 168, 211.

From station turn right. Guildhall across Parliament Square.

Eating out:

Sandwich bars in Bridge St. and Victoria St.

MILDENHALL MAGISTRATES' COURT,
WEST SUFFOLK MAGISTRATES' COURT,
WEST SUFFOLK COMBINED YOUTH COURT,
WEST SUFFOLK FAMILY COURT

Court House, Queensway, Mildenhall, Suffolk. Admin from Bury St. Edmunds.

Telephone: 01284 352300 (Bury St. Edmunds). 01638 712625 (Mildenhall—court days only). Fax: 01284 352345.

Court times: Doors open 9.30 a.m. Court sits 10.00 a.m.

Facilities: Advocates' room. Interview room. Vending machine.

Travel: NR Newmarket (Liverpool St. 1 hr. 50 min.) plus taxi (13 miles).

EC 179, 970–5, 977, 979.

Court in Main St.

Driving: M11–A11 beyond Newmarket to Barton Mills then turn left A1101 to Mildenhall.

Parking: Off-street parking.

MILTON KEYNES COUNTY COURT

351 Silbury Boulevard, Witan Gate East, Central Milton Keynes, Bucks. MK9 2DT.

Telephone: 01908 302800 for general enquiries, 01908 302801 for family matters.

DX: 136266 Milton Keynes 6.

Court times: Doors open 9.30 a.m. Court sits 10.00 a.m. Office hours: 10.00 a.m.–4.00 p.m. Bailiff's office open 8 a.m.– 10 a.m.

Facilities: Robing rooms. Conference room. Drinks machine. Mother and baby room. Children's suite for care and adoption proceedings. Disabled access.

MILTON KEYNES MAGISTRATES' COURT, MILTON KEYNES YOUTH COURT

301 Silbury Boulevard, Witan Gate East, Central Milton Keynes, Bucks. MK9 2AJ.

Telephone: 08702 412819. Fax: 01908 451146.

DX: 54462 Milton Keynes.

Court times: Doors open 9.00 a.m. Courts sit 10.00 a.m. Office hours Mon.–Thurs. 9.00 a.m.–5.00 p.m. Fri. 9.00 a.m.–4.30 p.m.

Facilities: WRVS tea room. Interview rooms. Baby changing facilities. Video link facilities.

Travel: NR Milton Keynes Central (Euston 40–71 min.) plus 10 min. walk or Milton Keynes Citybus.

From station proceed two blocks along Midsummer Boulevard. Turn left and proceed one block to Silbury Boulevard, and turn right. Courts 200 yds on left. Cty Ct. in adjacent building.

Driving: M1 to Junc. 14. Follow signs to Milton Keynes centre and proceed to Silbury Boulevard. Car park opposite courts.

Parking: Opposite front of courts.

Eating out:

The City Duck	bar food	Midsummer Boulevard
Brunches	restaurant	Deer Walk

NEWBURY COUNTY COURT

King's Road West, Newbury, Berks. RG14 5BY.

Telephone: 01635 40928. Fax: 01635 37704.

DX: 30816 Newbury 1.

Court times: Doors open 8.30. a.m. Court sits 10.00 a.m.

Travel: NR Newbury Rail Station plus 2 min. walk. Bus station plus 2 min. walk.

Driving: Junc. 13 off M4.

Parking: Town centre—ample parking.

Eating out: Sandwich shops, pizza restaurants, and numerous pubs within walking distance of court.

NEWBURY MAGISTRATES' COURT, NEWBURY YOUTH COURT

Court session only at: Court House, Mill Lane, Newbury, Berks. RG14 5QT. (Admin. from Reading Magistrates' Court, Civic Centre, Reading, Berks. RG1 7TQ.)

Telephone: 01189 552600. Fax: 01189 508173.

Court times: Doors open 9.30 a.m. Court sits 10.00 a.m.

Facilities: Advocates' room. Interview room. Drinks machine.

Travel: NR Newbury (Paddington 38 min.–1 hr. 30 min.) plus 15 min. walk.

For Mags Ct. from station cross bridge. Turn right and follow road to and cross dual carriageway to Cheap St. Turn right into King's Rd. West. Through underpass and turn right. Court next to police station.

NEWBURY MAGISTRATES' COURT—
CONTINUED

For Cty Ct. exit station via ticket office. Turn right up slope. Take 1st left towards town centre. Do *not* join main road. Take second right. King Charles Tavern on corner. Court in very small office, 50 yds on right.

Driving: M4 Junc. 13 then A34/A339 into Newbury. Follow signs to police station.

Parking: Newbury Station car park.

Eating out:

The Rising Sun	bar food	Mill Lane
King Charles Tavern	bar food	King's Rd. West

NORWICH COUNTY COURT,
NORWICH CROWN COURT

The Law Courts, Bishopgate, Norwich, Norfolk NR3 1UR.

Telephone: 01603 728200. Fax: 01603 760863.

DX: 97385 Norwich 5.

Court times: Doors open 9.00 a.m. Court sits 9.30 a.m. Office hours 10.00 a.m.–4.00 p.m.

Facilities: Robing room. Interview rooms. Public canteen. Disabled access. Separate advocates' dining area.

NORWICH EMPLOYMENT TRIBUNALS

Elliot House, 130 Ber St., Norwich, Norfolk NR1 3TZ.

Telephone: 01284 762171. Fax: 01284 706064.

Court times: Tribunal sits 10.00 a.m.

Facilities: Waiting rooms. Drinks machine.

Travel: Call for map.

NR Norwich station (10 min. walk). Bus station (10 min. walk).

Parking: Postwick and Airport park and ride buses every 10 min.

Eating out:

Close to town centre.

NORWICH MAGISTRATES' COURT,
NORWICH FAMILY PROCEEDINGS COURT,
NORWICH YOUTH COURT

Bishopgate, Norwich, Norfolk NR3 1UP.

Telephone: 01603 679500. Fax: 01603 663263. General Listings Fax: 01603 679567.

Court times: Doors open 8.30 a.m. Court sits 10.00 a.m. Office hours 9.00 a.m.–5.00 p.m. Timetabled courts 9.15 a.m.–4.15 p.m.

Facilities: Advocates' room. Interview room. Coffee shop.

Travel: NR Norwich Thorpe Station (Liverpool St. 2 hrs. 20 min.) plus 20 min. walk.

NORWICH MAGISTRATES' COURT—
CONTINUED

From station turn right into Riverside and over into Riverside Rd. Cross pedestrianized Bishops Bridge and follow road around. Law Courts next to Mags Ct.

Driving: M11–A11–Norwich. Through city one-way system to inner ring road and follow directions for Law Courts. Courts very close to Norwich Cathedral.

Parking: Pay and display next to Law Courts.

Eating out:

The Wig and Pen	bar food	Palace Plain
The Maid's Head Hotel	bar food	Tombland
Adam and Eve	bar food	Bishopgate

OXFORD COMBINED CROWN AND COUNTY COURT CENTRE,

St. Aldates, Oxford, Oxon. OX1 1TL.

Telephone: 01865 264200. Fax: 01865 790773.

DX: 96450 Oxford 4.

Court times: Mon.–Fri. 10.00 a.m.–4.00 p.m. Office hours 9.00 a.m.–5.00 p.m.

Facilities: Robing room. Dining room.

OXFORD MAGISTRATES' COURT,
OXFORD YOUTH COURT,
OXFORD FAMILY PROCEEDINGS COURT

The Courthouse, PO Box 37, Speedwell St., Oxford, Oxon. OX1 1RZ.

Telephone: 0870 2412808. Fax: 01865 448024.

DX: 96452 Oxford 4.

Court times: Doors open 9.00 a.m. Court sits 10.00 a.m. Office hours 8.15 a.m.–4.30 p.m.

Facilities: Interview rooms. Dedicated advocates' office. Drinks and light snacks available.

Travel: NR Oxford station (Paddington 1 hr. 5 min.–1 hr. 25 min.) plus taxi or 15 min. walk. Buses National: Oxford Gloucester Green Bus Station 10 min. walk. Local Service: 2, 2A, 2B, 4 4B, 4C.

For Combined Court Centre: From station approach turn left and cross to Park End St. 3rd right New Rd., 2nd right St. Aldates, Courts 300 yds on right. Mags Ct. is adjacent building on corner of Speedwell St. and Albion Place.

Driving: M40 into Headington or Hinksey Hill junction of A34, then onto A4144, Abingdon Rd. to town centre.

Parking: Blackfriars Rd. car park via Thames St. and Oxpens Rd.

Eating out: Many local restaurants 5 min. walk.

PETERBOROUGH CROWN COURT,
PETERBOROUGH COUNTY COURT

Crown Building, Rivergate, Peterborough, Cambs. PE1 1EJ.

Telephone: 01733 349161. Fax: 01733 557348.

DX: 702302 Peterborough 8.

Court times: 10.00 a.m.–4.00 p.m.

Facilities: Cafeteria 9.00 a.m.–2.00 p.m. Drinks vending machine. Disabled toilet. Interview rooms.

Travel: NR Peterborough (Kings Cross 44 min.–1 hr. 15 min.) plus 15 min. walk or taxi. From station turn right along Bourges Boulevard (A15). Follow main road for 500 yds. Crown Buildings are below to the right on the riverside on Rivergate.

Driving: Leave A1 at junction of A1139 follow A1139 past S-tanground exit and take exit marked City Centre/Eastern Industry. Left at first two roundabouts then follow signs for Courts/Key Theatre.

Parking: Public parking by side of court.

Eating out: Sandwich shops, etc. 10 min. walk from Court into city centre.

PETERBOROUGH MAGISTRATES' COURT,
PETERBOROUGH YOUTH COURT

Bridge St., Peterborough, Cambs. PE1 1ED.

Telephone: 0845 310 0575. Fax: 01733 313749.

DX: 702304 Peterborough 8.

Court times: Doors open 9.30 a.m. Court sits 10.00 a.m. Office hours 8.30 a.m.–5.00 p.m.

Facilities: Advocates' room. Interview rooms. Drinks machine.

Travel: As for Combined Court Centre. Follow A15 Bourges Boulevard. Bridge St. is next right after Vier Platz. Court on left.

POPLAR CORONER'S COURT,
HACKNEY CORONER'S COURT

127 Poplar High St., London E14 0AE.

Telephone: Poplar (020) 7987 3614. Fax: (020) 7538 0565. Hackney (020) 7538 0602.

Court times: By appointment.

Facilities: None.

Travel: DLR Poplar plus 5 min. walk.

From station cut through Simpson Rd. into Poplar High St. and turn right. Court 50 yds on left.

Driving: From A13 East India Dock Rd., eastbound, turn right into Newby Place by All Saints Station (DLR). At end turn right into Poplar High St. Court 100 yds on right, at junction with Cottage St.

Parking: Limited meters in side-streets.

READING COUNTY COURT

160–163 Friar St., Reading, Berks. RG1 1HE.

Telephone: 0118 9870 500. Fax: 0118 959 9827.

DX: 98010 Reading 6.

Court times: Doors open 9.30 a.m. Court sits 10.00 a.m. Office hours 10.00 a.m.–4.00 p.m.

Facilities: Robing room. Interview rooms. Drinks machine. Disabled access.

READING CROWN COURT

The Old Shire Hall, The Forbury, Reading, Berks. RG1 3EH.

Telephone: 0118 967 4400. Fax: 0118 967 4444.

DX: 97440 Reading 5.

Court times: Doors open 9.00 a.m. Court sits 10.00 a.m. Office hours 9.00 a.m.–5.00 p.m.

Facilities: Robing room. Advocates' room. Interview rooms. Public cafeteria. Vending machine. Advocates' dining area.

READING EMPLOYMENT TRIBUNALS

30/31 Friar St., Reading, Berks. RG1 1DY.

Telephone: 0118 959 4917. Fax: 0118 956 8066.

Court times: 9.45 a.m.

Facilities: Telephone.

Travel: NR Reading station (4 min. walk). Local buses in immediate vicinity.

Driving: Follow signs to railway station.

Parking: Large public car parks in the vicinity. No public parking at the building.

Eating out:

Many cafes and restaurants in the immediate vicinity of the Tribunal.

READING MAGISTRATES' COURT,
READING YOUTH COURT

Civic Centre, Reading, Berks. RG1 7TQ.

Telephone: 0118 980 1800. Fax: 0118 9801873.

DX: 151160 Reading 25.

Court times: Doors open 9.00 a.m. Court sits 10.00 a.m. Office hours 9.00 a.m.–4.00 p.m.

Facilities: Advocates' room. Interview room. Coffee bar. Drinks machine.

Travel: NR Reading (Paddington 37 min.) plus 10 min. walking to all courts. Crown: From station cross roundabout into Station Rd. Turn left at traffic lights and follow signs to Court and Forbury Gardens.

Cty: From station cross roundabout into Station Rd. Proceed until 1st set of traffic lights and turn left into Friar St.

Mags: From station cross roundabout into Station Rd. Proceed over set of traffic lights and turn right into Broad St. Turn left into St.

READING MAGISTRATES' COURT—

CONTINUED

Mary's Butts at junction towards the end of the street. Opposite the church on the left turn right into Hesien St. and proceed towards the Civic Centre. The Mags Ct. is on the left-hand side.

Driving: M4 Junc. 10 then A329M into Reading. Proceed into town for courts.

Parking: Crown: Town centre car parks—the nearest is Queens Rd. No parking at Shire Hall. Cty: Underground car park nearby. Mags: Butts shopping centre car park.

Eating out:

Civic Centre:

The Horn	bar food	Castle St.
The Sun	bar food	Castle St.
The Horse and Jockey	bar food	Castle St.
Sweeney Todd	restaurant	Castle St.
Friar's Walk:		
Tudor Tavern	bar food	Friar St.
Presto's	coffee lounge	Friar's Walk

REDBRIDGE MAGISTRATES' COURT,

REDBRIDGE YOUTH COURT (Tues. at 10.00 a.m. and 2.00 p.m., and Wed. and Fri. at 10.00 a.m.)

The Court House, 850 Cranbrook Rd., Barkingside, Ilford, Essex IG6 1HW.

Telephone: (020) 8551 4461. Fax: (020) 8550 2101.

e-mail: information@redbridge.olmcs-law.co.uk.

DX: 99327 Barkingside.

Court times: Doors open 9.00 a.m. Courts sit: Mags 10.00 a.m. Y Tues. 10.00 a.m. and 2.00 p.m., Wed. 10.00 a.m. Fri. 10.00 a.m. Early hearings start 9.45 a.m. on Tues. and Fri. Office hours 9.00 a.m.–4.45 p.m.

Facilities: Advocates' room. Interview room. Prosecution witness room. Court-based drug workers (Tues. and Fri. 10.00 a.m.). Disabled facilities. CCTV in operation. WRVS coffee.

Travel: Und. NB Barkingside (Liverpool St. 27 min., Oxford Circus 38 min.) plus 10 min. walk.

LRT 129, 150, 167, 169, 247.

From station approach cross junction turning left into Carlton Drive. Turn right into Tanners Lane. Court 400 yds on left, corner of Cranbrook Rd.

Driving: Court on A123 at Barkingside.

Parking: Car park to rear in Tanners Lane.

REDBRIDGE MAGISTRATES' COURT—
CONTINUED
Eating out:

Ye Old Sherlock Holmes	bar food	Cranbrook Rd.
Marino's	cafe	High St.
McDonald's	restaurant	High St.
Rossi's	restaurant	High St.
Tesco's	restaurant	Cranbrook Rd.

REIGATE COUNTY COURT
The Law Courts, Hatchlands Rd., Redhill, Surrey RH1 6BL.
Telephone: 01737 763637. Fax: 01737 766917.
DX: 98020 Redhill West.
Court times: Doors open 9.00 a.m. Court sits 10.00 a.m. Office hours 9.00 a.m.–4.00 p.m.

SOUTH EAST SURREY MAGISTRATES' COURT
(sitting at Redhill and Dorking),
REDHILL MAGISTRATES' COURT,
REDHILL YOUTH COURT
The Law Courts, Hatchlands Rd., Redhill, Surrey RH1 6DH.
Telephone: 01737 765581. Fax: 01737 764972/778372.
DX: 98021 Redhill West.
Court times: Doors open 9.00 a.m. Courts sit 10.00 a.m. Office hours 8.30 a.m.–4.30 p.m. (Mon. to Thurs.) 8.30 a.m.–4.15 p.m. (Fri.). Counter hours 9.00 a.m.–4.00 p.m.
Facilities: Robing room. Advocates' room. Interview rooms. Snack machines.
Travel: NR Redhill (Victoria 32–40 min.) plus 10 min. walk or <u>410</u>, <u>414</u>, <u>422</u>.
LC: Bus stop outside Law Courts. 405–6, <u>410</u>, 411, 411A, <u>414</u>, <u>422</u>, 440.
From station cross roundabout and proceed along Station Rd. for 800 yds. Continue up Hatchlands Rd. Courts 200 yds on right.
Driving: A23 into Redhill. Pass station and turn right onto one-way system at Cromwell Rd. then left into Station Rd. and follow walking directions.
Parking: Limited parking at front of court.
Eating out:

The Hatch	bar food	Hatchlands Rd.
Red Lion	bar food	Hatchlands Rd. roundabout
Peach Blossom	Chinese restaurant/ take-away	Hatchlands Rd.
Master Fryer	fish restaurant	Hatchlands Rd.

RICHMOND MAGISTRATES' COURT,

RICHMOND YOUTH COURT (Tues. 10.00 a.m.) Parkshot, Richmond, Surrey TW9 2RF.

Telephone: (020) 8271 2300. Fax: (020) 8271 2330.

DX: 100257 Richmond 2.

Court times: Doors open 8.30 a.m. Court sits 10.00 a.m. and 2.00 p.m.

Facilities: Advocates' room. Consultation rooms. Food kiosk.

Travel: NR, Und. Richmond (Waterloo 15–25 min., Embankment 32 min.).

LRT 7, 27, 33, 37, 65, 371, 90B, 202, 270, 290.

From station cross High St. and proceed down path by Oriel House. Turn right. Court 50 yds on left.

Driving: Court off A307 in Richmond town centre. Parkshot off A316.

Parking: Domestic car park for counsel. Meters. NCP multi-storey car park by station.

Eating out:

Edwards	bar food	Parkshot/High St.
Sun Inn	bar food	Parkshot
Emendal's	pizzeria	The Quadrant
Don Fernandos	Spanish	The Quadrant
McDonald's	restaurant/take-away	The Quadrant
The Orange Tree	bar food	Kew Rd.

ROMFORD COUNTY COURT

2A Oakland Avenue, Romford, Essex RM1 4DP.

Telephone: 01708 775555. Fax: 01708 756653.

DX: 97530 Romford 2.

Court times: Doors open 9.00 a.m. Court sits: Circuit Judge 10.30 a.m. District Judge 10.00 a.m. Office hours 10.00 a.m.–4.00 p.m.

Facilities: Robing room. Three interview rooms. Drinks machine. Disabled access.

HAVERING MAGISTRATES' COURT,

HAVERING YOUTH COURT (Wed. 10.00 a.m.)

Main Rd., Romford, Essex RM1 3BH.

Telephone: 01708 771771. Fax: 01708 771777.

DX: 131527 Romford 8.

Court times: Doors open 8.30 a.m. Court sits 10.00 a.m. Office hours 8.00 a.m.–4.00 p.m.

Facilities: Interview room. Vending machine. Witness waiting area. CPS room. Duty solicitor room. Disabled toilet. Baby changing facilities.

Travel: NR Romford (Liverpool St. 17–28 min.) plus 15 min. walk.

LRT 87, 248.

From station turn left and proceed up South St. Turn right at Market Place and proceed complete length of market square to pedestrian subway under roundabout at Main Rd. Mags Ct. 150 yds on left up Main Rd. Cty Ct. 250 yds on left.

Driving: A12 s/p Romford. On entering town centre take inner ring road (St. Edwards Way) to roundabout by library. Turn left up Main Rd. and follow walking directions.

Parking: Large public car park opposite via Junction Rd. Multi-storey car park on inner ring road. Some meters by Cty Ct.

Eating out:

The Bull	bar food	Market Place
Littlewoods	restaurant	Market Place
Debenhams	restaurant	Market Place
British Home Stores	restaurant	Market Place

ROYAL COURTS OF JUSTICE BUILDING,
COURT OF APPEAL,
HIGH COURT OF JUSTICE

Strand, London WC2A 2LL.

Telephone: (020) 7947 6000.

DX: 44450 Strand.

Court times: Doors open 9.00 a.m. Court sits 10.30 a.m. Office hours 10.00 a.m.–4.30 p.m.

Facilities: Male/female advocates' robing room. Solicitors' robing room. Consultation rooms. Public cafeteria. Book/Souvenir shop.

Annexes

Technology and Construction Court, Admiralty Court:
St. Dunstan's House, Fetter Lane, London EC4A 1HD.

Telephone: (020) 7936 6000.

Patents Court and overflow Queen's Bench Division Courts:
Field House, 15–25 Breams Buildings, London EC4A 1DZ.

Telephone: Clerk to the Patents Judge: (020) 7073 4251 Fax: (020) 7073 4253.

Supreme Court Costs Office

Clifford's Inn, Fetter Lane, London EC4A 1DQ.

Telephone: (020) 7936 6000. Fax: (020) 7936 6344/6247.

DX: 45444 Strand.

Family Division Principal Registry, Probate Registry,
First Avenue House, 42–49 High Holborn, London WC1V 6NP.

Telephone: (020) 7936 6000.

Travel: Und. Chancery Lane plus 5 min. walk.

LRT 4, 6, 9, 11, 15, 23, 171, 176, 502, 513.

Eating out:

Chez Gerrard	restaurant	Chancery Lane
Hodgson's	wine bar	Chancery Lane
Corts	wine bar	Chancery Lane
The Old Bank of England	bar food	The Strand

ST. ALBANS CROWN COURT

Bricket Rd., St. Albans, Herts. AL1 3JW.
Telephone: 01727 753220. Fax: 01727 753221.
DX: 99700 St. Albans 3.
e-mail: stalbans.crn.cm@courtservice.gsi.gov.uk.

ST. ALBANS COUNTY COURT

Victoria House, 117 Victoria St., St. Albans, Herts. AL1 3TJ.
Telephone: 01727 856925. Fax: 01727 852484.
DX: 97770 St. Albans 2.

CENTRAL HERTFORDSHIRE MAGISTRATES' COURT, CENTRAL HERTFORDSHIRE FAMILY COURT, CENTRAL HERTFORDSHIRE YOUTH COURT

The Courthouse, Civic Centre, St. Peter's St., St. Albans, Herts. AL1 3LB.
Telephone: 01727 816822. Fax: 01727 816829.
DX: 6172 St. Albans.
Court times: Doors open 9.15 a.m. Courts sit: Cty 10.00 a.m., Crown 10.30 a.m., Mags 10.00 a.m.
Facilities: Mags: Robing rooms. Consultation rooms. Cty: Consultation rooms. Vending machines. Crown: Advocates' robing room. Consultation rooms. Cafeteria a.m. only.
Travel: NR St. Albans City (Kings Cross 21–39 min. Thameslink service) plus 15 min. walk to Crown/Mags, 5 min. walk to Cty Ct. From City station turn right into Victoria St. Cty Ct. offices and D. J. 250 yds on right. Turn into Bricket Rd. (5th on right) for Crown Ct. Mags Ct. on left among Civic Centre buildings.
Driving: A5 or A6 to St. Albans. A1081 or A414 into town centre. Mags Ct. in Civic Centre area off main street. Crown Ct. at rear of Civic Centre near police station. For Cty Ct. offices turn into Victoria St. from main street. Court half mile on left.
Parking: Pay and display car parks in vicinity and multi-storey in The Maltings shopping centre.
Eating out: District Judge:

Victoria Cafe	cafe	Victoria St.
Crown Mags:		
Waterend Barn	restaurant and bar	Civic Centre precinct
Pizzaland	restaurant	St. Peter's St.

ST. PANCRAS CORONER'S COURT

Camley St., London NW1 0PP.
Telephone: (020) 7387 4884. Fax: (020) 7383 2485.
Court times: Doors open 8.00 a.m.–4.00 p.m. Court sits from 10.00 a.m.
Facilities: Interview room. No on-premises catering.
Travel: NR, Und. King's Cross plus 10 min. walk; Mornington Crescent plus 10 min. walk.

ST. PANCRAS CORONER'S COURT—
CONTINUED
LRT 46, 214, C11.

From Kings Cross station proceed up Pancras Rd. to traffic lights at junction of six roads. Turn right into Goods Way and left into Camley St. Court 600 yds on left beyond bridge.

From Mornington Crescent (Northern line) second right from station, down Crowndale Rd., into Pancras Rd., and through St. Pancras Gardens.

Driving: Take Euston Rd. to King's Cross and A5202 Pancras Rd. Follow walking directions.

Eating out:

The College Arms	bar food	Royal College St.

SEVENOAKS MAGISTRATES' COURT, SEVENOAKS YOUTH COURT

The Court House, Morewood Close, London Rd., Sevenoaks, Kent TN13 2HU.

Telephone: Admin. from Maidstone: 01622 671041. Fax: 01622 691800.

DX: 51951 Maidstone 2.

Court times: Doors open 9.15 a.m. Courts sit 10.00 a.m.

Facilities: Advocates' room. Interview room. Drinks machine.

Travel: NR Sevenoaks (Charing Cross 33–40 min.) plus 10 min. walk.

From station turn left. Continue down London Rd. Court in Morewood Close on right.

Driving: From London A21 via Bromley to Sevenoaks. Proceed into town s/p station and follow walking directions.

Parking: Limited parking at court. Car parks at South Park/British Rail Station.

Eating out:

The Half Way House	bar food	London Rd.
Harvester	bar food	London Rd.
Alpino	restaurant	London Rd.
The Farmer's	bar food	London Rd.
Tom Bell's	fish and chips	London Rd.

SHOREDITCH COUNTY COURT

19 Leonard St., London EC2A 4AL.

Telephone: (020) 7253 0956. Fax: (020) 7490 5613.

DX: 121000 Shoreditch 2.

Court times: Doors open 9.00 a.m. Court sits 10.00 a.m. Office hours 10.00 a.m.–4.00 p.m.

Facilities: Robing room. Three interview rooms.

Travel: NR, Und. Old St. (Moorgate 10 min.).

LRT 5, 43, 55, 76, 141, 214, 243, 271.

SHOREDITCH COUNTY COURT—
CONTINUED

Old St. Station, City Rd. South exit (exit 4). 50 yds down City Rd. Leonard St. on left. Court 100 yds down on left.

Driving: Court by Old St. roundabout, junction of A5201, A501, and A1202.

Parking: Meters in vicinity. NCP car park opposite.

Eating out:

Superchef	restaurant	Old St. Station
Lord Nelson	bar food	Old St.
Gluepot	bar food	Old St.
London Apprentice	bar food	Old St.
Dandy Snacks	sandwich bar	Old St.

SITTINGBOURNE MAGISTRATES' COURT

The Magistrates' Court, 1 Park Rd., Sittingbourne, Kent ME10 1DP.

Telephone: Admin. from Maidstone: 01622 671041. Fax: 01622 691800.

DX: 51951 Maidstone 2.

Court times: Doors open 9.00 a.m. Court sits 10.00 a.m.

Facilities: Advocates' room. Interview rooms. WRVS.

Travel: NR Sittingbourne (Victoria 57 min.–1 hr. 17 min.) plus 5 min. walk.

From station cross car park and take footpath into High St. Cross and turn right along High St. Court on corner on left.

Driving: Court situated on A2 in Sittingbourne town centre.

Parking: Car parks in Central Ave. and Avenue of Remembrance.

Eating out: Many places in town centre.

SLOUGH COUNTY COURT

Law Courts, Windsor Rd., Slough, Berks. SL1 2HE.

Telephone: 01753 690300. Fax: 01753 575990.

DX: 98030 Slough 3.

Court times: Doors open 9.30 a.m. Court sits 10.00 a.m. Office hours 10.00 a.m.–4.00 p.m.

Facilities: Robing room. Advocates' room. Drinks machine.

EAST BERKSHIRE MAGISTRATES' COURT (also sits at Bridge Rd., Maidenhead and Court House, Town Sq., Bracknell), EAST BERKSHIRE YOUTH COURT (Tues. and Thurs.), EAST BERKSHIRE FAMILY PROCEEDINGS COURT (Fri. and by arrangement)

The Law Courts, Chalvey Park, off Windsor Rd., Slough, Berks. SL1 2HJ.

Telephone: 0870 2412820 (Gen. enquiries). Fax: 01753 232190.

DX: 98033 Slough 3.

EAST BERKSHIRE MAGISTRATES' COURT—
    CONTINUED

Court times: Doors open 8.45 a.m. Courts sit 10.00 a.m. Office hours 8.45 a.m.–5.00 p.m.

Facilities: Disabled access.

Travel: NR Slough (Paddington 14 min.) plus 10 min. walk. Turn right out of station. Walk to roundabout and take underpass to Windsor Rd. Courts by police station on corner of Windsor Rd. and Chalvey Park.

Driving: M4 to Junc. 5, A4 Bath Rd. to A332 s/p Windsor. Courts behind police station near town centre.

Parking: Multi-storey car park near station.

Eating out:

| McDonald's | restaurant | High St. |
| Lotus Garden | Chinese restaurant | High St. |

SNARESBROOK CROWN COURT

75 Hollybush Hill, London E11 1QW.

Telephone: (020) 8530 0000. Fax: (Reception) (020) 530 0072 (List office) (020) 530 0071.

DX: 9824 Wanstead 2.

Court times: Doors open 9.00 a.m. Court sits 10.00/10.30 a.m. Floaters 10.15 a.m.

Facilities: Five robing rooms. Consultation rooms. Bar mess. Public cafeteria. Disabled access.

Travel: Und. Snaresbrook (Liverpool St. 18 min., Oxford Circus 29 min.).

LRT W12, W13, W14, 101, 108.

From station proceed to traffic lights and turn left. Court 150 yds on right.

Driving: Court on A11 north of Green Man roundabout at Leytonstone, junction of A114, A113, and A12.

Parking: Car park to rear.

Eating out:

| The Eagle | bar food and restaurant | Hollybush Hill |

SOUTH WESTERN MAGISTRATES' COURT, BALHAM, LAMBETH, AND WANDSWORTH YOUTH COURTS

176a Lavender Hill, Clapham Junction, London SW11 1JU.

Telephone: (020) 7228 9201. Warrant office: (020) 7228 3575. Fax: (020) 7924 2704.

DX: 58559 Clapham Junction.

Court times: Doors open 9.30 a.m. Court sits 10.30 a.m.

Facilities: Interview room.

Travel: NR Clapham Junction (Victoria 6 min., Waterloo 7–12 min.).

Und. Vauxhall (Victoria 3 min., King's Cross 13 min.) plus 77, 77A.
LRT 45, 77, 77A.
From NR station turn left up Lavender Hill. Court 300 yds on left.
Driving: Court on A3036 near junction with A3220.
Parking: Side-streets, pay and display; car park for Asda supermarket.

Eating out:

The Cornet	bar food	Lavender Gardens
Effe's	doner kebab snack bar	Lavender Hill
Arding & Hobbs	restaurant	Lavender Hill

SOUTHEND COUNTY COURT

Tylers House, Tylers Ave., Southend-on-Sea, Essex SS1 2AW.
Telephone: 01702 601991. Fax: 01702 603090.
DX: 97780 Southend 2.
Court times: Doors open 8.00 a.m. Court sits at 10.00 a.m. Office hours 10.00 a.m.–4.00 p.m.
Facilities: Vending machines. Waiting rooms. Advocates' and consultation rooms.
Travel: NR Southend Central (Fenchurch St. approx. 50 min.) plus 5 min. walk from main entrance. Proceed to High St. pedestrian precinct. Tylers Ave. on left side at pedestrian lights, Tylers House is 80 yds on the left.
NR Southend Victoria (Liverpool St. 1 hr. 8 min.) plus 10 min. walk. Cross over to main shopping precinct and proceed along pedestrianized High St. Proceed under Railway Bridge and turn left into Tylers Ave. Tylers House is 80 yds on the left.
Driving: A127 follow 'Town Centre' (Victoria Ave.). At town centre proceed straight over large roundabout 2nd exit is the underpass and 1st right at traffic lights, carry straight on over two sets of traffic lights, car park on left next to traffic lights. Turn left, left again and then left into car park (one-way system).
Eating out:
A number of cafes and snack bars within easy walking distance.

SOUTHEND CROWN COURT (Admin. from Basildon Crown Ct.),
SOUTHEND CORONER'S COURT,
SOUTHEND (SOUTH EAST ESSEX) MAGISTRATES' COURT,
SOUTH EAST ESSEX YOUTH COURT

Hearings only: The Court House, 80 Victoria Ave., Southend-on-Sea, Essex SS2 6EG. Correspondence etc. to The Gore, Basildon, Essex SS14 2EU.

SOUTHEND CROWN COURT—
CONTINUED

Telephone: Crown: 01268 458000. Fax: 01268 458100. Mags: 01702 283800. Fax: 01702 283830 (general).

DX: Crown: 97633 Basildon 5. Mags: 97583 Southend 3 (general), 97585 Southend 3 (accounts/family).

Court times: Doors open 9.00 a.m. Courts sit: Y 10.00 a.m., Mags 10.00 a.m., Crown 10.30 a.m., Coroner's by appointment.

Facilities: Robing room. Solicitors' room. Interview rooms. Bar library. Public snack bar. Drinks machine.

Travel: NR Southend Victoria (Liverpool St. 1 hr. 8 min.) plus 5 min. walk to Crown Ct.

Crown/Mags: From station turn right and right again into Victoria Avenue. Court 200 yds on right.

Driving: A127 becomes Victoria Ave. Crown/Mags Ct. on left on entry into town centre.

Parking: Pay and display car park to rear of court.

Eating out:

A number of restaurants, public houses, and sandwich bars nearby.

SOUTHWARK CORONER'S COURT

Tennis St., Southwark, London SE1 1YD.

Telephone: (020) 7089 6380. Fax: (020) 7378 8401

Court times: Doors open 8.30 a.m. Court sits 10.30 a.m.

Facilities: Interview rooms. Hot drinks machine.

Travel: Und. Borough plus 2 min. walk. Elephant and Castle plus half a mile walk.

LRT 35, 40, 68, P3.

From station cross Borough High St. in front of church and turn left into Long Lane, Tennis St. is second left. Court is first building on left.

Driving: Cross London Bridge to Borough High St. (A3) and follow walking directions.

Parking: Multi-storey at Guy's Hospital.

Eating out: As for Inner London Crown Court (10 min. walk).

SOUTHWARK CROWN COURT

1 English Grounds, off Battle Bridge Lane, Southwark, London SE1 2HU.

Telephone: (020) 7522 7200. Fax: (020) 7522 7300.

DX: 39913 London Bridge South.

Court times: Doors open 8.00 a.m. Court sits 9.30 a.m. Office hours 9.00 a.m.–5.00 p.m.

Facilities: Male/female robing rooms. Interview rooms. Pre-trial video facilities. Video conferencing facilities. Bar mess. Bar library. Public cafeteria.

Travel: NR, Und. London Bridge plus 5 min. walk.

LRT 42, 47, 78, 188.

SOUTHWARK CROWN COURT—
CONTINUED

From station through passage down to Tooley St. s/p HMS Belfast. Turn right along Tooley St. Court on riverside down Battle Bridge Lane, 300 yds on left.

Driving: From London Bridge turn left into Tooley St. Court half a mile on left at Battle Bridge Lane.

Parking: Small domestic car park for counsel by arrangement with the mess. Otherwise limited meters.

Eating out: Restaurants and bars at Hay's Galleria.

STAINES COUNTY COURT,
STAINES MAGISTRATES' COURT,
STAINES YOUTH COURT

The Law Courts, Knowle Green, Staines, Middx. TW18 1XH.

Telephone: Mags: 01784 459261. Fax: 01784 466257. Cty: 01784 459175. Fax: 01784 460176.

DX: 98040 Staines 2.

Court times: Doors open 9.00 a.m. Courts sit: Cty 10.00 a.m., Mags 10.00 a.m. Office hours: Mags 9.00 a.m.–4.00 p.m.; Cty 10.00 a.m.–4.00 p.m.

Facilities: Male/female robing rooms. Interview rooms. Kiosk facility for beverages and sandwiches 9.30 a.m.–2.00 p.m.

Travel: NR Staines Central (Waterloo 25–34 min.) plus 10 min. walk.

LRT 117, 290.

Ar 436, 441–3, 451, 460.

From station (Surrey-bound platform) turn left and proceed to Kingston Rd. Continue on Kingston Rd. Knowle Green 1st right. Courts immediately on left.

Driving: A30 or A308 to Staines then B376 s/p Knowle Green.

Parking: Domestic car park.

Eating out:

| North Star | bar food | Kingston Rd. |
| Old Red Lion | bar food | Leacroft |

STEVENAGE MAGISTRATES' COURT,
NORTH HERTFORDSHIRE MAGISTRATES' COURT,
NORTH HERTFORDSHIRE YOUTH COURT

The Court House, Danesgate, Stevenage, Herts. SG1 1JQ.

Telephone: 01438 219440. Fax: 01438 219450.

DX: 122187 Old Stevenage.

Court times: Doors open 9.30 a.m. Court sits 10.00 a.m. Office hours 9.00 a.m.–4.00 p.m. The office for both North and East Herts. is now at Bayley House, Sish Lane, Stevenage, Herts. SG1 3SS.

Facilities: Advocates' room. Interview room. Witness rooms. Victim support rooms. Induction loop system. Disabled facilities. Refreshments.

Travel: NR Stevenage (New Town) (King's Cross 20–38 min., Moorgate 37–47 min.) plus 5 min. walk.

Ar SB1, SB2, 285; or 44, 323, 379, 382, 384, 794, to New Town. Bus station opposite Danesgate.

From station take footbridge across ring road and through the Leisure Centre. Turn right after leaving the covered walkway and the Court is down the steps and across the car park.

Driving: A1(M) s/p Stevenage (New Town). At roundabout take B197 Great North Rd. to Six Hills roundabout. First exit into Lytton Way, straight on to Tesco roundabout. Double back along Lytton Way to Danesgate. Court is 100 yds on left.

Parking: Two pay car parks in Danesgate beyond court.

Eating out:

Numerous bars and restaurants in the Retail Park and the town centre.

Edward the Confessor	bar food	New Town Sq.
McDonald's	restaurant	New Town Sq.
Wimpy	restaurant	New Town Sq.
Hertford Park Hotel	restaurant and bar food	New Town Sq.

STRATFORD EMPLOYMENT TRIBUNALS

44 Broadway, Stratford, London E15 1XH.

Telephone: (020) 8221 0921. Fax: (020) 8221 0398.

Court times: Tribunal sits 10.00 a.m.

Facilities: Waiting rooms. Drinks machine. Cardphone. Baby changing facilities.

Travel: Call for map.

NR Stratford (2 min. walk).

Buses: Bus station (2 min. walk). Buses: 257, 158, 69, 25, S2, 108, D8, 262, 473.

Parking: Stratford Centre (entrance opposite station).

Eating out: Variety of facilities in Stratford Centre and in Broadway.

STRATFORD MAGISTRATES' COURT,
STRATFORD YOUTH COURT

389–397 High St., Stratford, London E15 4SB.

Telephone: (020) 8522 5000. Warrant office: (020) 8522 5007. Fax: (020) 8519 9214. Minicom: (020) 8534 7966.

DX: 5417 Stratford.

Court times: Doors open 9.00 a.m. Courts sit 10.00 a.m.

Facilities: Restaurant. Advocates' room. Interview rooms. Witness rooms.

Travel: NR, DLR Stratford (Liverpool St. 8 min.) plus 5 min. walk.
Und. Stratford (Liverpool St. 10 min., Oxford Circus 21 min.)
LRT 25, <u>69</u>, 86, 108, 238, 241, <u>262</u>, 276.

From station through shopping centre, cross Stratford Broadway to the High St. Turn right and Court is 200 yds on left. Entrance to Youth Court via Chant St. at back of building.

Driving: Court on A11 opposite entrance to one-way system.

Parking: Multi-storey car park opposite station on one-way system.

Eating out:

The Swan	bar food	High St.
King Edward VII	bar food	High St.
Colours	restaurant	High St.

SUDBURY AND HAVERHILL MAGISTRATES' COURT, WEST SUFFOLK COMBINED FAMILY COURT, WEST SUFFOLK COMBINED YOUTH COURT

(Cts. sit Tues. to Fri.)

Court House, Acton Lane, Sudbury, Suffolk CO10 6ED.

Telephone: 01284 352300 (Bury St. Edmunds). Fax: 01284 352345.

Court times: Doors open 9.30 a.m. Courts sit 10.00 a.m.

Facilities: Vending machine. Interview room. Witness room.

Travel: NR Sudbury (Liverpool St. 1 hr. 31 min. via Colchester) plus 20 min. walk.

From station, proceed uphill and right to roundabout. Continue left uphill then right and continue into East St. Acton Lane is 300 yds on left s/p Health Centre. Proceed to top of hill. Court at police station.

Driving: For Mags: A12 to Chelmsford then A131 to Sudbury. Follow one-way system in town s/p Health Centre and proceed uphill to police station.

Parking: Off-street parking.

Eating out:

The Horse and Groom	bar food	East St.
Black Horse	bar food	East St.

SUTTON MAGISTRATES' COURT,

SUTTON YOUTH COURT (Tues. 10.00 a.m. and 2.00 p.m., Thurs. 10.00 a.m.)

Shotfield, Wallington, Surrey SM6 0JA.

Telephone: (020) 8770 5950. Fax: (020) 8770 5977.

DX: 59957 Wallington.

Court times: Doors open 9.00 a.m. Court sits 10.00 a.m. and 2.00 p.m. Office hours 9.00 a.m.–4.30 p.m.

Facilities: Advocates' room. Three witness rooms. Drinks machine.

SUTTON MAGISTRATES' COURT—
CONTINUED

Travel: NR Wallington (Victoria 34 min., London Bridge 30 min.) plus 5 min. walk.

LRT: 127, 151, 154, 157, 301, 407.

From station turn right uphill. Proceed up Woodcote Rd. Turn right at footpath before Town Hall. Mags Ct. immediately ahead.

Driving: Court on Shotfield near junction of A237 Woodcote Rd. with B271, Stanley Pk Rd./Stafford Rd.

Parking: Pay and display car parks opposite and next to Mags Ct.

Eating out:

Whispering Moon	bar food	Woodcote Rd.
Coughlans	bakery, hot snacks	Woodcote Rd.
Three Cooks	bakery	Woodcote Rd.
Toppers	sandwiches	Woodcote Rd.

SWAFFHAM (CENTRAL NORFOLK) MAGISTRATES' COURT

The Court House, Westacre Rd., Swaffham, Norfolk PE27 7NH.

Telephone: Admin. from King's Lynn: 01553 770120. Fax: 01553 775098.

Court times: Doors open 9.30 a.m. Court sits 10.00 a.m. Court sits Tues. and Fri. for adult work; Wed. for Youth work.

Facilities: Advocates' room. Interview room. Vending machine.

Travel: NR Thetford/King's Lynn (**NB** 20 and 24 miles, respectively) plus taxi. **NB** Cannot be reached from London before Court sits. Court next to police sation, just off the King's Lynn Rd.

Driving: A10 via Cambridge, Ely to Downham Market then A1122 to Swaffham via A47 and A1065.

Parking: Domestic car park.

Eating out:

Jan's Pantry	restaurant	Market Place
The George	bar food	off Market Place
The Horse and Groom	bar food	Lynn St.

THAMES MAGISTRATES' COURT,

58 Bow Rd., London E3 4DJ.

INNER LONDON YOUTH COURTS CENTRE 1

66 Bow Rd., London E3 4DH. Dealing with youth cases arising in the boroughs of Islington, Camden, Tower Hamlets, Hackney, and the City of London.

Telephone: (020) 8271 1270. Fax: (020) 8271 1263 (gen. office). (020) 8271 1235. Fax: (020) 8271 1241 (public funding). (020) 8271 1200. Fax: (020) 8271 1251 (listing). (020) 8271 1239.

DX: 55654 Bow.

Court times: Doors open 9.00 a.m. Court sits at 10.00 a.m. Y 10.00 a.m. Office hours 9.00 a.m.–5.00 p.m.

THAMES MAGISTRATES' COURT—
CONTINUED

Facilities: Advocates' room. Interview rooms. Cafeteria (snacks). Staff canteen available for advocates.

Travel: Und. Bow Rd. (Embankment 18 min.). Turn right out of station. Court 20 yds on right.

DLR: Bow Church. Turn left out of station. Court 150 yds on left.

LRT 25.

Parking: Side-streets (restricted).

Eating out:

Little Driver	bar food	Bow Rd.

THANET COUNTY COURT

Courthouse, 2nd Floor, Cecil Sq., Margate, Kent CT9 1RL.

Telephone: 01843 221722. Fax: 01843 222730.

DX: 98210 Cliftonville 2.

Court times: Doors open 10.00 a.m. Court sits 10.30 a.m. Office hours 10.00 a.m.–4.00 p.m.

Facilities: Robing/advocates' room. Interview rooms. Drinks machine.

THANET (MARGATE) MAGISTRATES' COURT, THANET (MARGATE) YOUTH COURT

The Court House, Cecil Sq., Margate, Kent CT9 1RL.

Telephone: 01843 291775. Fax: 01843 231613.

Court times: Doors open 9.00 a.m. Court sits 10.00 a.m. Office hours 9.00 a.m.–4.00 p.m. (3.30 p.m. Fridays).

Facilities: Advocates' room. Interview room. Drinks machine.

Travel: NR Margate (Victoria 1 hr. 35 min. Charing Cross 1 hr. 50 min.) plus 20 min. walk.

From station follow Marine Parade but bear right past Clock Tower into Marine Gardens and across to Cecil Square. Courthouse next to library.

Driving: A2–M2–A2 to Canterbury then A28 to Margate via Birchington. Proceed to seafront then follow walking directions.

Parking: Car park in Hawley St. off Cecil Square.

Eating out:

The Eastcliffe	bar food	Northdown Rd.
Peter's	fish bar	Marine Parade
The Cottage	snacks	High St.
Bouquetts	restaurant	Marine Parade

THETFORD (SOUTH NORFOLK) MAGISTRATES' COURT, CENTRAL, SOUTH, AND WEST NORFOLK YOUTH COURT

The Court House, Old Bury Rd., Thetford, Norfolk IP24 3AQ.

THETFORD (SOUTH NORFOLK) MAGISTRATES' COURT—CONTINUED

Telephone: Admin. from King's Lynn: 01553 770120. Fax: 01553 775098.

Court times: Doors open 9.30 a.m. Court sits 10.00 a.m. Office admin. at King's Lynn. Court sits for adult work on Mon. and Thurs.; Youth work on Thurs. a.m. only

Facilities: Interview rooms. Vending machine.

Travel: NR Thetford (Liverpool St. 2 hrs. 30 min.) plus 15 min. walk.

From station turn left into Station Rd. Cross to and proceed down White Hart St. Cross traffic lights to Bridge St. Turn left at Bell Hotel and take public footpath across river to court.

Driving: M11–A11 to Thetford. Court on riverside on approach to town.

Parking: Domestic car park.

Eating out:

The Anchor Hotel	bar food	Bridge St.
Bell Hotel	bar food/restaurant	Bridge St.
Thomas Paine Hotel	bar food/restaurant	King St.

TRANSPORT TRIBUNAL

Procession House, 55 Ludgate Hill, London EC4M 7JW.

Telephone: 0207 029 9789. Fax: 0207 029 9781.

DX: 149065 Ludgate Hill.

TUNBRIDGE WELLS COUNTY COURT

Merevale House, 42–46 London Rd., Tunbridge Wells, Kent TN1 1DP.

Telephone: 01892 515515. Fax: 01892 513676.

DX: 98220 Tunbridge Wells 3.

Court times: Office hours 10.00 a.m.–4.00 p.m.

Travel: NR Tunbridge Wells (Charing Cross 50 min.–1 hr.) plus 5 min. walk.

From station over bridge to Safeway. Bear left past Safeway and PPP House. Turn right into London Rd. Pass sorting office. Merevale House is building on 'stilts'.

Driving: From London A21 then A26/A264 into Tunbridge Wells town centre. Cty Ct. on main London Rd.

TUNBRIDGE WELLS MAGISTRATES' COURT, TUNBRIDGE WELLS YOUTH COURT

The Court House, Police Station, Crescent Rd., Tunbridge Wells, Kent TN1 2LU.

Telephone: Admin. from Maidstone: 01622 671041. Fax: 01622 691800.

DX: 51951 Maidstone.

TUNBRIDGE WELLS MAGISTRATES' COURT—
CONTINUED

Court times: Doors open 9.00 a.m. Courts sit 10.00 a.m.

Facilities: Advocates'/interview room. No on-premises catering.

Travel: NR Tunbridge Wells (Charing Cross 50 min.–1 hr.) plus 10 min. walk. From station turn left up Mount Pleasant Rd. At traffic lights, top of hill, turn right into Crescent Rd. Court in police station on left.

Driving: From London A21 then A26/A264 into Tunbridge Wells town centre. Court in upper part of town at police station.

Parking: Multi-storey in Crescent Rd.

Eating out:

Calverley Hotel	restaurant/coffee bar	Crescent Rd.
Honeymoon Chinese	restaurant	Mount Pleasant Rd.

UXBRIDGE COUNTY COURT

501 Uxbridge Rd., Hayes, Middx. UB4 8HL.

Telephone: (020) 8561 8562. Fax: (020) 8561 2020.

DX: 44658 Hayes (Middx).

Court times: Doors open 9.00 a.m. Court sits 10.00 a.m. Office hours 10.00 a.m.–4.00 p.m.

Facilities: Advocates' room. Consultation rooms. Hot and cold drinks machine. Disabled access.

Travel: NR Hayes and Harlington (Thames trains from Paddington) then buses 90, 195, or H98, or taxi (1.5 miles).

LRT 204, 207, 222, 224.

Und. Northolt on Central line (3 miles), then bus 90, or Uxbridge on Piccadilly line, then bus 427, 607. Buses 427 and 607 run along Uxbridge Rd. via Southall to Ealing Broadway. Bus 90 runs from Northolt.

Driving: Court at junction of A4020 Uxbridge Rd. (westbound carriageway) and Grange Rd. s/p Beck Theatre.

Parking: Domestic car park.

UXBRIDGE MAGISTRATES' COURT,
UXBRIDGE FAMILY COURT (Mon. and Wed. 10.00 a.m.),
UXBRIDGE YOUTH COURT (Tues. and Thurs. 10.00 a.m.)
Harefield Rd., Uxbridge, Middx. UB8 1PQ.

Telephone: 01895 814646. Fax: 01895 274280.

DX: 95110 Uxbridge.

Court times: Doors open 9.00 a.m. Court sits 10.00 a.m. Office hours 9.00 a.m.–4.00 p.m.

Facilities: Advocates' room. Interview rooms. Refreshments.

Travel: Und. Mags/Y: Uxbridge (Baker St. 38 min., Piccadilly Circus 53 min.) plus 10 min. walk.

From station turn right into High St. (from bus station cut through into High St. and turn right). Proceed to junction with Harefield Rd. Mags Ct. opposite.

UXBRIDGE MAGISTRATES' COURT—
CONTINUED

Driving: From London A40 to B483 s/p Uxbridge then B467 Harefield Rd. to Court. From south or west A4020/A4007/A408 to Uxbridge town centre.

Parking: Multi-storey car park at 'The Cedars' by shopping centre.

Eating out:

Nonna Rosa	Italian restaurant	High St.
Crown and Sceptre	bar food	High St.
Bermuda Bar	restaurant	Cook's Yard
McDonald's	restaurant	High St.

WALTHAM FOREST MAGISTRATES' COURT,
WALTHAM FOREST FAMILY PROCEEDINGS COURT
(alt. Wed. a.m./ p.m.),
WALTHAM FOREST YOUTH COURT (alt. Tues. and Thurs. 2.00 p.m. Remands, Wed. 10.00 a.m.)

Court House, 1 Farnan Ave., Walthamstow, London E17 4NX.

Telephone: (020) 8527 8000. Fax: (020) 8527 9063.

DX: 124542 Waltham Forest.

Court times: Doors open 8.45 a.m. Court sits 10.00 a.m.

Facilities: Advocates' room. Interview rooms. Lift. Telephones. Toilets for disabled. Witness service.

Travel: NR Walthamstow Central (Liverpool St. 15 min.) plus 275 bus or 15 min. walk.

Und: Walthamstow Central (King's Cross 16 min., Victoria 24 min.) plus 275 bus or 15 min. walk.

LRT 34, 69, 97, 123, 275.

Turn right out of station forecourt then left into Hoe St. (North) and continue 10 min. to The Bell traffic lights. Turn right up Forest Rd. Court 200 yds on left with municipal buildings.

Driving: Court on A503 Forest Rd. east of junction with A112 Hoe St. in Waltham Forest Civic Centre complex.

Parking: Large free car park to rear.

Eating out:

The Bell	bar food/restaurant	Forest Rd.
Adam Sandwich Bar	sandwich bar	Forest Rd.
Ristorante La Notte	licensed restaurant	Forest Rd.

WALTHAMSTOW CORONER'S COURT

Queen's Rd., London E17 8QP.

Telephone: (020) 8520 7246. Fax: (020) 8521 0896.

Court times: Doors open 8.00 a.m. Court sits 10.00 a.m. Close 3.30 p.m.

Facilities: No on-premises catering.

Travel: NR, Und. Walthamstow Central (Liverpool St. 15 min., King's Cross 16 min., Victoria 24 min.) plus 10 min. walk.

LRT 20, 34, 48, 69, 97, 206, 275.

WALTHAMSTOW CORONER'S COURT—
CONTINUED

LC 502–3.

EN 251.

From station turn right along Hoe St. Queen's Rd. 4th right. Court 500 yds on left by cemetery.

Driving: Take A104 Lea Bridge Rd. or A503 Ferry Lane. From A104 turn left into A1006 Markhouse Rd. Queen's Rd. 3rd right by leisure centre. From A503 turn right at Blackhorse Rd. Und. station into Blackhorse Rd. Proceed past St James's St. NR station and bear left and right. Queen's Rd. 3rd left.

Parking: Large domestic car park.

Eating out:

McDonald's	restaurant	Hoe St.
Law Arms	bar food	Queen's Rd.
Nag's Head	bar food	Orford Rd.

WANDSWORTH COUNTY COURT

76–78 Upper Richmond Rd., Putney, London SW15 2SU.

Telephone: (020) 8333 4351/2. Fax: (020) 8877 9854.

DX: 97540 Putney 2.

Court times: Doors open 9.00 a.m. Court sits 10.30 a.m. Office hours 10.00 a.m.–4.00 p.m.

Facilities: Male/female robing rooms. Consultation rooms. Hot and cold drinks machines.

Travel: NR Putney (Waterloo 11–13 min.).

Und. East Putney (Embankment 40 min.).

LRT 14, 37, 39, 74, 85, 93, 337.

From NR station turn left and left at lights into Upper Richmond Rd. Court 300 yds on left. From underground turn right. Court 50 yds on left past station.

Driving: Court on A205 immediately beyond East Putney und. station.

Parking: Meters in side-streets.

Eating out:

Bayee House	Chinese restaurant	Upper Richmond Rd.
Mini Bar	snacks/sandwiches	Upper Richmond Rd.
Pizza Express	pizza and pasta	Upper Richmond Rd.
Prince of Wales	bar food	Upper Richmond Rd.

WANTAGE (SOUTHERN OXFORDSHIRE) MAGISTRATES' COURT (Wed.), SOUTHERN OXFORDSHIRE FAMILY PROCEEDINGS COURT (third Mon. in month)

The Court House, Church St., Wantage, Oxon. OX12 8EQ.

Telephone: All admin. from Oxford: 0870 2412808.

DX: 96452 Oxford 4.

Court times: Doors open 9.00 a.m. Court sits 10.00 a.m.–1.00 p.m. 2.00 p.m.–4.30 p.m. Trials only: all enquiries to Oxford Magistrates' Court.

Facilities: Interview room. Drinks machine.

Travel: NR Didcot Parkway (Paddington 48–55 min.) plus taxi 3 miles. Local bus: X31, 31 from Oxford. National Bus: To Oxford Gloucester Green then Local bus X31, 31.

Driving: From A34 Marcham interchange, A338 for 2 miles direct to Market Place. First exit left is Church St.

Parking: Public car park, Wantage Civic Hall next to the Court. Market Place limited to 30 min. Short stay.

Eating out: Many within 4 min. walk.

WATFORD COUNTY COURT

3rd Floor, Cassiobury House, 11–19 Station Rd., Watford, Herts. WD1 1E2.

Telephone: 01923 249666. Fax: 01923 251317.

Court times: Doors open 9.00 a.m. Court sits 10.00 a.m. District Judges 10.00 a.m. Office hours 9.30 a.m.–4.00 p.m.

Facilities: Robing rooms. Interview rooms. Drinks machine. Disabled access.

WATFORD EMPLOYMENT TRIBUNALS

2nd Floor, Radius House, 51 Clarendon Rd., Watford, Herts. WD17 1HU.

Telephone: 01923 281750. Fax: 01923 281781.

Court times: Tribunal sits 10.00 a.m.

Facilities: Waiting rooms. Drinks machines.

Travel: Call for map.

NR Watford Junction (5 min. walk).

Parking: Sutton car park.

Eating out:

Town centre 5 min. walk.

WATFORD MAGISTRATES' COURT

The Court House, Clarendon Rd., Watford, Herts. WD1 1ST.

Telephone: 01923 297500. Fax: 01923 297528.

DX: 51509 Watford 2.

Court times: Doors open 9.00 a.m. Courts sit 10.00 a.m. and 2.00 p.m.

Facilities: Advocates' room. Duty solicitors' room. Refreshments machine.

Travel: NR Watford Junction (Euston 17–19 min. (fast)).

LRT 142, 258.

Ar 322, 336.

WATFORD MAGISTRATES' COURT—
CONTINUED

Cty: Turn right out of Station Rd. Court in office block building 250 yds on left. Mags: Turn left from station into Clarendon Rd. Court 500 yds on right.

Driving: M1 Junc. 5 then A41 to North Watford. Follow signs to Watford Junction Station. Both courts in vicinity of station.

Parking: Station car park. NCP in Wellington Rd. (right and left behind Mags Ct.).

Eating out:

The Pennant	bar food	Station Rd.
The White Lion	bar food	St. Albans Rd.

WEST LONDON COUNTY COURT

181 Talgarth Rd., London W6 8DN.

Telephone: (020) 8600 6868. Fax: (020) 8600 6860.

DX: 97550 Hammersmith 8.

Court times: Doors open 9.30 a.m. Court sits 10.30 a.m. Office hours 10.00 a.m.–4.00 p.m.

Directions and facilities etc. as Mag Ct.

WEST LONDON CORONER'S COURT,
WESTERN DISTRICT CORONER'S COURT

2nd Floor, 25 Bagleys Lane, London SW6 2QA.

Telephone: (020) 88753 6800. Fax: (020) 88753 6803.

Court times: Doors open 9.30 a.m. Court sits 10.00 a.m.

Facilities: Advocates' room. Interview room.

Travel: Und. Fulham Broadway or Parsons Green (Embankment 18 min.) plus 20 min. walk.

LRT C4 from Fulham Town Hall (Harwood Rd.) to Chelsea Harbour plus 10 min. walk.

11, 22, 28, 91, 295 to New Kings Rd. (Eel Brook Common) plus 10 min. walk.

From Fulham Broadway cross over to Harwood Rd. to New Kings Rd. Cross over turning right and left into Bagleys Lane. Court 1,000 yds on left.

From Parsons Green turn right and proceed down to New Kings Rd. Turn left, Bagleys Lane 500 yds on right.

Driving: Take Wandsworth Bridge Rd. From the north turn left before bridge into Townmead Rd. Bagleys Lane half mile on left. Court 150 yds on right.

Parking: Side-streets to front of Court.

Eating out:

Queen Elizabeth	bar food	Bagleys Lane
Just so Bar	bar food	Stephendale Rd.
Jury Inn	hotel restaurant	Townmead Rd.

WEST LONDON MAGISTRATES' COURT,
HAMMERSMITH AND FULHAM YOUTH COURT,
KENSINGTON and CHELSEA YOUTH COURT,
WESTMINSTER YOUTH COURT

181 Talgarth Rd., London W6 8DN.

Telephone: Listing: (020) 8700 9350. Fax: (020) 8700 9344 Central switchboard 0845 601 3600

DX: 124800 Hammersmith 8.

Court times: Doors open 9.30 a.m. Adult Courts sit 10.30 a.m. Youth Court sits at 10.00 a.m. Applications heard 10.15 a.m.

Facilities: Disabled access and facilities. Pay phones. Refreshments servery. Advocates' room. Interview rooms.

Travel: Und. Barons Court and Hammersmith (5 min. walk). From Hammersmith station exit 14, emerge onto Talgarth Rd. Court diagonally opposite on right (2 min. walk).

Buses: 9, 10, 26, 33, 72, 190, 211, 220, 283, 295, and 391.

Parking: None except Orange Badge holders by prior arrangement. NCP and parking meters at Hammersmith Broadway and Queen Caroline St.

WESTMINSTER CORONER'S COURT

65 Horseferry Rd., London SW1P 2ED.

Telephone: (020) 7834 6515. Fax: (020) 7828 2837.

Court times: Doors open 9.00 a.m. Court sits by appointment.

Facilities: Waiting rooms.

Travel: Und. St. James's Park plus 10 min. walk. Turn right into Broadway and proceed to Victoria St. and cross over into Strutton Ground which becomes Horseferry Rd. Court 500 yds on right (past second bend in road).

Driving: As for Horseferry Rd. Mags Ct.

Parking: Meters, Vincent Sq. As for Horseferry Rd. Mags Ct.

Eating out:

| The Bishops | cafe/restaurant | Horseferry Rd. |
| Alexander's | wine bar | Horseferry Rd. |

For travel and eating out see also Horseferry Rd. Mags Ct.

WEST SUFFOLK MAGISTRATES' COURT,
WEST SUFFOLK COMBINED FAMILY COURT,
WEST SUFFOLK COMBINED YOUTH COURT

Court House, Acton Lane, Sudbury, Suffolk CO10 6ED.

Admin by Bury St. Edmunds Magistrates' Court.

Telephone: 01284 352300. (Bury St. Edmunds) 01787 379073 (Sudbury court days only).

Court times: Doors open 9.30 a.m. Court sits 10.00 a.m.

Facilities: Witness room. Interview room. Vending machine.

WEST SUFFOLK MAGISTRATES' COURT—
CONTINUED

Travel: NR Sudbury (Liverpool St. 1 hr. 31 min. via Colchester) plus 20 min. walk. From station, proceed uphill and right into Eastern Road. At roundabout turn right into East St. Acton Lane is 300 yds on left s/p Health Centre. Proceed to top of hill. Court at police station.

Driving: For Mags: A12 to Chelmsford then A131 to Sudbury. Follow one-way system in town s/p Health Centre and proceed past it uphill to police station.

Parking: Off-street parking.

Eating out:

| Black Horse | bar food | East St. |
| The Horse and Groom | bar food | East St. |

WILLESDEN COUNTY COURT

9 Acton Lane, Harlesden, London NW10 8SB.

Telephone: (020) 8963 8200. Fax: (020) 8453 0946.

DX: 97560 Harlesden 2.

Court times: Doors open 9.30 a.m. Court sits 10.30 a.m. Office hours 10.00 a.m.–4.00 p.m.

Facilities: Male/female robing rooms. Interview room. No on-premises catering.

Travel: NR, Und. Willesden Junction (Euston 13 min., Liverpool St. 26 min., Embankment 24 min.) plus 10 min. walk.

LRT 18, 187, 205, 220, 226, 260, 266.

From station turn right and right again. Court at junction with Acton Lane, 600 yds on left.

Driving: A404 to Willesden. Court at junction of A404 and B4492 by Harlesden Jubilee Clock.

Parking: Limited parking in side-streets to rear.

Eating out:

| McDonald's | restaurant | High St. |

WIMBLEDON MAGISTRATES' COURT,
WIMBLEDON FAMILY COURT (daily 10.00 a.m.),
WIMBLEDON YOUTH COURT (Mon. and Thurs. 10.00 a.m.)

The Law Courts, Alexandra Rd., Wimbledon, London SW19 7JP.

Telephone: (020) 8946 8622. Fax: (020) 8946 7030.

DX: 116610 Wimbledon 4.

Court times: Doors open 9.00 a.m. Court sits 10.00 a.m. Office hours 9.30 a.m.–3.30 p.m.

Facilities: Advocates'/interview room. On-premises catering.

Travel: BR, Und. Wimbledon (Waterloo 12–14 min., London Bridge 27 min., Embankment 28 min.) plus 5 min. walk.

LRT 57, 93, 131, 155–6, 164.

From station turn right into Wimbledon Hill Rd. First right Alexandra Rd. Court on right by B & Q.

WIMBLEDON MAGISTRATES' COURT—
CONTINUED
Driving: Court off Wimbledon Broadway A219 before station.

Parking: Domestic car park.

Eating out:

Ely's	department store restaurant	St. George's Rd.
Smart Alex	wine bar/restaurant	St. Mark's Place
The Alexandra	bar food	Wimbledon Hill Rd.

WISBECH (FENLAND) MAGISTRATES' COURT (Tues., Wed.),
WISBECH YOUTH COURT (Thurs. or Fri.)
The Court House, Lynn Rd., Wisbech, Cambs. PE13 3AP.

Telephone: Admin. from Peterborough: 0845 3100575.

Court times: Doors open 9.30 a.m. Court sits 10.00 a.m.

Facilities: Interview room.

Travel: NR King's Lynn (King's Cross or Liverpool St. via Peterborough 2 hrs) plus bus or taxi 12 miles.

Driving: A1/A141/A47 to A1101 into town centre. At bridge over River Nene follow signs for police station. Court to rear.

Parking: Side-streets to rear. Car park close by.

Eating out:

Within town centre and by riverside.

WITHAM (MID-NORTH ESSEX) MAGISTRATES'
COURT (to include business of Braintree Magistrates' Courts),
MID-NORTH ESSEX YOUTH COURT,
The Court House, Newland St., Witham, Essex CM8 2AS.

Telephone: Admin. from Harlow: 01279 693200. 01245 313300. Fax: 01245 313399.

Court times: Doors open 9.30 a.m. Court sits 10.00 a.m.

Facilities: Advocates' room. Victim/witness support service. Interview room. Refreshment room. Video link/conferencing.

Travel: NR Witham (Liverpool St. 40–50 min.) plus 10 min. walk. From station turn left from Albert Rd. and left again into Collingwood Rd. Take second left Avenue Rd. and immediately bear right into The Avenue, proceed to end. Court across main road (Newland St.) 50 yds to left immediately behind police station.

Driving: A12 via Chelmsford then B1389 s/p Witham. Court behind police station in main road at eastern end of town centre.

Parking: Very small domestic car park on first left, The Grove.

Eating out:

The Red Lion	bar food	Newland St.
The George	bar food	Newland St.
The White Hart	bar food	Newland St.
Barton's Bakery	take-away	Newlands Precinct

WITNEY (NORTHERN OXFORDSHIRE) MAGISTRATES' COURT

The Court House, Welch Way, Witney, Oxon. OX29 7HX.
Telephone: 01295 452000. Fax: 01295 452050.
DX: 24221 Banbury.
Court times: Mon. and Thurs. 10.00 a.m. Adult 2nd Wed. in month 10.00 a.m. Office hours 8.15 a.m.–4.30 p.m. (4.00 p.m. Fri.)
Facilities: Vending machine. Interview rooms.
Travel: NR Oxford (Paddington 1 hr.) plus bus/taxi 12 miles.
Driving: From east take A40(T) to Witney. B4022 into town down Oxford Hill which becomes Newland. Turn left into Bridge St. and continue into High St. Turn right into Welch Way and park opposite court. From west take A40(T) to Witney. Following road anti-clockwise via Witan Way to High St. Turn left and right into Welch Way.
Parking: No parking at court. Car park opposite (free).
Eating out: Town centre within 5 min. walking distance.

WOKING MAGISTRATES' COURT,
NORTH WEST SURREY MAGISTRATES' COURT,
NORTH WEST SURREY YOUTH COURT

Station Approach, Woking, Surrey GU22 7YL.
Telephone: 01483 714950. Fax: 01483 723698.
DX: 135090 Woking 5.
Court times: Doors open 9.00 a.m. Court sits 10.00 a.m. Office hours 9.00 a.m.–4.30 p.m.
Facilities: Interview rooms. Refreshments (morning only). Telephones. Mother and baby changing room. Help desk.
Travel: NR Woking (Waterloo 30–42 min.) plus 5 min. walk.
Exit from south side of station and turn right into Station Approach.
Driving: M25 Junc. 11, then A320 into Woking. Follow Victoria Way ring road under railway bridge, bearing left into Station Approach.
Parking: Limited side-streets. Car park Heathside Crescent.
Eating out:

The Sovereigns	bar food	Guildford Rd.
Duvals Wine Bar		Goldsworth Rd.
Woking Tandoori	restaurant	Goldsworth Rd.
Peacocks Centre	food hall	Woking Centre

WOOD GREEN CROWN COURT

Woodall House, Lordship Lane, London N22 5LF.
Telephone: (020) 8826 4100. Fax: (020) 8881 4802. Listing (020) 8826 4131.
DX: 130346 Wood Green 3.
Court times: Doors open 9.00 a.m. Court sits 10.15 a.m. Office hours 9.00 a.m.–5.00 p.m.
Facilities: Robing room. Interview rooms. Public cafeteria. Bar mess. Witness support. Child liaison officer. Video link facilities.

WOOD GREEN CROWN COURT—
CONTINUED

Travel: NR Alexandra Palace (Moorgate 17 min.) plus 15 min. walk.
Und. Wood Green (King's Cross 13 min., Piccadilly Circus 21 min.) plus 5 min. walk.
LRT 29, 67, 84A, 121, 123, 141, 144, 221, 243, 243A, 298, W2, W3.
From Alexandra Palace Station take right-hand exit s/p Wood Green town centre into Station Rd. Follow Station Rd. to end past mini-roundabout (800 yds) to lights by Wood Green underground station. Cross at lights. From underground station turn left into Lordship Lane. Court 400 yds on left.
Driving: From London take A105 Green Lanes North through Manor House, Turnpike Lane, Wood Green, to Wood Green Station. At junction with Lordship Lane (A109) turn right. Court 400 yds on left.
Parking: Domestic car park via Winkfield Rd. Parking is limited and residential parking only within half a mile of the court.
Eating out:

The Lordship	bar food	Lordship Lane
Avenida	restaurant	Wood Green Broadway
Pizza Hut	restaurant	Wood Green Broadway
Kossoff's	bakery/take-away	Wood Green Broadway
Freemasons Arms	bar food	Lordship Lane

WOOLWICH COUNTY COURT
The Court House, Powis St., London SE18 6JW.
Telephone: (020) 8854 2127. Fax: (020) 8316 4842.
DX: 123450 Woolwich 8.
Court times: Doors open 9.00 a.m. Court sits 10.00 a.m. Office hours 10.00 a.m.–4.00 p.m.
District Judge's appointments: Doors open 9.00 a.m. Court sits 10.00 a.m.
Facilities: Male/female robing rooms. Consultation rooms. Vending machine. Baby changing facilities. Children's area.
Travel: NR Woolwich Arsenal (Charing Cross 28 min., Waterloo East 26 min., London Bridge 19 min.) plus 5 min. walk.
LRT 51, 53, 54, 96, 99, 122, 161, 177, 180.
From station cross over General Gordon Place. Turn right and left into Powis St. Court 500 yds on left.
Driving: Court by roundabout for Woolwich ferry at junction of A206 with A205.
Parking: NCP car park by court.
Eating out:

| The Castle | bar food | Powis St. |
| Starburger | restaurant | Hare St. |

WOOLWICH CROWN COURT

2 Belmarsh Rd., Western Way, Thamesmead SE28 0EY.

Telephone: (020) 8312 7000. Fax: (020) 8312 7078.

DX: 117650 Woolwich 7.

Court times: Doors open 8.30 a.m. Court sits 10.00 a.m. or 10.30 a.m. Office hours 9.00 a.m.–5.00 p.m.

Facilities: Robing rooms. Conference rooms. Public canteen.

Travel: NR Woolwich Arsenal (Charing Cross 28 min., London Bridge 19 min.) plus taxi or bus.

LRT 244.

Driving: Take A206 s/p Woolwich Ferry. At roundabout by ferry follow s/p Woolwich Royal Arsenal East past Waterfront Centre into Woolwich High St. At mini-roundabout 2nd exit into Beresford St. which becomes Plumstead Rd. Bear left at 2nd traffic lights s/p Royal Arsenal East into Pettman Crescent. Follow road around to right and bear left into Western Way s/p Belmarsh. At lights marked Intersection B (Belmead) take left-hand filter lane then cross lights s/p Belmarsh and Court. Keep in left-hand lane and cross dual carriageway at lights going directly ahead into approach road for Belmarsh Prison and Court. Turn right into car park.

Parking: Domestic car park.

Eating out: None.

WOOLWICH MAGISTRATES' COURT

Market St., Woolwich, London SE18 6QY.

Telephone: (020) 8271 9000. Fax: (020) 8271 9002.

DX: 35203 Greenwich West.

Court times: Doors open 9.30 a.m. Court sits 10.15 a.m., 1.45 p.m.

Facilities: Advocates' room. Interview room. Vending machine.

Travel: NR as for Cty Ct. plus 10–15 min. walk.

From station cross over General Gordon Place. Turn left and cross over into Wellington St. Market St. is 2nd on right. Court 100 yds on right.

Driving: Court off A205 in Woolwich town centre by police station.

Parking: Meters. Multi-storey car park in Monk St. (opposite).

Eating out:

Wimpy	restaurant	Thomas St.
Earl of Chatham	bar food	Thomas St.
Littlewoods	restaurant	Powis St.
McDonald's	restaurant	Powis St.
Director General	bar food	Wellington St.

WORTHING COUNTY COURT,
WORTHING MAGISTRATES' COURT,
WORTHING YOUTH COURT

The Law Courts, Christchurch Rd., Worthing, West Sussex BN11 1JE (Mags) BN11 1JD (Cty).

WORTHING COUNTY COURT—
  CONTINUED

Telephone: Cty: 01903 206721. Fax: 01903 235559. Mags: 01903 210981. Fax: 01903 820746.

DX: Cty: 98230 Worthing 4. Mags: 98233 Worthing 4.

Court times: Doors open 9.00 a.m. Court sits 10.00 a.m. Office hours: Cty: 9.30 a.m.–4.00 p.m., Mags: 9 a.m.–4.30 p.m.

Facilities: Advocates' room. Interview room. Vending machines for hot/cold drinks, snacks. Public telephone.

Travel: NR Worthing (Victoria 1 hr. 20 min.) plus 5 min. walk.

Buses: 208, 210, 229, 230, 700, 900.

From station walk south along station approach. Turn left into Teville Rd. then right into Christchurch Rd. Courts are at far end on the left.

Driving: A24 to Worthing town centre. Turn right past town hall. Christchurch Rd. is 1st right.

Parking: Multi-storey at Teville Gate or Stoke Abbott Rd.

Eating out:

The Wheatsheaf	bar food	Richmond Rd.
Trenchers		Portland Rd.

The
Western Circuit

AGRICULTURAL LAND TRIBUNALS (SOUTH WEST AREA)

Government Buildings, Burghill Road, Westbury-on-Trym, Bristol BS10 6NJ.

Telephone: 0117 959 8648. Fax: 0117 950 5392.

e-mail: Tony.Collins@Defra.gsi.gov.uk.

Website: www. defra.gov.uk/rds/alt/default.htm.

Travel: NR Bristol Temple Meads (Paddington 1 hr. 45 min.) plus taxi 3 miles.

Driving: From M4 Junc. 19, M32 Junc. 1 onto A4174 s/p Filton. At Filton take B4056 to Westbury-on-Trym. At junction with A4018 turn left into Falcondale Rd. Second right is Burghill Rd.

ALDERSHOT AND FARNHAM COUNTY COURT

84–86 Victoria Rd., Aldershot, Hants. GU1 1SS.

Telephone: 01252 796 800. Fax: 01252 345 705.

DX: 98530 Aldershot 2.

Court times: Doors open 9.15 a.m. Court sits 10.30 a.m. Office hours 10.00 a.m.–4.00 p.m. District Judge's appointments from 9.30 a.m.

Facilities: Robing room. Consultation rooms.

Travel: NR Aldershot (Waterloo 60 min.) plus 5 min. walk.
From station into Station Rd., right into Arthur St. Continue to end. Court opposite, across Victoria Rd., in modern red brick building.

Driving: M3 Junc. 4, then A325 to Aldershot town centre via Wellington Ave. right after police station into Barrack Rd. Left-hand fork into Grosvenor Rd. Left into Victoria Rd., Court 450 yds on left after post office.

Parking: Off Victoria Rd. Public car parks.

Eating out and Accommodation:

George	hotel	Victoria Rd.

ALDERSHOT MAGISTRATES' COURT,

The Court House, Civic Centre, Aldershot, Hants. GU11 1NY.

Telephone: 01252 366000. Fax: 01252 330877.

DX: 145110 Aldershot 4.

Court times: Doors open 9.00 a.m. Court sits 10.00 a.m. Office hours 8.30 a.m.–5.00 p.m.

Facilities: Advocates' room. Interview rooms. Vulnerable witness video link.

Travel: NR Aldershot plus walking 15 min.
S/p to health centre which is next to police station. Court on left between police station and health centre.

Driving: Follow Cty Ct. directions, court next to police station.

Parking: Public car park behind court.

Eating out and Accommodation:

The Goose	bar food	High St.
The Queen's	bar food	High St.

ALTON MAGISTRATES' COURT (Mon. and Thurs.),
ALTON FAMILY PROCEEDINGS COURT (alt. Fri.),
ALTON YOUTH COURT (alt. Mon.)

The Court House, Normandy St., Alton, Hants. GU34 1AQ.
Telephone: 01252 366000. Fax: 01252 330877.
DX: 145110 Aldershot 4.
Court times: Doors open 9.00 a.m. Court sits 10.00 a.m.
Facilities: Advocates' room. Interview room. Vulnerable witness video link.
Travel: NR Alton (Waterloo 1 hr. 10 min.) plus 5 min. walk.
From Station Rd. turn left into Normandy St. Court 100 yds on left next to police station.
Driving: M3 Junc. 6, A339 Basingstoke Rd. to Alton. Continue through Lenten St. and Market St. and turn left into High St. Continue through into Normandy St. Court on right next to police station.
Parking: Pay and display by Court, off Orchard St. Side-streets.
Eating out and Accommodation:

| Alton House | hotel | Normandy St. |
| Crown | bar food | Normandy St. |

ANDOVER MAGISTRATES' COURT (Tues., Wed., Thurs., and Fri.),
ANDOVER FAMILY PROCEEDINGS COURT (alt. Tues. 10.00 a.m.),
ANDOVER YOUTH COURT (alt. Fri. 10.00 a.m.)

The Court House, West St., Andover, Hants. SP10 1EU.
Telephone: 01252 366000. Fax: 01252 330877.
DX: 145110 Aldershot 4.
Court times: Doors open 9.00 a.m. Court sits 10.00 a.m.
Facilities: Advocates' room. Interview room. Vulnerable witness video link.
Travel: NR Andover (Waterloo 1 hr. 15 min.) plus 15–20 min. walk.
Mags: From station approach cross the Cross Ways into Charlton Rd., right at roundabout into Western Ave. Court 400 yds, next to theatre and sports centre.
Driving: M3 Junc. 8, A303 to Andover. Follow bypass round and take A343 Northern Ave.
Mags: From Northern Ave. take 2nd left at roundabout into Western Ave. First left into West St. Court on the left-hand corner.
Parking: Multi-storey off Western Ave.
Eating out and Accommodation:

| White Hart | bar food | Bridge St. |

BARNSTAPLE COUNTY COURT,
BARNSTAPLE CROWN COURT (admin from Exeter Combined Court Centre),
BARNSTAPLE (NORTH DEVON) MAGISTRATES' COURT,
BARNSTAPLE (NORTH DEVON) YOUTH COURT (Thurs. 10.00 a.m.)

The Law Courts (Mags: 8th Floor, Cty: 7th Floor), Civic Centre, North Walk, Barnstaple, Devon EX31 1DX.

Telephone: Cty: 01271 372252. Fax: 01271 322968. Crown when sitting: 01271 373286. When not sitting: 01392 210655. Fax: 01271 22968. Mags: 01271 340410. Fax: 01271 340415.

DX: (Cty) 98560 Barnstaple 2.

Court times: Doors open 9.00 a.m. Court sits 10.00 a.m. Office hours 10.00 a.m.–4.00 p.m. Court sits at the Town Hall, Bideford on Tues. at 10.00 a.m.

Facilities: Robing room. Solicitors' room. Interview rooms. Canteen in Civic Centre (6th floor).

Travel: NR Barnstaple (Paddington via Exeter 4 hrs.) plus 20–5 min. walk.

From Station Rd. right into Sticklepath Terrace. Over roundabout and across Long Bridge. Left into Strand. Along Castle St., Court ahead in Civic Centre.

Driving: M5 Junc. 27 and A361 to Barnstaple. Continue along Eastern Ave., over roundabout, follow road round to left Victoria Rd. Right at roundabout into Barbican Way. Right at roundabout, straight on at traffic lights and straight over next roundabout. Left at 2nd roundabout and almost immediately straight across next. Civic Centre, tallest building in Barnstaple, is 300 yds on right.

Parking: No car park in Civic Centre but several short- and long-stay car parks within easy walking distance. Facilities for disabled persons available.

Eating out and Accommodation:

Cawardines	coffee house	Holland Walk
Lynwood House	hotel	Bishop's Tawton Rd.

BASINGSTOKE COUNTY COURT

Third Floor, Grosvenor House, Basing View, Basingstoke, Hants. RG21 4HG.

Telephone: 01256 318200. Fax: 01256 318225.

DX: 98570 Basingstoke 3.

Court times: Doors open 10.00 a.m. Court sits 10.30 a.m. Office hours 10.00 a.m.–4.00 p.m.

Facilities: Robing room. Interview rooms.

BASINGSTOKE MAGISTRATES' COURT,
BASINGSTOKE FAMILY PROCEEDINGS COURT (Thurs. 10.00 a.m.),
BASINGSTOKE YOUTH COURT (Tues.)
The Court House, London Rd., Basingstoke, Hants. RG21 4AB.
Telephone: 01252 366000. Fax: 01256 811447.
DX: 145110 Aldershot 4.
Court times: Doors open 9.00 a.m. Court sits 10.00 a.m. Office hours 9.30 a.m.–3.00 p.m.
Facilities: Advocates' room. Interview rooms. WRVS. Duty solicitor's room. Prosecution witness room.
Travel: NR Basingstoke (Waterloo 50 min.) plus 10–20 min. walk. Cty: From Station Approach and Bunnian Place left into Alencon Link. At roundabout left into Basing View.
Mags: From Station Hill through Porchester Sq., Hollins Walk, Queen Annes Walk, Wote St. into Market Place. Left to London Rd. Cross New Rd., Court on left, corner of New Rd. and London Rd.
Driving: M3 Junc. 6, A30 to Ringway South. Straight across the Hackwood Rd. and take the next exit, London Rd. Follow road round and at end turn right into New Rd. Mags Ct. on right at corner. For Cty Ct. continue straight along New Rd. Left into Timberlake and the one-way system. Follow road round and at Victory roundabout turn right into Churchill Way. Take 2nd left at Eastrop roundabout into Basing View.
Parking: Mags: Public car park. Cty: Domestic car park.
Eating out and Accommodation:

Magnum's	wine bar	Basing View
The White Hart	bar food	London Rd.
Red Lion	bar food	London St.

BATH COUNTY COURT
Cambridge House, Henry St., Bath, Somerset BA1 1DJ.
Telephone: 01225 310282. Fax: 01225 480915.
DX: 98580 Bath 2.
Court times: Doors open 9.00 a.m. Court sits 10.00 a.m. Office hours 10.00 a.m.–4.00 p.m.
Facilities: Advocates' room. Consultation rooms.

BATH AND WANSDYKE MAGISTRATES' COURT,
BATH FAMILY PROCEEDINGS COURT (Wed. 10.00 a.m.)
BATH YOUTH COURT (Thurs. 10.00 a.m.)
North Parade Rd., Bath, Somerset BA1 5AF.
Telephone: 01225 463281. Fax: 01225 420255.
DX: 138142 Bath 5.
Court times: Doors open 9.00 a.m. Court sits 10.00 a.m. Office hours 9.00 a.m.–4.30 p.m.
Facilities: One general room. Pay phone. Refreshments.

BATH AND WANSDYKE MAGISTRATES' COURT—
CONTINUED

Travel: NR Bath Spa (Paddington 1 hr. 25 min.) plus 10 min. walk.
Cty: From station walk up Manvers St. Take 2nd left, Henry St. Court
on left in building beyond car park.

Mags: From station walk up Manvers St. into Pierrepont St. Turn
right at traffic lights into North Parade Rd. Court at end on left.

Driving: M4 Junc. 18, A46 and A4 London Rd. Bear left at end of
London Rd. into London St. Continue along Ladymead, Walcot St.,
and Northgate St. Left into Bridge St., round one-way system, right
into Grand Parade, right again into Orange Grove, and right into High
St. Mags: From Grand Parade left into Pierrepont St. First left into
North Parade Rd. Court at end on left.

Parking: Multi-storey car parks in Walcot St. and Broad St. and at
sports centre adjacent to Court. Some side-street parking.

Eating out and Accommodation:

Davids	restaurant	Bridge St.
Moon and Sixpence	bar food	Broad St.
Pump Rooms	restaurant	Abbey Church Yd.
Bath	hotel	Widcombe Basin

BLANDFORD FORUM MAGISTRATES'
COURT (Mon., Tues., Wed., Fri.),
DORSET COMBINED YOUTH PANEL (Mon.)

The Law Courts, Salisbury Rd., Blandford Forum, Dorset DT11
7HR.
(Correspondence to be sent to The Law Courts, Park Rd., Poole,
Dorset BH15 2RH.)

Telephone: All admin. from Poole: 01202 745309/01305 783891.
Fax: 01305 761418.

Court times: Doors open 9.30 a.m. Court sits 10.00 a.m.

Facilities: Refreshments. Interview room. Disabled facilities.

Travel: NR Salisbury plus bus (66 min.) or Poole plus bus (14
miles).

Driving: M27, A31, and A350 to Blandford. Take Blandford Forum
bypass and follow round taking left at 2nd roundabout into Salisbury
Rd. Turn right into Peel Close. Court on left next to police and
ambulance stations.

Parking: Domestic car park.

Eating out and Accommodation:

D'Armory Arms	bar food	Salisbury Rd.
The Crown	hotel	West St.

BODMIN COUNTY COURT

Cockswell House, Market St., Bodmin, Cornwall PL31 2HJ. (Also
sits at Launceston).

Telephone: 01208 74224. Fax: 01208 77255.

BODMIN COUNTY COURT—
    CONTINUED
DX: 136846 Bodmin 2.
Court times: Doors open 9.30 a.m. Court sits 10.00 a.m. Office hours 10.00 a.m.–4.00 p.m.
Facilities: Interview rooms.

BODMIN (EAST CORNWALL) MAGISTRATES' COURT (Tues., Wed., Thur., and Fri.),
EAST CORNWALL YOUTH COURT (Mon. 10.00 a.m.)
The Magistrates' Court, PO Box 2, Launceston Rd., Bodmin, Cornwall PL31 1XQ.
Telephone: 01208 262700. Fax: 01208 77198.
Court times: Doors open 9.00 a.m. Courts sit 10.00 a.m. Office hours 8.45 a.m.–4.30 p.m.
Facilities: Advocates' room. Refreshment bar/vending machine. Interview rooms. Disabled facilities.
Travel: NR Bodmin Parkway (Paddington 4 hrs.) plus Steam Railway (30 min.) or bus (15 min.).
Driving: Mags Ct.: A38 to Bodmin, Priors Barn Rd. Right into Launceston Rd., Court. 150 yds on right.
Cty Ct.: Continue along Priors Barn Rd. into Priory Rd. Right at roundabout into Dennison Rd., 3rd left into Market St. Court entrance on right.
Parking: Domestic car parks.
Eating out and Accommodation:

| Weavers Inn | bar food | Honey St. |
| Westbury | hotel | Rhind St. |

BOURNEMOUTH COUNTY COURT,
BOURNEMOUTH CROWN COURT
The Courts of Justice, Deansleigh Rd., Bournemouth, Dorset BH7 7DS.
Telephone: 01202 502800. Fax: 01202 502801.
DX: 98420 Bournemouth 4.
Court times: Doors open 9.00 a.m. Court sits at 10.30 a.m. (occasionally 10.00 a.m.) Office hours 10.00 a.m.–4.00 p.m.
Facilities: Advocates' robing room. Consultation rooms. Disabled facilities. Witness waiting areas. Public dining room. Advocates' dining room.
Travel: NR to Bournemouth Travel Interchange (Waterloo 1 hr. 45 min.). The Courts of Justice are 3 miles from town centre. The Wessex Fields development on which the Courts of Justice are located, is served by the Yellow Buses, and Hants and Dorset bus companies.
Driving: M27, A31, A338, A3060 from the Cooper Dean roundabout, Deansleigh Rd. is 1st exit from the Littledown roundabout. The Courts of Justice are at the furthermost point of Deansleigh Rd.

BOURNEMOUTH COUNTY COURT—
CONTINUED

Parking: Parking at the Court is limited.

Eating out and Accommodation: Harvester Restaurant on exit from Cooper Dean roundabout. Brewers Fayre Restaurant one exit from Iford roundabout. The nearest hotel accommodation is in Bournemouth town centre. A Travel Inn is located 5 min. walk from the Court.

BOURNEMOUTH MAGISTRATES' COURT

The Law Courts, Stafford Rd., Bournemouth, Dorset BH1 1LA.

Telephone: 01202 745309. Fax: 01202 711999.

Court times: Doors open 9.00 a.m. Court sits: 10.00 a.m. Office hours: 8.30 a.m.–5.00 p.m.

Facilities: Interview rooms. Disabled facilities. Refreshment area. Witness room. Advocates' room.

Travel: NR Bournemouth (Waterloo 1 hr. 30 min.) plus 15 min. walk.

From station exit to St. Pauls Rd. Cross into Oxford Rd. and continue to end, straight across roundabout into Madeira Rd. First left into Stafford Rd. Court 50 yds on left.

Driving: M27, A31, and A338 into Bournemouth. Along Wessex Way, over railway. At roundabout left into St. Pauls Rd. Right at next roundabout into Holdenhurst Rd. Fourth exit at roundabout into Christchurch Rd. First right into Stafford Rd. Courts on right.

Parking: Car park in Madeira Rd.

Eating out and Accommodation:

| Casanova's | Italian restaurant | Old Christchurch Rd. |
| Carlton | hotel | East Overcliff |

BRIDGWATER (SEDGEMOOR) MAGISTRATES' COURT,

SEDGEMOOR YOUTH COURT (Fri. 10.00 a.m.)

The Court House, Northgate, Bridgwater, Somerset TA6 3EU.

Telephone: 01278 423723. Fax: 01278 453667.

DX: 80616 Bridgwater.

(Admin from The Courthouse, St. John's Rd. Taunton, Somerset TA1 4AX. Tel: 01823 257084. Fax: 01823 335795. DX: 122473 Taunton 7.)

Court times: Doors open 9.30 a.m. Court sits 10.00 a.m. Office hours at Taunton 8.35 a.m.–4.45 p.m. (4.00 p.m. on Fri.).

Facilities: Advocates' room. Interview room. Children's playroom. Canteen. TV and video facilities.

Travel: NR Bridgwater (Paddington 3 hrs.) plus 30–40 min. walk. From station proceed along St. John St. Cross over the Broadway into Eastover, across Town Bridge and into Fore St. to end. Turn towards King Sq. At end cross over Northgate. Court is ahead.

BRIDGWATER (SEDGEMOOR) MAGISTRATES'
   ## COURT—CONTINUED

Driving: Bridgwater M5 Junc. 23, A38 Bristol Rd. At end of Bristol Rd. right at roundabout into The Clink. Follow road round to the left into Northgate. Court on right opposite King Sq.

Parking: Pay and display behind court.

Eating out and Accommodation:

Cobblestone Inn	bar food	Eastover
The Great Escape	bar food	Castle Moat
Piggy's	sandwich bar	High St.
The Old Vicarage	bar food	St. Mary St.

BRIDPORT (WEYMOUTH) COUNTY COURT

The Law Courts, Mountfield, Bridport, Dorset DT6 3JL.

Telephone: All admin. from Weymouth: 01305 752510. Fax: 01305 788293.

BRIDPORT MAGISTRATES' COURT (Tues.)

The Court House, Mountfield, Bridport, Dorset. All correspondence to be sent to: The Law Courts, Westwey Road, Weymouth DT4 8BS.

Telephone: All admin. from Weymouth: 01305 783891. Fax: 01305 761418.

Court times: Doors open 9.30 a.m. Court sits 10.00 a.m.

Facilities: Advocates' room. Interview room.

Travel: NR Dorchester (Waterloo 2 hrs. 10 min.) plus bus (45 min., 12 miles).

Driving: A35 from Weymouth to Bridport. Along East Rd., straight across roundabout to East St. Second right into Downes St. Continue to end. Court opposite across Rax Lane.

Parking: Domestic car park.

Eating out and Accommodation: A variety of restaurants, cafes, and pubs in the town centre.

BRISTOL COUNTY COURT

1. Greyfriars, Lewins Mead, Bristol BS1 2NR.
2. The Guildhall, Small St., Bristol BS1 2NR.

Telephone: 0117 910 6700. Fax: 0117 910 6729 (High Court and Family Division 0117 925 0912).

DX: 95903 Bristol 3.

Court times: 1. Court office 9.00 a.m. District Judge's waiting area 9.00 a.m. Court sits 10.00 a.m. or 10.30 a.m. Office hours: 9.30 a.m.–4.00 p.m. 2. Court sits 10.00 a.m.

Facilities: Robing rooms. Interview rooms. Vending machines. Coffee shop at the Law Courts.

BRISTOL CROWN COURT

The Law Courts, Small St., Bristol BS1 1DA.

Telephone: 0117 976 3030. Fax: 0117 976 3074/3026.

BRISTOL CROWN COURT—
CONTINUED

DX: 78128 Bristol.

Court times: Doors open 8.30 a.m. Court sits 10.00 a.m. or 10.30 a.m. Office hours 8.30 a.m.–5.00 p.m.

Facilities: Robing rooms. Interview rooms. Coffee shop/restaurant.

BRISTOL EMPLOYMENT TRIBUNALS

The Crescent Centre, Temple Back, Bristol BA1 6EZ.

Telephone: 0117 9298261. Fax: 0117 9253452.

Court times: Tribunal sits 10.30 a.m.

Facilities: Waiting rooms. Drinks machine.

Travel: Call for map.

NR Bristol Temple Meads (10 min. walk). Bus station (30 min. walk).

Parking: Spaces can be reserved in advance for visitors with disabilities. Car parks within walking distance: Bristol Temple Meads Rail station, Avon St., Temple Gate, Portwall Lane, and Queen Sq.

Eating out:
Cafes etc. in Victoria St.

BRISTOL MAGISTRATES' COURT,
BRISTOL YOUTH COURT

PO Box 107, Nelson St., Bristol BS99 7BJ.

Telephone: 0117 943 5100. Fax: 0117 925 0443.

DX: 78126 Bristol 1.

Court times: Doors open 9.00 a.m. Court sits 10.00 a.m. Office hours 8.30 a.m.–5.00 p.m. (Fri. 4.30 p.m.).

Facilities: Interview rooms. Small cafeteria.

Travel: NR Bristol Temple Meads (Paddington 1 hr. 30 min.) plus bus/taxi or 20 min. walk.

Guildhall: From station along Temple Gate to underpass system. Under flyover and left to Victoria St., straight across roundabout and over Bristol Bridge. Straight on into High St. turn left into Corn St., first right into Small St. Court 50 yds on left.

For Lewins Mead: at end of High St. proceed along Broad St. Cross over Rupert St. using passage. Turn right along Lewins Mead. Greyfriars is 300 yds on left.

Crown: As to Guildhall. Court 50 yds on left.

Mags: As for Guildhall to High St. continue to end of Broad St. Turn right into Nelson St. Court on left.

Driving: M4 Junc. 19 (or M5 Junc. 18) to Bristol. Inner Ring Rd. At St. James Barton roundabout turn into Haymarket and left into Bridewell St.

Crown: Take Victoria St. exit at junction system near station. Continue on to Bristol Bridge, turn left into Baldwin St., first right into St. Stephen's St., first right into Corn St. and first left into Small St.

NB Corn St. is a pedestrian precinct.

Parking: Car park off Nelson St.

Eating out and Accommodation:

The Glass Boat	restaurant	Welsh Lock, nr. Bristol Bridge
Harvey's	restaurant	Denmark St.
Jamesons	restaurant	Upper Maudlin St.
Grand	hotel	Broad St.
Oakene	hotel	Oakfield Rd.

CHELTENHAM COUNTY COURT

Kimbrose Way, Gloucester GL1 2DE.

Telephone: 01452 834991. Fax: 01452 834923.

DX: 98630 Cheltenham 4.

Court times: Doors open 9.00 a.m. Court sits 10.00 a.m. Office hours 10.00 a.m.–4.00 p.m.

Facilities: Robing room. Interview room.

CHELTENHAM MAGISTRATES' COURT,
CHELTENHAM YOUTH COURT (Fri. 10.00 a.m.)

St. George's Rd., Cheltenham, Glos. GL50 3PF.

Telephone: 01242 532323. Fax: 01242 532400.

DX: 134021 Cheltenham 9.

Court times: Doors open 9.00 a.m. Court sits 10.00 a.m. Office hours 8.30 a.m.–5.00 p.m. (Fri. 4.30 p.m.)

Facilities: Interview room. Disabled toilet. Witness waiting room.

Travel: NR Cheltenham (Paddington 2 hrs.) plus taxi or 30–40 min. walk.

Mags: From station (Lansdown) exit into Gloucester Rd. Straight over roundabout. Continue along road. Turn right into St. George's Rd. Continue along road towards town centre. Mags Ct. is on right-hand side (pay and display car park adjacent).

Cty: As for Mags, continue to end of St. George's Rd. Left into the Promenade, right into Ormond Place, and left into Regent St. Court on left at corner of County Court Rd.

Driving: M5 Junc. 11, A40 Golden Valley bypass. Continue along A40 Gloucester Rd. Follow Gloucester Rd. left after police station, past Lansdown Station and straight over roundabout. Continue along Gloucester Rd. and left into St. George's Rd. Mags Ct. 400 yds on left. Cty: As above but right in St. George's Rd. into Royal Well Rd. Continue into Clarence Rd. Follow one-way system into Clarence St. and North St. Right into Albion St. and right into Pittville St. Continue with one-way system round and into County Court Rd.

Parking: Mags: Domestic car park and pay and display in St. George's Rd. Cty: Pay and display off Oriel Rd.

Eating out and Accommodation:

Regency Fayre	restaurant	Regent Rd.
Thatchers	tea shop	Montpellier St.
George	hotel	St. George's Rd.

CHIPPENHAM (NORTH WEST WILTSHIRE) MAGISTRATES' COURT,
NORTH WEST WILTSHIRE (CHIPPENHAM) YOUTH COURT (Every Weds.)

The Court House, Pewsham Way, Chippenham, Wilts. SN15 3BF.

Telephone: 01249 463473. Fax: 01249 444319.

DX: 34213 Chippenham.

Court times: Doors open 8.45 a.m. Court sits 10.00 a.m. Office hours 8.30 a.m.–5.00 p.m. (4.30 p.m. on Fri.).

Facilities: Advocates' room. Coffee shop. Full facilities for disabled persons and baby changing.

Travel: NR Chippenham (Paddington 1 hr. 10 min.) plus 20 min. walk.

From station into Station Hill. Left into New Rd. Over the bridge into High St., and then Causeway until roundabout with Avenue la Fleche. Turn right and court is 200 yds on left.

Driving: M4 Junc. 17, A429 to Chippenham. Follow signs to Town Centre, and then signs to Calne. Court is at the junction of Avenue la Fleche and Pewsham Way.

Parking: Car parking at court.

Eating out and Accommodation: Numerous coffee shops.

| Angel | hotel | Market Place |
| Bear | hotel | Market Place |

CIRENCESTER MAGISTRATES' COURT

(Swindon County Court also sits here last Fri. of month.) The Court House, The Forum, Cirencester, Glos. GL7 2PL.

Telephone: Admin. from Gloucester: 01452 420100. Fax: 01242 532400. Family 01452 423610.

DX: 98665 Gloucester 5.

Court times: Doors open 9.00 a.m. Court sits 10.00 a.m.

Facilities: Advocates' room. Disabled toilet. Refreshments.

Travel: NR Kemble plus bus (12 min., 4 miles).

Driving: M4 Junc. 15, A429 to Cirencester through town centre past Market Place. Court on right next to police station.

CIRENCESTER MAGISTRATES' COURT—
CONTINUED

Parking: Pay and display opposite Court.

Eating out and Accommodation:

The Bear Inn	bar food	Market Place
Shepherds	hotel/restaurant	Market Place

CULLOMPTON (CENTRAL DEVON) MAGISTRATES' COURT (Mon.),
CENTRAL DEVON FAMILY PROCEEDINGS COURT (Tues. and Thurs.)

The Court House Exeter Hill, Cullompton, Devon EX15 1OJ.

Telephone: 01884 32308 (when sitting). All admin. from Exeter: 01392 814814. Fax: 01392 814811.

e-mail: dcmcc.centraldevon@dcmcc.mcs.gsi.gov.uk.

Court times: Doors open 9.15 a.m. Court sits 10.00 a.m. Office hours 8.30 a.m.–5.00 p.m.

Facilities: Advocates' room. Interview room. Refreshments. Disabled facilities.

Travel: NR Tiverton Parkway (Paddington 2 hrs.) plus bus (30 min., 4.5 miles), or bus from Exeter (60 min.).

Driving: M5 Junc. 28 and B3181 Station Rd. Continue into Lower St. Left at end into High St., continue into Fore St. Court on right next to health centre.

Parking: Car park available for court users.

Eating out and Accommodation:

Culm Vale Bakers	sandwiches	High St.
White Hart	restaurant/bar food	High St.
Little Holwell	B&B	Collipriest, Tiverton

DORCHESTER COUNTY COURT

County Hall, Dorchester, Dorset DT1 1XJ.

Telephone: All admin. from Weymouth: 01305 752510.

DORCHESTER CROWN COURT (also sits at Bournemouth),
DORCHESTER MAGISTRATES' COURT (Mon. and Thurs.),
DORSET COMBINED YOUTH PANEL (alt. Fri.)

County Hall, Dorchester, Dorset DT1 1XJ.

(Correspondence for Magistrates' Court and Youth Panel to be sent to The Law Courts, Westwey Rd., Weymouth, Dorset DT4 8BS.)

Telephone: Crown: 01305 265867. Fax: 01305 788293. Admin. from Weymouth: 01305 778684. Mags: 01305 783891. Fax: 01305 761418. Admin. from Weymouth: 01305 752510 (Mags).

Court times: Doors open 9.45 a.m., Mags: 9.00 a.m. Court sits 10.30 a.m., Mags 10.00 a.m.

Facilities: Robing room. Interview room. Coffee machine.

DORCHESTER CROWN COURT—
CONTINUED

Travel: NR Dorchester South (Waterloo 2 hrs. 20 min.) plus 20 min. walk.

From station cross Weymouth Ave. into Fairfield Rd. Right into Maumbury Rd. Continue straight along Cornwall Rd. and Albert Rd., across roundabout into The Grove. Court 50 yds on right in County Hall.

Driving: A35 to Dorchester bypass. Turn into B3150 Stinsford Rd. Continue along London Rd. into High East St. and High West St. Right at roundabout into The Grove. Immediate right turn into small road. County Hall on left.

Parking: Plenty around Court.

Eating out and Accommodation:

The Mock Turtle	restaurant	High St.
The Old Tea House	restaurant	High St.
The Casterbridge	hotel	East St.
King's Arms	hotel	High St

EXETER CROWN COURT,
EXETER COUNTY COURT

Exeter Combined Court Centre, Southernhay Gardens, Exeter, Devon EX1 1UH.

Telephone: Crown: 01392 415330. Fax: 01392 415644. Cty: 01392 415300. Fax: 01392 413642.

DX: 98440 Exeter 2.

Court times: Doors open Crown 9.00 a.m. Cty 9.00 a.m. Courts sit: Crown: 10.30 a.m. Cty: 10.00 a.m. Office hours 10.00 a.m.–4.00 p.m.

Facilities: Robing room. Interview room. Snack bar.

EXETER (CENTRAL DEVON) MAGISTRATES' COURT,
CENTRAL DEVON YOUTH COURT (Wed., Thurs., and Fri.)

The Court House, Heavitree Rd., Exeter, Devon EX1 2LS. (All correspondence to First Floor, Exeter Trust House, Blackboy Rd., Exeter EX4 6TZ.)

Telephone: 01392 814814. Fax: 01392 814830. Finance: 814811.

e-mail: dcmcc.centraldevon@dcmcc.mcs.gsi.gov.uk.

Court times: Doors open 9.30 a.m. Court sits 10.00 a.m. Office hours 8.30 a.m.–5.00 p.m.

Facilities: Advocates' room. Interview room. Tea bar.

Travel: NR Exeter Central (Waterloo 3 hrs. 30 min.) plus 5 min. walk, Exeter St. Davids (Paddington 2 hrs. 10 min.) plus a taxi ride. Buses from Exeter St. Davids to Exeter Central (1 mile).

EXETER (CENTRAL DEVON) MAGISTRATES' COURT—
CONTINUED

Crown/Cty: From Central Station walk towards city centre. Turn right, take first left. Go through two sets of traffic lights, left at third set. Parking opposite Southgate Hotel.

Mags/Y: From Central station left into Queen St. At end left into High St. Right into Paris St. At roundabout straight across into Heavitree Rd. Court on left next to police station.

Driving: M5 Junc. 29. B3183 Fore St., into Heavitree Rd. Court on right next to Police HQ.

Parking: Pay and display off Queen St. and Musgrave Rd. Mags/Y: pay and display in Russel St.

Eating out and Accommodation:

The Hole in the Wall	bar food	Castle St.
Tinleys Tea Shoppe	restaurant	Cathedral Close
Turks Head	bar food	High St.
Royal Clarence	hotel	Cathedral Yard

EXETER EMPLOYMENT TRIBUNALS

2nd Floor, Keble House, Southernhay Gardens, Exeter, Devon EX1 1UH.

Telephone: 01392 279665. Fax: 01392 430063.

Court times: Tribunal sits 10.30 a.m.

Facilities: Waiting rooms. Drinks machine.

Travel: Same as for Cty Ct.

NR Exeter St. Davids (20 min. walk). Bus station (15 min. walk).

Parking: Town centre car parks 5 mins. walk.

Eating out:

Cafes and pubs within walking distance.

FAREHAM MAGISTRATES' COURT,
FAREHAM YOUTH COURT

Trinity St., Fareham, Hants. PO16 7SB.

Telephone: Admin. from Portsmouth: (023) 9281 9421. Fax: (023) 9229 3085.

Court times: Doors open 9.00 a.m. Court sits 10.00 a.m.

Facilities: Advocates' room. Lift. WRVS.

Travel: NR Fareham (from Waterloo 1 hr. 10 min.) and 10 min. walk. From station turn left and bear left along Gordon Rd. Turn left at end. Court 50 yds on right.

Driving: M27/A27 to Fareham. A27 becomes ring road The Avenue. At roundabout by station turn into West St. Trinity St. is 2nd left.

Parking: Car park by court 150 yds on right.

FLAX BOURTON (LONG ASHTON) MAGISTRATES'
COURT

The Court House, Old Weston Rd., Flax Bourton, Bristol BS48 1UL.

Telephone: 01275 462957. Admin. from Weston-Super-Mare: 01934 621503.

**FLAX BOURTON (LONG ASHTON) MAGISTRATES'
   COURT**—CONTINUED

Court times: Doors open 9.30 a.m. Court sits 10.00 a.m.

Facilities: Advocates' room. Interview room. Coffee machine.

Travel: NR Yatton or Bristol plus taxi.

Driving: M4 Junc. 19, M32 A370 to Flax Bourton town centre.
Signposted to Mags Ct. on right.

Parking: Domestic car park.

Eating out and Accommodation:

Jubilee Inn	bar food	Weston Rd.
The George	bar food	Weston Rd.

**FOREST OF DEAN MAGISTRATES' COURT,
FOREST OF DEAN YOUTH COURT** (alt. Mon.)

The Courthouse, Gloucester Rd., Coleford, Glos. GL16 8BQ.

Telephone: 01452 420100. Fax: 01452 833555.

DX: 98665 Gloucester 5.

Court times: Doors open 9.30 a.m. Court sits 10.00a.m (Tues.–Fri.).
All correspondence to Gloucester Magistrates' Court.

Facilities: Interview room. Disabled access.

Travel: NR Lydney (8 miles) or Gloucester plus bus (67 min., 20
miles).

Driving: M4 Junc. 22 and B4228 to Coleford. Proceed to town
centre. Continue across roundabout to Market Place and Gloucester
Rd. Court immediately opposite next to police station.

Parking: Public car park opposite Court.

Eating out and Accommodation:

Bay of Bengal	Tandoori restaurant	Gloucester Rd.
Angel	hotel	Gloucester Rd.

FROME MAGISTRATES' COURT (Thurs. 10.00 a.m.),
FROME YOUTH COURT (every fortnight on Wed. 10.00 a.m.)

The Court House, Oakfield Rd., Frome, Somerset BA11 4JG.

Telephone: 01225 463281/463306. Fax: 01225 420255.

DX: 138142 Bath 5.

Court times: Doors open 9.30 a.m. Court sits 10.00 a.m.

Facilities: Advocates' room. Interview room. WRVS.

Travel: NR Frome (Paddington via Bath or Westbury 2 hrs.
30 min.) plus 35 min. walk. Taxi office at station.
From station approach left into Portway. Continue into Christchurch
and into Bancox. Left before the roundabout into Nunney Rd. Third
right into Oakfield Rd. Court 300 yds on right.

Driving: M4 Junc. 18, A46 to Bath, A36 and A361 to Frome.
Continue to town centre along Bath Rd., into Fromfield, North
Parade, and Market Place. Continue into Bath St. and right
into Christchurch St. Continue straight across roundabout and into
Broadway. Second left into Oakfield Rd. Court on left.

FROME MAGISTRATES' COURT—
CONTINUED

Parking: Car park in Nunney Rd.

Eating out and Accommodation:

The George	bar food	Nunney
The Old Bath Arms	bar food	Palmer St.

GLOUCESTER COUNTY COURT AND FAMILY PROCEEDINGS COURT

Kimbrose Way, Gloucester, Glos. GL1 2DE.

Telephone: 01452 834900. Fax: 01452 834923.

DX: 98660 Gloucester 5.

Court times: Doors open 8.30 a.m. Court sits 10.00 a.m. or 10.30 a.m. Office hours 9.45 a.m.–4.00 p.m.

Facilities: Robing room. Conference rooms. Vending machine for coffee, soft drinks, snacks. Child witness room. Lift to all floors.

GLOUCESTER CROWN COURT

Longsmith St., Gloucester, Glos. GL1 2TS.

(Admin. from Criminal Courts Section, 2nd Floor, Southgate House, Southgate St., Gloucester GH1 1UB.)

Telephone: 01452 420100. Fax: 01452 833556.

Court times: Doors open 8.30 a.m. Court sits 10.30 a.m.

Facilities: Robing room. Interview rooms. Child witness room. Vending machine for hot/cold drinks, snacks.

GLOUCESTER MAGISTRATES' COURT, GLOUCESTER YOUTH COURT

The Courthouse, Barbican Way, Gloucester, Glos. GL1 2JH.

(Admin. as Crown Ct.)

Telephone: 01452 420100. Fax: 01452 833557.

DX: 98665 Gloucester 5.

Court times: Doors open 9.00 a.m. Court sits 10.00 a.m.

Facilities: Interview room. WRVS.

Travel: NR Gloucester Central (2 hrs.) plus 5–15 min. walk.

Cty: From station, into George St., past Wellington Hotel and across Bruton Way up to roundabout at Station Rd. Turn right at roundabout and left into Clarence St. At end of street turn right into Eastgate St. Turn left at The Cross (by traffic lights) into Southgate St. Continue to junction by Severn Sound Radio. Cross junction and Court building is just to the right (on the corner of the Docks).

Crown: As for Cty but continue up Eastgate. Left at traffic lights into Southgate St. Right into Longsmith St. Court 400 yds on right.

Mags: Continue along Longsmith St. Left into Barbican Rd. and right into Barbican Way. Court between police station and prison.

Driving: M5 Junc. 11, A40 Golden Valley bypass to Gloucester. Follow signs to Gloucester Historic Quay and park at the Quay. Court building is on the corner of the Docks.

GLOUCESTER MAGISTRATES' COURT—

Crown: Left at end of Eastgate St. into Southgate St. Right into Longsmith.

Mags: Continue along Longsmith, left into Barbican Rd. and first right into Barbican Way.

Parking: City centre car parks or in the Docks.

Eating out and Accommodation:

Butties	sandwiches	Westgate St.
College Green	restaurant	College St.
Crown and Thistle	bar food	Eastgate St.
Rotherfield House	hotel	Horton Rd.
Windmill	restaurant	Eastgate St.
Roma	restaurant	Westgate St.

HONITON (CENTRAL DEVON) MAGISTRATES' COURT
(Wed.)

The Court House, Dowell St., Honiton, Devon EX14 1LZ.

Telephone: Honiton 01404 42777. Admin. from Exeter: 01392 814814.

Court times: Doors open 9.30 a.m. Court sits 10.00 a.m. Office hours 8.30 a.m.–5.00 p.m.

Facilities: Advocates' room. Interview room. WRVS.

Travel: NR Honiton (Waterloo 2 hrs. 10 min.) plus 10–15 min. walk. From station left into New St. At end left into High St. Right into Dowell St. Court on left.

Driving: M5 Junc. 28 and A373 Cullompton Rd. Continue into Dowell St. Court at end on right.

Parking: Pay and display next to court.

Eating out and Accommodation:

Honeybee	restaurant	High St.
The Dolphin	hotel	High St.

ISLES OF SCILLY (WEST CORNWALL) MAGISTRATES' COURT

Town Hall, St. Mary's, Isles of Scilly, Cornwall TR21 0JD.

Telephone: Admin. from Truro: 01872 274075. Fax: 01872 276227.

Court times: Doors open 9.30 a.m. Court sits 10.00 a.m.

Facilities: Advocates' room. Informal coffee arrangements by Methodist Ladies.

Travel: NR Penzance (Paddington 5 hrs.), helicopter from Heliport and airport bus to town. Ferry from Penzance to St. Mary's and 5 min. walk.

Driving: Ferry from Penzance to St. Mary's (2 hrs. 30 min.). Continue to town centre. Ask for Town Hall.

Parking: Side-streets.

ISLES OF SCILLY (WEST CORNWALL) MAGISTRATES' COURT—CONTINUED

Eating out and Accommodation:

Atlantic House	restaurant	Church St., Hugh Town
Mermaid Inn	bar food	
Godolphin	hotel	

LAUNCESTON (BODMIN) COUNTY COURT

The Court House, 'Hendra', Dunheved Rd., Launceston, Cornwall. PL15 9JE.

Telephone: Admin. from Bodmin: 01208 74224.

Court times: Doors open 9.30 a.m. Court sits 10.00 a.m. or 10.30 a.m.

Facilities: Interview room.

LAUNCESTON (EAST CORNWALL) MAGISTRATES' COURT (Tues.)

The Court House, Dunheved Rd., Launceston, Cornwall. PL15 9JE. (Correspondence to Magistrates' Court, PO Box 2, Launceston Rd., Bodmin PL31 1XQ.)

Telephone: Admin. from Bodmin: 01208 262700.

Court times: Doors open 9.30 a.m. Court sits 10.00 a.m. Office hours 8.45 a.m.–4.30 p.m.

Facilities: WRVS. Interview room.

Travel: NR Liskeard (Paddington 4 hrs.) or Plymouth plus bus.

Driving: M5 Junc. 31, A30 to Launceston bypass. Left into Western Rd. At fork right into Westgate St. and immediately right again into Dunheved Rd. Court on right.

Parking: Restricted parking in court.

Eating out and Accommodation:

Westgate	bar food	Westgate St.
The Coffee House	cafe	Westgate St.
Sutton Farm	B&B	Boyton, Launceston
(or see entry for Liskeard)		

LISKEARD (EAST CORNWALL) MAGISTRATES' COURT (Mon., Weds., Thues., and Fri.),
EAST CORNWALL YOUTH COURT (every Mon. at Bodmin)

The Magistrates' Court, Trevecca, Liskeard, Cornwall PL14 6RF. (Correspondence to The Magistrates, PO Box 2, Launceston Rd., Bodmin PL31 1XQ.)

Telephone: 01579 347133. Fax: 01579 344958. On court days only. (Admin. from Bodmin: 01208 262700.)

Court times: Doors open 9.15 a.m. Court sits 10.00 a.m. Office hours (Bodmin) 8.45 a.m.–4.30 p.m.

LISKEARD (EAST CORNWALL) MAGISTRATES' COURT—CONTINUED

Facilities: Advocates' room. Interview rooms. WRVS. Disabled facilities. Refreshment bar.

Travel: NR Liskeard (Paddington 4 hrs.) plus 20–30 min. walk. From station right into Station Rd. Continue into Barn St. through Windsor Place and into Barras St. Continue to end. At The Parade right into Greenbank. Court on left. For Trevecca, continue into Callington Rd. Left into St. Cleer Rd. Court on left.

Driving: A38 from Plymouth. Continue to town centre and follow signposts to Callington. From Callington Rd. follow signposts to Mags Ct., St. Cleer Rd.

Parking: Domestic car park.

Eating out and Accommodation:

Purdys	bakery/coffee shop	Baytree Hill Rd.
Country Castle	hotel	Station Rd.

MINEHEAD (WEST SOMERSET) MAGISTRATES' COURT (Fri. 10.00 a.m.),
TAUNTON DEANE AND WEST SOMERSET YOUTH COURT (2nd Tues. each month 10.00 a.m.)

The Court House, Townsend Rd., Minehead, Somerset TA24 5RJ.

Telephone: Admin. from Taunton: 01823 257084. Fax: 01823 335195. Accounts: 01278 423723.

DX: 122473 Taunton 7.

Court times: Doors open 9.30 a.m. Court sits 10.00 a.m. Office hours at Taunton 8.30 a.m.–5.00 p.m. (4.30 p.m. Fri.).

Facilities: Advocates' room. Interview room. Refreshments.

Travel: NR Taunton (25 miles) plus bus (60 min.) or West Somerset Railway.

Driving: M5 Junc. 25, A358 and A39 Bircham Rd. Continue into Alcombe Rd. and through to Townsend Rd. Court on left next to police station.

Parking: Street parking.

Eating out and Accommodation:

Kildare Lodge	hotel	Townsend Rd.
Benares	hotel	Northfield Rd.

NEW FOREST (LYNDHURST) MAGISTRATES' COURT,
NEW FOREST FAMILY PROCEEDINGS COURT (Tues.)

The Court House, Pikes Hill, Lyndhurst, Hants SO43 7AY.

Telephone: Admin. from Southampton: 023 8038 4200. Fax: 023 8023 4203.

Court times: Doors open 9.00 a.m. Court sits 10.00 a.m.

Facilities: Advocates' room. Interview rooms. Drinks vending machine.

Travel: NR Brockenhurst (Waterloo 1 hr. 45 min.) plus taxi 4 miles.

NEW FOREST (LYNDHURST) MAGISTRATES' COURT—
   CONTINUED

Driving: From London/Southampton M27 Junc. 1 then A337 to Lyndhurst. Follow one-way system around town s/p A35 Christchurch/Bournemouth, turning left into High St. On leaving Lyndhurst, courthouse is one of the last remaining buildings set back on the left.

Parking: Small car park.

NEWPORT (IOW) COUNTY COURT,
NEWPORT (IOW) CROWN COURT

1 Quay St., Newport, Isle of Wight PO30 5YT.

Telephone: Cty: 01983 535100. Crown: 01983 535100. Fax: 01983 821039.

DX: 98460 Newport (IOW) 2.

Court times: Doors open 9.30 a.m. Courts sit 10.30 a.m. Office hours: 9.45 a.m.–4.00 p.m.

Facilities: Interview rooms. WRVS.

NEWPORT (IOW) MAGISTRATES' COURT,
NEWPORT (IOW) FAMILY PROCEEDINGS COURT (Wed.),
NEWPORT (IOW) YOUTH COURT (Wed.)

Court House, Quay St., Newport, Isle of Wight PO30 5BB.

Telephone: 01983 535100. Fax: 01983 554977.

Court times: Doors open 9.15 a.m. Courts sit 10.00 a.m. Office hours 9.15 a.m.–4.30 p.m. (4.00 p.m. Fri.).

Facilities: Advocates' room. Interview room. WRVS.

Travel: Passenger ferry, Southampton to West Cowes and then bus to Newport. Hovercraft Southsea to Ryde and bus to Newport. Portsmouth Harbour to Ryde and bus to Newport.

Driving: Lymington car ferry to Yarmouth and then follow signs to Newport. Right at roundabout and then left. Portsmouth car ferry to Fishbourne and follow signs to Newport. Southampton car ferry to East Cowes and follow signs to Newport.

Parking: Coppins Bridge car park on roundabout plus 10 min. walk. Cross roundabout into Sea St. and court on left, corner of Sea St. and Quay St.

Eating out and Accommodation:

Wheatsheaf Inn	bar food	St Thomas Sq.
Calverts	hotel	Quay St.
God's Providence House	restaurant	St Thomas Sq.

NEWTON ABBOT (SOUTH DEVON) MAGISTRATES'
   COURT (Mon., Tues., and Thurs.),
SOUTH DEVON YOUTH COURT (2nd, 3rd, and 4th Fri. in month and every Wed. 10.00 a.m.)

The Court House, Newfoundland Way, Newton Abbot, Devon TQ12 1NG.

NEWTON ABBOT (SOUTH DEVON) MAGISTRATES' COURT—CONTINUED

Telephone: Torquay Mags: 01803 612211. Fax: 01803 618618.

Court times: Doors open 9.00 a.m. Court sits 10.00 a.m. Office hours 9.00 a.m.–3.30 p.m.

Facilities: Robing room. Consulting rooms. Drinks machine.

Travel: NR Newton Abbot (Paddington 2 hrs. 30 min.) plus 15 min. walk.

From station left into Station Rd. and Courtlands Rd. Right into Torquay Rd. and continue into East St. which becomes Newfoundland Way. Court on left.

Driving: M5 Junc. 31, A38 and A382 Exeter Rd. Straight over roundabout into Bovey Rd. continue into Highweek St. Over next roundabout into Bank St. Continue straight and turn right into Newfoundland Way. Court on left.

Parking: Pay and display next to court.

Eating out and Accommodation:

Austin's	restaurant	Newfoundland Way
Jaspers	restaurant	Newfoundland Way
The Ship	bar food	Newfoundland Way

NORTH AVON MAGISTRATES' COURT, NORTH AVON YOUTH COURT (Tues.)

The Magistrates' Court, Kennedy Way, Yate, Avon BS37 4PY.

Telephone: 01454 310505. Fax: 01454 319404. Family: 01454 315745.

e-mail: yate.mc@avonsom.mcs.gsi.gov.uk.

DX: 47260 Yate.

Court times: Doors open 9.00 a.m. Court sits 10.00 a.m. Office hours 8.30 a.m.–4.30 p.m.

Facilities: Advocates' room. Interview rooms. Refreshments (a.m. only).

Travel: NR Bristol Temple Meads and local train from Bristol to Yate (10 min.) plus 10 min. walk, or bus from Bristol (35–45 min.).

From station along Station Rd. and continue straight into Kennedy Way Court 50 yds on right opposite sports centre.

Parking: Free car park adjacent to court.

Eating out and Accommodation: Cafes and public houses in vicinity, also hotels and B&Bs. (See entry for Bristol.)

NORTH SOMERSET MAGISTRATES' COURT, NORTH SOMERSET FAMILY PROCEEDINGS COURT (Thurs.), NORTH SOMERSET YOUTH COURT (Weds.)

The Court House, Walliscote Rd., Weston-Super-Mare, Avon BS23 1UX.

NORTH SOMERSET MAGISTRATES' COURT—
CONTINUED

Telephone: 01934 621503. Fax: 01934 625766. Call-box 01934 624702.

DX: 8424 Weston-Super-Mare 1.

Court times: Doors open 9.00 a.m. Court sits 10.00 a.m. Office hours 9.00 a.m.–4.30 p.m. (Fri. 4.00 p.m.)

Facilities: Advocates' room. Interview room. WRVS.

Travel: NR Weston-Super-Mare (Paddington 2 hrs.) plus 5 min. walk.

From station west exit into Station Approach and left into Station Rd. At end turn left, Mags Ct. on left next to police station. For Cty Ct. turn left out of Station Rd. into the Centre. Left into Regent St. and left into High St. Court in Regent House.

Driving: M5 Junc. 21 and follow A370 to town centre. Mags: on left next to police station. Cty: 3rd left into High St. Court on left.

Parking: Public car parks.

Eating out and Accommodation:

| Town Crier | bar food | Walliscote Rd. |
| Reflections | restaurant | The Boulevard |

OKEHAMPTON (CENTRAL DEVON) MAGISTRATES'
COURT (Once a month on a Thurs.)

The Council Chambers, Oaklands Drive, Okehampton, Devon EX20 1LH.

Telephone: Admin. from Exeter: 01392 814814.

e-mail: dcmcc.centraldevon@dcmcc.mcs.gsi.gov.uk.

Court times: Doors open 9.30 a.m. Court sits 10.00 a.m.

Facilities: Waiting room. Interview room.

Travel: NR Exeter St. David's and bus (45–60 min., 20 miles).

Driving: A30 and B3260 Exeter Rd. Continue into East St. and Fore St. Right into Market St. At end left into Oaklands Drive. Court on right, signposted.

Parking: Domestic car park.

Eating out and Accommodation:

| Plume of Feathers | bar food | West St. |
| White Hart | hotel/bar food | West St. |

PENZANCE COUNTY COURT

Trevear, Alverton St., Penzance, Cornwall TR18 4GH.

Telephone: 01736 62987. Fax: 01736 330595.

DX: 136900 Penzance 2.

Court times: Doors open 10.00 a.m. (flexible). Courts sits 10.00 a.m. or 10.30 a.m. Office hours 10.00 a.m.–4.00 p.m.

Facilities: Robing room. Interview room. Public toilets. Baby changing facilities. Payphone.

**WEST CORNWALL MAGISTRATES' COURT
  (PENZANCE),**
**WEST CORNWALL COMBINED FAMILY PROCEEDINGS
  COURT,**
WEST CORNWALL COMBINED YOUTH COURT
The Guildhall, Penzance, Cornwall TR18 2QD.
Telephone: Admin. from Truro: 01872 321900. Fax: 01872 276227.
Court times: Doors open 9.00 a.m. Court sits 10.00 a.m. Office
hours 9.00 a.m.–1.00 p.m. on court days only.
Facilities: Advocates' room. WRVS.
Travel: NR Penzance (Paddington 6 hrs.) plus 10 min. walk.
Cty: From station left into Market Jew St. Continue into Alverton St.
Court 200 yds on right.
Mags: As for Cty Ct., Mags Ct. 50 yds further on right.
Driving: A30 Chyandour Cliff past Station and into Market Jew St.
Continue into Alverton St. Courts on right.
Parking: Pay and display next to Courts.
Eating out and Accommodation:

Mount Prospect	hotel	Britons Hill
The Buttery	restaurant	Morrab Rd.
Sir Humphry Davy	bar food	Alverton St.

PLYMOUTH COUNTY COURT,
PLYMOUTH CROWN COURT
Plymouth Combined Court Centre, The Law Courts, Armada Way,
Plymouth, Devon PL1 2ER.
Telephone: 01752 677400. Fax: Cty 01752 208286. Crown 01752
208292.
DX: 98740 Plymouth 7.
e-mail: plymou.cmb.cm@courtservice.gsi.gov.uk.
Court times: Security officers on duty from 9.00 a.m. and will allow
entry from then. Courts sit 10.00 a.m. or 10.30 a.m. Office hours
10.00 a.m.–4.00 p.m.
Facilities: Advocates' robing room. Interview rooms. Witness
service. Public canteen. Lift.

PLYMOUTH MAGISTRATES' COURT,
PLYMOUTH YOUTH COURT (Daily)
The Magistrates' Court, St. Andrews St., Plymouth, Devon
PL1 2DP.
Telephone: 01752 206200. Fax: 01752 206194.
Court times: Doors open 9.15 a.m. Court sits 10.00 a.m. Office
hours 9.00 a.m.–5.00 p.m.
Facilities: Advocates' room. Interview rooms. WRVS tea bar.
Travel: NR Plymouth (Paddington 3 hrs. 15 min.) plus 10–15 min.
walk.

PLYMOUTH MAGISTRATES' COURT—
CONTINUED

Cty and Crown: From Station Rd. turn left into Penny-Come-Quick Hill. Right at roundabout into Western Approach. Left into Union St. Straight across Derry Cross into Royal Parade. Other side of dual carriageway via top roundabout. Court is on left.

Mags: As for Cty but continue along Royal Parade to next roundabout. Right into Whimpole St., right at the end and right again into Palace St. St. Andrews St. at the end, turn right. Court at end of dead end.

Driving: M5 Junc. 31, A38 to Plymouth. Follow A374 Exeter St. to town centre. At St. Andrews Cross roundabout (fountains in centre), continue straight for Royal Parade. Crown/Cty Cts. on left.

Mags: Take 2nd left to Whimpole St. Follow road right into Buckwell St. and right into Palace St. Turn right into St. Andrews St. Court at end.

Parking: Large multi-storey behind Cty Ct. Meters in side-streets next to Mags Ct.

Eating out and Accommodation:

The Abbey	bar food	St Andrews St.
Bigwigs	bar food	St Andrews St.
The Bank	bar food	Royal Parade
Theatre Royal	coffee/restaurant	Royal Parade,
Plymouth Moat House	hotel	Plymouth Hoe,
		Armada Way

POOLE COUNTY COURT,
POOLE MAGISTRATES' COURT,
DORSET COMBINED YOUTH PANEL (Wed.)

The Law Courts, Park Rd., Poole, Dorset BH15 2NS.

Telephone: Cty: 01202 741150. Fax: 01202 747245. Mags: 01202 745309. Fax: 01202 711996.

DX: (Mags): 123822 Poole 7. (Cty): 98700 Poole 4.

Court times: Security on duty from 8.30 a.m. and will allow access. Court sits: Cty 10.00 a.m. or 10.30 a.m., Mags 10.00 a.m. Office hours: Cty 10.00 a.m.–4.00 p.m., Mags 8.30 a.m.–5.00 p.m. (Fri. 4.30 p.m.).

Facilities: Advocates' room. Interview rooms. Vending machine for food and drink.

Travel: NR Poole (Waterloo 2 hrs.) plus 30 min. walk, or taxi.
From Poole station come out from under Towngate Bridge. At roundabout straight across into Parkstone Rd. Civic Centre on next roundabout.

Driving: M27 Junc. 1, A31, A348 into Poole. At roundabout left into Parkstone Rd. Court on right at next roundabout.

Parking: On-road parking nearby.

POOLE COUNTY COURT—
CONTINUED

Eating out and Accommodation:

| The Conjuror's Half Crown | bar food | Commercial Rd. |
| The Mansion House | dining club/hotel | Thames St. |

PORTSMOUTH COUNTY COURT,
PORTSMOUTH CROWN COURT

The Courts of Justice, Winston Churchill Ave., Portsmouth, Hants. PO1 2EB.

Telephone: (023) 9282 3000. Fax: (023) 9282 6385.

DX: 98490 Portsmouth 5.

Court times: Doors open 8.30 a.m. Court sits 10.00 a.m. or 10.30 a.m. Office hours 10.00 a.m.–4.00 p.m.

Facilities: Robing room. Barristers' lounge. Barristers' dining room. Interview rooms. Public canteen.

PORTSMOUTH MAGISTRATES' COURT

The Law Courts, Winston Churchill Ave., Portsmouth, Hants. PO1 2DQ.

Telephone: (023) 9281 9421. Fax: (023) 9229 3085.

Court times: Doors open 8.30 a.m. Court sits 10.00 a.m. Office hours 10.00 a.m.–5.00 p.m. (Fri. 4.30 p.m.).

Facilities: Advocates' room. Interview rooms. WRVS.

Travel: NR Portsmouth & Southsea (Waterloo 1 hr. 40 min.) plus 5 min. walk.

From station left into Isambard Brunel Rd. Right at roundabout. Law Courts on right after police station. Courts of Justice third building on right.

Driving: M25 Junc. 10, A3, A3(M), A27. Follow signposts to the station. Continue along Isambard Brunel Rd. Right at roundabout. Courts on right.

Parking: NCP off Alec Rose St. (behind Courts).

Eating out and Accommodation:

Becketts Wine House	wine bar	Bellevue Terrace
Cellar	wine bar	High St.
Crest	hotel	Pembroke Rd.

SALISBURY COUNTY COURT,
SALISBURY CROWN COURT

The Courts of Justice, Alexandra House, St. John's St., Salisbury, Wilts. SP1 2PN.

Telephone: 01722 325444. Fax: 01722 412991.

DX: 98500 Salisbury 2.

SALISBURY COUNTY COURT—
    CONTINUED

Court times: Security officer on duty from 7.00 a.m. and will allow access from 8.30 a.m. Court sits 10.00 a.m. or 10.30 a.m. Office hours 10.00 a.m.–4.00 p.m.

Facilities: Advocates' room. Solicitors' room. Interview rooms. Drinks machine. Mother and baby facilities.

SALISBURY (SOUTH EAST WILTSHIRE) MAGISTRATES' COURT, SOUTH EAST WILTSHIRE YOUTH COURT
(Tues. 10.00 a.m.)

The Guildhall, Market Place, Salisbury, Wilts.

Court Offices: 43/55 Milford St., Salisbury, Wilts. SP1 2BP.

Telephone: 01722 333225. Fax: 01722 413395.

DX: 58022 Salisbury.

Court times: Doors open 9.30 a.m. Court sits 10.00 a.m. Office hours 9.00 a.m.–4.30 p.m. (4.00 p.m. Fri.)

Facilities: Refreshments available. Access for disabled persons by prior arrangement (tel: 01722 414921).

Travel: NR Salisbury (Waterloo 1 hr. 35 min.) plus 10 min. walk.
Combined Ct.: From station turn right into Mill Rd. Follow road over Crane Bridge and to the end of Crane St. Cross High St. into New St. Court at end on right opposite the White Hart Hotel.
Mags: From station into South Western Rd. and right into Fisherton St. Cross over bridge and continue straight into Silver St. Left into Castle St. 1st right into Blue Boar Row. Continue to end. Court at end in Market Sq.

Driving: M4 Junc. 15, A345, A338, and A30 London Rd. Right at roundabout into Churchill Way North. Left at next roundabout into Castle St. Left at end into Blue Boar Row. Court at end on right. For Combined Ct. continue to end of Castle St., right into Silver St. and 1st left into High St. Left into New St.. Court at end on right.

Parking: Culver St. car park (10 min. walk from Combined Ct., very reasonable all-day rate). Public parking in Market Sq.

Eating out and Accommodation (all within 2 min. of the Court):

The Cloisters	bar food	Catherine St.
The Wig and Quill	bar food	New St.
White Hart	hotel	St John St.
Kings Arms	hotel	St John St.
New Inn (non-smoking)	bar food	New St.

SHERBORNE MAGISTRATES' COURT (some Wed.)
The Court House, Digby Rd., Sherborne, Dorset DT9 3NL.
Correspondence to be sent to: The Law Courts, Westwey Rd., Weymouth DT4 8BS.

SHERBORNE MAGISTRATES' COURT—
CONTINUED

Telephone: Admin. from Weymouth: 01305 783891. Fax: 01305 761418.

Court times: Doors open 9.30 a.m. Court sits 10.00 a.m.

Facilities: Refreshment. Interview room. Disabled facilities.

Travel: NR Sherborne (Waterloo 2 hrs. 15 min.) plus 5 min. walk.

From station left into Digby St., Court on left next to police station.

Driving: Follow directions as for Shepton Mallet but continue on A371 and B3145 Bristol Rd. At end turn right into Greenhill, left into Higher Cheap and continue down Cheap St. and into South St. Follow road round to the right in front of station and continue right into Digby St. Court on left by police station.

Parking: Limited domestic parking. Side-streets.

Eating out and Accommodation:

Church House Gallery	restaurant	Half Moon St.
Plume of Feathers	bar food	Half Moon St.
Eastbury	hotel	Long St.
Half Moon Toby Inn	bar food	Half Moon St.

SOUTH EAST WILTSHIRE MAGISTRATES' COURT, DEVIZES MAGISTRATES' COURT (Tues. and Thurs.)

The Magistrates' Court, Northgate Gardens, Devizes, Wilts. SN10 1JW.

Telephone: 01380 727802. Fax: 01380 726142. Admin. from Salisbury: 01722 333225. Fax: 01722 413395.

DX: 58022 Salisbury.

Court times: Doors open 9.20 a.m. Court sits 10.00 a.m. Salisbury office hours 9.00 a.m.–4.30 p.m. (4.00 p.m. Fri.)

Facilities: Advocates' room. Interview rooms. Coffee machines.

Travel: NR Chippenham plus bus (35 min., 10 miles) or Swindon plus bus (52 min., 20 miles).

Driving: M4 Junc. 17, A429 to Chippenham, A4 and A342 to Devizes. Continue along Devizes Rd. and Dunkirk Hill into Bath Rd. and The Nursery. Proceed into Northgate St. Northgate Gardens are on the right next to Wadworth's Brewery.

Parking: Side-streets and public car park. Parking not available at courthouse.

Eating out and Accommodation: 5 min. walk to town centre.

SOUTH GLOUCESTERSHIRE MAGISTRATES' COURT (Mon.–Fri.)

The Court House, Parliament St., Stroud, Glos. GL5 1ET.

Telephone: Admin. from Gloucester: 01452 420100. Fax: 01452 762756.

Court times: Doors open 9.00 a.m. Court sits 9.30 a.m.

SOUTH GLOUCESTERSHIRE MAGISTRATES'
COURT—CONTINUED

Facilities: Two general rooms.

Travel: NR Stroud (Paddington 1 hr. 30 min.) plus 10 min. walk. From station right into Rowcroft, continue into King St. Right into High St. Continue to end, Court on left next to police station.

Driving: M5 Junc. 13, A419. Follow signs to town centre. Court at top of High St. next to police station.

Parking: Pay and display opposite Court.

Eating out and Accommodation:

The Retreat	bar food	Church St.
The Imperial	hotel	Station Rd.
Mills'	cafe	Withy's Yard

SOUTHAMPTON COUNTY COURT,
SOUTHAMPTON CROWN COURT

The Courts of Justice, London Rd., Southampton, Hants. SO15 2XQ.

Telephone: (023) 8021 3200. Fax: Listings office: (023) 8021 3232. Cty: (023) 8021 3222. Crown: (023) 8021 3234. Bailiff's office: (023) 8023 3227.

DX: 111000 Southampton 11.

Court times: Doors open 9.00 a.m. Court sits 10.00 a.m. or 10.30 a.m. Office hours 10.00 a.m.–4.00 p.m.

Facilities: Barristers' robing room. Solicitors' robing room. Interview rooms. Restaurant. Separate dining room for Bar. Baby changing facilities. Disabled access.

SOUTHAMPTON EMPLOYMENT TRIBUNAL

4th Floor, Dukes Keep, Marsh Lane, Southampton, Hants. SO14 3EX.

Telephone: (023) 8071 6400. Fax: (023) 8063 5506.

Court time: 10.00 a.m.

Facilities: Hot drinks machine. Telephone. Consultation rooms.

Travel: NR Southampton Central (15 min. walk). Local buses (7 min. walk).

Driving: s/p City centre and Ocean Village.

Parking: Large public car parks in the vicinity. No public parking at the building.

Eating out: Cafes and restaurants in East St. 3 min. walk and city centre 10 min. walk.

SOUTHAMPTON MAGISTRATES' COURT,
SOUTHAMPTON AND NEW FOREST COMBINED
YOUTH COURT (daily)

100 The Avenue, Southampton, Hants. SO17 1EY.

Telephone: (023) 8038 4200. Fax: (023) 8038 4023.

DX: 135986 Southampton.

SOUTHAMPTON MAGISTRATES' COURT—
CONTINUED

Court times: Doors open 9.30 a.m. Court sits 10.00 a.m. Office hours 9.00 a.m.–4.30 p.m.

Facilities: Advocates' room. Interview room. WRVS.

Travel: NR Southampton (Waterloo 1 hr. 10 min.) plus 5–15 min. walk. Court is next to Cty Ct.

Driving: See Cty Ct. directions.

Parking: West Park car park off Havelock Rd. Public car park in Brunswick Place.

Eating out and Accommodation:

Kutis		London Rd.
Simons	wine bar	Vernon Walk
Southampton Park	hotel	Cumberland Place

SOUTHAMPTON (EASTLEIGH) MAGISTRATES' COURT,
SOUTHAMPTON FAMILY PROCEEDINGS COURT

The Court House, Leigh Rd., Eastleigh, Hants. SO5 4ZN.

Telephone: Admin. from Southampton: (023) 8063 5911. Fax: (023) 8023 3882.

Court times: Doors open 9.00 a.m. Court sits 10.00 a.m.

Facilities: Advocates' room. Interview room. Witness rooms. WRVS.

Travel: NR Eastleigh (Waterloo 1 hr. 25 min.) plus 25 min. walk or short bus ride from station.

From station cross into Leigh Rd. Court 400 yds on left.

Driving: M27 Junc. 5, A335 to Eastleigh. Follow s/p to station. Turn left at station into Leigh Rd. Court on left.

Parking: Domestic car park.

Eating out and Accommodation:

Crest	hotel	Leigh Rd.

SWINDON COUNTY COURT,*
SWINDON CROWN COURT

The Law Courts, Islington St., Swindon, Wilts. SN1 2HG.

*Also sits at The Court House, The Forum, Cirencester, Glos., on last Fri. of month.

Telephone: Cty and Crown: 01793 690500. Fax: Cty: 01793 690555 Crown: 01793 670535

DX: 98430 Swindon 5.

Court times: Doors open 7.30 a.m. Court sits 9.15 a.m./10.30 a.m. Office hours 10.00 a.m.–4.00 p.m. Information desk 9.30 a.m.–4.00 p.m.

Facilities: Advocates' robing room. Interview rooms. Dining facilities for public and advocates. Children's playroom.

SWINDON MAGISTRATES' COURT

Princes St., Swindon, Wilts. SN1 2JB.

Telephone: 01793 699800. Fax: 01793 433740.

DX: 118725 Swindon 7.

Court times: Doors open 9.00 a.m. Court sits 10.00 a.m. Office hours 9.00 a.m.–5.00 p.m. (4.30 p.m. Fri.)

Travel: NR Swindon (Paddington 1 hr.) plus 10 min. walk.

From station cross Station Rd. into Wellington St. At end right into Milford St. Left at roundabout into Fleming Way. Right at next roundabout into Princes St., Court on right by police station. For Cty and Crown Cts. continue into Princes St., 1st right, Gordon St. and then left into Islington St. Court at end.

Driving: M4 Junc. 16, follow signs to town centre, A4311 County Rd. At roundabout right into Fleming Way. Left at next roundabout into Princes St. First right and then left into Islington St.

Parking: Public car parks either side of the Courts.

Eating out and Accommodation: Regent St. pedestrian precinct The Goddards hotel High St.

TAUNTON COUNTY COURT,
TAUNTON CROWN COURT

Shire Hall, Taunton, Somerset TA1 4EU.

Telephone: Cty: 01823 335972. Fax: 01823 351337. Crown: 01823 326685. Fax: 01823 322116.

DX: Cty: 98410 Taunton 2.

DX: Crown: 98411 Taunton 2.

Court times: Doors open 8.00 a.m. Court sits 10.00 a.m. or 10.30 a.m. Office hours 10.00 a.m.–4.00 p.m.

Facilities: Advocates' room. Interview room. Vending machines. Lift for disabled.

TAUNTON DEANE AND WEST SOMERSET
MAGISTRATES' COURT,
TAUNTON DEANE AND WEST SOMERSET YOUTH
COURT (Tues., except 2nd Tues. in month)

The Magistrates' Court, St. John's Rd., Taunton, Somerset TA1 4AX.

Telephone: 01823 257084. Fax: 01823 335195. Accounts: 01278 423723.

DX: 122473 Taunton 7.

Court times: Doors open 9.15 a.m. Court sits 10.00 a.m. Office hours 8.30 a.m.–5.00 p.m. (4.30 p.m. Fri.).

Facilities: Advocates' room. Interview room. Refreshments.

Travel: NR Taunton (Paddington 2 hrs.) plus 30 min. walk/taxi/yellow shuttle bus.

From station into Station Rd. and follow it to the left. At second set of traffic lights turn left into Bridge St. and over bridge. Keep right and continue straight into North St. and right at end, into Corporation St.

Pass County Hall on left and turn right after church into St. John's Rd.
Shire Hall is beyond County Hall on Shuttern.

Driving: M5 Junc. 25, A38 Hamilton Rd. Continue into East Reach.
Left at Hurdle Way and follow one-way system into Mary St. and
Upper High St. Continue to end into one-way system, taking right-
hand lane and then left-hand lane into Park St. Court is first turning on
left, before the church.

Parking: Mags: Tangier car park. Cty: Crescent North and South
NCP off Upper High St.

Eating out and Accommodation:

Pen and Quill	bar food	Shuttern
The Vivary Inn	bar food	Vivary Rd.
Corner House	hotel	Park St.

TORQUAY AND NEWTON ABBOT COUNTY COURT

The Willows, Nicholson Rd., Torquay, Devon TQ2 7AZ.

Telephone: 01803 616791. Fax: 01803 616795.

DX: 98740 Torquay 4 (receive only).

Court times: Doors open 9.00 a.m. Court sits 10.00 a.m. or 10.30
a.m. Office hours 10.00 a.m.–4.00 p.m.

Facilities: Advocates' room. Interview rooms. Drinks machine. Payphone. Baby changing facilities.

Travel: NR Torre Station is nearest but services are limited (see
below). Torquay NR is 2 miles and Newton Abbot NR 4 miles from
Court. Both have taxi ranks and are on main bus routes.

Driving: M5 Junc. 31, A38 and A380 Newton Rd., Court s/p from
dual carriageway (turn left at Willows retail development).

Parking: Car park for court users with approx. 25 spaces.

TORQUAY (SOUTH DEVON) MAGISTRATES' COURT,

The Court House, Union St., Torquay, Devon TQ1 4BP.

(Admin. Centre, Riviera House, The Willows, Nicholson Rd.,
Torquay, Devon TQ2 7TT.)

Telephone: 01803 202211. Fax: 01803 618618.

Court times: Doors open 9.00 a.m. Court sits 10.00 a.m. Office
hours 9.00 a.m.–3.30 p.m.

Facilities: Advocates' room. Interview rooms. Drinks machine.

Travel: BR Torquay (Paddington 2 hrs. 40 min.) plus taxi or Torre
(Paddington 3 hrs. 10 min. and change) plus 10 min. walk.

From Torre station right into Newton Rd., continue on left into
Upton Rd. (s/p town centre). Turn right at mini-roundabout onto
Lymington Rd. Pay and display car park on right. Mags building at top
of steps to rear of car park.

TORQUAY (SOUTH DEVON) MAGISTRATES' COURT—
CONTINUED

Driving: M5 Junc. 31, A38 and A380 Newton Rd. Right into Avenue Rd., left into Falkland Rd. Continue across into Lucius St. and right into Tor Church. Straight over into Tor Hill Rd. Left into Union St. (one-way). Courts on right. Mags Ct before Trematon Ave. Cty Ct.: 10 The Willows, Nicholson Rd., Torquay.

Parking: Public car park behind courts in Lymington Rd.

Eating out and Accommodation:

| Jolly Judge | bar food | Union St. |
| Homers | hotel | Warren Rd. |

TOTNES (SOUTH DEVON) MAGISTRATES' COURT
(Mon., Tues., and Fri.),
SOUTH DEVON FAMILY PROCEEDINGS COURT (Wed. and some Fri.)

The Court House, Ashburton Rd., Totnes, Devon TQ9 5JY.

Telephone: Admin. from Torquay (when court is sitting).

Court times: Doors open 9.00 a.m. Court sits 10.00 a.m. Office hours 9.00 a.m.–3.30 p.m.

Facilities: Advocates' room. Interview room. Drinks machine.

Travel: NR Totnes (Paddington 3 hrs.) plus 5 min. walk.

From station right into Station Rd. and straight across into Ashburton Rd. Court on left next to police station.

Driving: A381 from Newton Abbot. Right at roundabout over Brutus Bridge. Continue straight over next roundabout into Station Rd. Straight ahead into Ashburton Rd. Court on left after police station.

Parking: Domestic car park.

Eating out and Accommodation:

Anne of Cleves	tea room	Fore St.
The Elbow Room	bar food	Fore St.
Royal Seven Stars	hotel	Fore St.

TROWBRIDGE COUNTY COURT,
NORTH WEST WILTSHIRE (TROWBRIDGE) MAGISTRATES' COURT,
NORTH WEST WILTSHIRE (TROWBRIDGE) YOUTH COURT (Fri.)

Town Hall, Market St., Trowbridge, Wilts. BA14 8EQ.

County Court Office: Ground Floor, Clarks Mill, Stallard St., Trowbridge, Wilts. BA14 8DB.

Telephone: Cty: 01225 752101. Fax: 01225 776638. Mags: 01225 765844. Fax: 01225 763897. Admin. from Chippenham: 01249 463473. Fax: 01249 444319.

DX: Cty: 98750 Trowbridge 2. Mags: 116890 Trowbridge 3.

Court times: Doors open 9.30 a.m. Courts sit: 10.00 a.m. Office hours 8.30 a.m.–5.30 p.m.

TROWBRIDGE COUNTY COURT—
CONTINUED

Facilities: Advocates' room. Interview rooms. Drinks machine. Disabled toilet. Baby changing facilities.

Travel: NR Trowbridge (Paddington 2 hrs.) plus 15 min. walk.
Mags: From station left into Stallard St. Over Town Bridge, along Wicker Hill, and right into Fore St. Right again into Castle St. and left into Market St. Court on right in Town Hall. Cty Ct. office: turn left out of station. Court 100 yds on right.

Driving: M4 Junc. 17, A350 and A361 Devizes Rd. to Town Centre. Straight over roundabout into Roundstone St. Continue into Silver St. and Market St. Court on left in Town Hall.

Parking: Multi-storey behind Town Hall.

Eating out and Accommodation:

| Dickens | restaurant | Market St. |
| Polebarn | hotel | Roundstone St. |

TRURO COUNTY COURT,
TRURO CROWN COURT
Courts of Justice, Edward St., Truro, Cornwall TR1 2PB.
Telephone: Cty: 01872 222340 Crown: 01872 222328. Fax: Cty: 01872 222348. Crown: 01872 261550.
DX: 135396 Truro 2.
Court times: Doors open 9.00 a.m. Court sits 10.00 a.m. or 10.30 a.m. Office hours 9.00 a.m.–4.00 p.m.
Facilities: Robing room. Solicitors' room. Interview rooms. Public canteen. Bar mess. Witness support service, tel: 01872 260333.
Travel: NR Truro (Paddington 4 hrs.) plus 5 min. walk.
From station left down Richmond Hill. Straight over roundabout into Ferris Town. Bear right into Frances St. and left into Edward St. Court at top of street.
Driving: A39 westwards to Truro. Right at roundabout into St. Austell St. Bear left along St. Clement. Turn left at roundabout, into Union St. Bear left at end into Castle St. Right into Frances St. and 1st right into Edward St. Court at top at the end.
Parking: Pay and display in Edward St.

Eating out and Accommodation:

The City Inn	bar food	Kenwyn St.
The Famous Old Globe Inn	bar food	Frances St.
Wig and Pen	bar food	Castle St.
Alverton Manor	hotel	Tregolls Rd.
Royal	hotel	Lemon St.

WAREHAM MAGISTRATES' COURT (every 4th Wed.)
The Court House, Worgret Rd., Wareham, Dorset. (Correspondence to be sent to: The Law Courts, Park Rd., Poole, Dorset BH15 2RH.)

WAREHAM MAGISTRATES' COURT—
  CONTINUED
Telephone: All admin. from Poole: 01202 745309.
DX: 123822 Poole 7.
Court times: Doors open 9.30 a.m. Court sits 10.00 a.m.
Facilities: Interview rooms. Disabled facilities. Drinks machine.
Travel: NR Wareham (Waterloo 2 hrs.) plus 25 min. walk.
From station right into North Causeway. Straight over roundabout.
Turn right into West St. Continue straight into Worgret Rd. Court
50 yds on left next to police and fire stations.
Driving: A351 Wareham bypass. Proceed to town centre, left into
North Causeway. Continue along North St. Right at Town Hall into
West St. Continue into Worgret Rd. Court on left.
Parking: Domestic car park.
Eating out and Accommodation:

Antelope	bar food	North St.
Red Lion Inn	bar food	North St.
Priory	hotel	Church St.

WELLS MAGISTRATES' COURT (Mon. and Tues. Bristol
County Court also sits here),
WELLS YOUTH COURT (alt. Wed. at 10.00 a.m.)
Town Hall, Market Place, Wells, Somerset BA5 1SE.
Telephone: 01225 463281/463306. Fax: 01225 420255.
DX: 138142 Bath 5.
Court times: Doors open 9.30 a.m. Court sits 10.00 a.m.
Facilities: Vending machine.
Travel: NR Bath plus bus (81 min., 20 miles).
Driving: A37 and A39 from Bristol. From New St. left into Sadler St.
and right into Market Place. Court in Town Hall.
Parking: Pay and display car parks by Cathedral and Moat.
Eating out and Accommodation:

| Cloister | restaurant | Cathedral precinct |
| Crown | hotel | Market Place |

(WEST CORNWALL) MAGISTRATES' COURT
  (CAMBOURNE),
WEST CORNWALL COMBINED FAMILY PROCEEDINGS
  PANEL,
WEST CORNWALL COMBINED YOUTH COURT
  PANEL
The Basset Centre, Basset Rd., Cambourne, Cornwall TR14 8SZ.
Telephone: Admin. from Truro: 01872 274075. Fax: 01872 276227.
Court times: Doors open 9.00 a.m. Court sits 10.00 a.m. Office
hours 9.00 a.m.–1.00 p.m. on court days only.
Facilities: Interview room. Advocates' room.

(WEST CORNWALL) MAGISTRATES' COURT—
CONTINUED

Travel: NR Camborne (Paddington 5 hrs. 10 min.) plus 10 min. walk. From Station to Trevu Rd., cross into Basset St. At end turn left into Basset Rd.

Driving: A30 to Camborne. A3047 to town centre, Wesley St. Continue, bearing to right into Trelowarren St. Mags Ct. on corner of 1st turning left.

Parking: Behind shops. Car park in Rosewarne Rd. Side-streets.

Eating out and Accommodation:

Lowenac	restaurant	Basset Rd.
White Hart	bar food	Trelowarren St.
Inn for All Seasons	bar food	Treleigh, Redruth

**WEST CORNWALL MAGISTRATES' COURT (TRURO),
WEST CORNWALL COMBINED FAMILY PROCEEDINGS
COURT** (Wed.),
WEST CORNWALL COMBINED YOUTH COURT (Fri.)

The Magistrates' Court, Tremorvah Wood Lane, Mitchell Hill, Truro, Cornwall TR1 2HQ.

Telephone: 01872 321900. Fax: 01872 276227.

Court times: Doors open 9.00 a.m. Court sits 10.00 a.m. Office hours 8.30 a.m.–4.30 p.m.

Facilities: Advocates' room. Interview rooms. WRVS. Babies' room.

Travel: NR Truro (Paddington 5 hrs.) plus 40 min. walk.
From station left into Station Rd. and down Richmond Hill. Over roundabout into Ferris Town, bear right into Frances St. and River St. Left into Victoria Place and continue straight into Boscawen. Over bridge, cross St. Austell St. into Mitchell Hill.

Driving: A39 to Truro. Right at roundabout into St. Austell St. First right into Mitchell Hill.

Parking: Domestic car park.

Eating out and Accommodation:

Ann's Pantry	restaurant	Little Castle St.
The City Inn	bar food	Kenwyn St.

See entry for Truro County/Crown Court.

WESTON-SUPER-MARE COUNTY COURT

2nd Floor, Regent House, High St., Weston-Super-Mare, North Somerset BS23 1JF.

Telephone: 01934 626967/627787. Fax: 01934 643028.

Court times: Doors open 9.30 a.m. Court sits 10.00 a.m. or 10.30 a.m. Office hours 10.00 a.m.–4.00 p.m.

Facilities: Robing room.

WESTON-SUPER-MARE COUNTY COURT—
CONTINUED
Travel: BR Weston-Super-Mare (Paddington 2 hrs.) plus 5 min. walk. From station west exit into Station Approach and left into Station Rd. At end turn left, into the Centre. Left into Regent St. and left into High St. Court in Regent House.

Driving: M5 junction 21 and A370 Bristol Rd. Left into Locking Rd. Second left after the station into The Centre. Cty: third left into High St. Court on left.

Parking: Public car parks.

Eating out and Accommodation:

Town Crier Public House	Walliscote Rd.
Reflections	The Boulevard

WEYMOUTH COUNTY COURT (also sits at County Hall, Dorchester and Mountfield, Bridport),
WEYMOUTH AND PORTLAND MAGISTRATES' COURT
(Mon., Tues., Thurs., and Fri.),
DORSET COMBINED YOUTH PANEL (alt. Fri.)
The Law Courts, Westwey Rd., Weymouth, Dorset DT4 8TE.
Telephone: Cty: 01305 752510. Fax: 01305 788293. Mags: 01305 783891. Fax: 01305 761418.

Court times: Doors open 9.30 a.m. Court sits: Cty: 10.00 a.m. or 10.30 a.m. Mags: 10.00 a.m. Office hours: Cty: 10.00 a.m.–4.00 p.m. Mags: 9.00 a.m.–5.00 p.m.

Facilities: Advocates' room. Interview rooms. WRVS.

Travel: NR Weymouth (Waterloo 2 hrs. 30 min.) plus 10 min. walk. From station into King St. Over roundabout and over bridge. Left at roundabout into Westwey Rd. Court on right next to sports centre.

Driving: A354 Dorchester Rd. Right at Manor roundabout into Weymouth Way. Straight over this roundabout and next into Westwey Rd. Court on right.

Parking: Domestic car park.

Eating out and Accommodation:

Squash Centre	bar food	Westwey Rd.
Crown	hotel	St. Thomas St.

WIMBORNE MAGISTRATES' COURT (Mon. and Fri.)
The Law Courts, Hanham Rd., Wimborne, Dorset BH21 1JW.
(Correspondence to be sent to: The Law Courts, Park Rd., Poole BH15 2RH.)
Telephone: Admin. from Poole: 01202 745309.
Court times: Doors open 9.00 a.m. Court sits 10.00 a.m.
Facilities: Advocates' room. Interview rooms. Drinks machine.
Travel: NR Poole plus bus (40 min., 5 miles).

WIMBORNE MAGISTRATES' COURT—
CONTINUED

Driving: M27 Junc. 1, A31 and B3073 Leigh Rd. Right at first roundabout, left at next roundabout, right at third roundabout. Court on left next to police station.

Parking: Car park behind Court.

Eating out and Accommodation:

The Dormers	hotel	The Square
The King's Head	hotel	The Square

WINCHESTER COUNTY COURT,
WINCHESTER CROWN COURT,

The Law Courts, Winchester, Hants. SO23 9EL.

Telephone: Cty and Crown: 01962 814100. Fax: 01962 853821.

DX: 98520 Winchester 3.

Court times: Doors open 8.30 a.m. Courts sit: Cty and Crown: 10.00 a.m. or 10.30 a.m. Office hours: Cty: 10.00 a.m.–4.00 p.m. Crown: 9.00 a.m.–5.00 p.m.

Facilities: Robing room. Solicitors' room. Buffet. Bar mess.

Travel: NR Winchester (Waterloo 1 hr.) plus 5 min. walk. From station right into Station Rd. Left into High St., Court 400 yds on right, next to Great Hall.

Driving: M3 Junc. 9. Follow one-way into town along St. Georges St. Left at end into Jewry St. and right into High St. Courts on left after Trafalgar St.

Parking: Multi-storey car park off Sussex St.

Eating out and Accommodation:

Mr So	Chinese restaurant	Jewry St.
Royal	hotel	St. Peter St.

YEOVIL COUNTY COURT,[*]

22 Hendford, Yeovil, Somerset BA20 2QD.

[*]Occasionally sits at The Town Hall, Shaftesbury, Dorset, and The Court House, Axminster, Devon.

Telephone: 01935 382150. Fax: 01935 410004.

DX: 98830 Yeovil 2.

Court times: Doors open 9.30 a.m. Court sits 10.00 a.m. or 10.30 a.m. Office hours: 10.00 a.m.–4.00 p.m.

Facilities: Robing room. Interview rooms. Public telephone. Lift and disabled access.

Travel: NR See Mags Ct.

Driving: From Frome A359 Mudford Rd. into Yeovil. Left at roundabout.

Parking: There is no public parking at the court. Pay and display in West Hendford.

YEOVIL MAGISTRATES' COURT (Mon.–Fri.),
SOUTH SOMERSET MAGISTRATES' COURT,
SOUTH SOMERSET YOUTH COURT
The Law Courts, Petters Way, Yeovil, Somerset BA20 1SW.
Telephone: Mags: 01935 426281. Fax: 01935 431022.
DX: 100357 Yeovil.
Court times: Doors open 9.00 a.m. Court sits: 10.00 a.m. Office hours: 8.30 a.m.–5.00 p.m./4.30 p.m. Fri.
Facilities: Advocates' room. Coffee machine. WRVS (on Mon., Tues., Thurs.)
Travel: NR Yeovil Pen Mill (Paddington 3 hrs.) or Yeovil Junction (Waterloo 2 hrs. 30 min.) plus buses and taxis to town centre.
Driving: From outskirts of town follow signs for Tourist Information Centre. Court is situated opposite.
Parking: Pay and display in Petter's Way.
Eating out and Accommodation:

Manor	hotel	Hendford Rd.

Index

142

Alterations and Additions

The publishers of *The Court Guide 2004* would be pleased to receive details of any alterations and additions to the text by users of the Guide.

COURT . . . .
Page No. in this edition . . . .
Alteration or addition . . . .

. . . .
. . . .
. . . .
. . . .
. . . .
. . . .
. . . .
. . . .
. . . .
. . . .
. . . .
. . . .
. . . .
. . . .
. . . .
. . . .
. . . .
. . . .
. . . .
. . . .
. . . .
. . . .
. . . .
. . . .
. . . .
. . . .
. . . .
. . . .
. . . .
. . . .
. . . .
. . . .
. . . .
. . . .

Your name and address:

. . . .
. . . .

Please detach and send to Academic and Professional Law Department
Oxford University Press, Great Clarendon St., Oxford OX2 6DP.
email: law.uk@oup.com

154

O Interchange stations
⇌ Connections with National Rail
⇌ Connections with riverboat services
🚋 Connection with Tramlink
✈ Airport interchange   ● Closed Sundays
▲ Served by Piccadilly line trains early
  morning and late evening
† For opening times see poster journey planners.
Certain stations are closed on public holidays.

i 24 hour travel information
020 7222 1234

Textphone
020 7918 3015

Website
www.tfl.gov.uk

UNDERGROUND

LTM FA(a) 09.05   Reg. user No. 05/E/1583

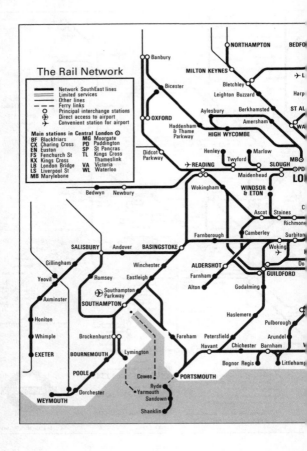

The Rail Network

Main stations in Central London ⊖
BF Blackfriars   MG Moorgate
CX Charing Cross   PD Paddington
EN Euston   SP St Pancras
FS Fenchurch St   TL Kings Cross
KX Kings Cross   Thameslink
LB London Bridge   VA Victoria
LS Liverpool St   WL Waterloo
MB Marylebone

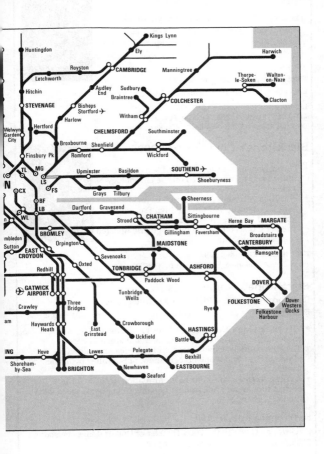

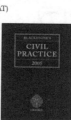